SEC...

...OUT OF LINE
by Michele Dunaway

From the opening green flag at Daytona to the final checkered flag at Homestead, the competition will be fierce for the NASCAR Sprint Cup Series championship.

The **Grosso** family practically has engine oil in their veins. For them racing represents not just a way of life but a tradition that goes back to NASCAR's inception. Like all families, they also have a few skeletons to hide. What happens when someone peeks inside the closet becomes a matter that threatens to destroy them.

The **Murphys** have been supporting drivers in the pits for generations, despite a vendetta with the Grossos that's almost as old as NASCAR itself! But the Murphys have their own secrets... and a few indiscretions that could cost them everything.

The **Branches** are newcomers, and some would say upstarts. But as this affluent Texas family is further enmeshed in the world of NASCAR, they become just as embroiled in the intrigues on and off the track.

The **Motor Media Group** are the PR people responsible for the positive public perception of NASCAR's stars. They are the glue that repairs the damage. And more than anything, they feel the brunt of the backlash....

These NASCAR families have secrets to hide, and reputations to protect. This season will test them all.

Dear Reader,

Have you ever fallen for a person because at the time you thought he or she was so right, only to find out later you were so very wrong? That's Lucy Gunter's current problem. The former girlfriend of driver Justin Murphy plans to give up men and NASCAR racing, her favorite sport, until she meets Sawyer Branch, brother of two NASCAR Sprint Cup Series drivers.

Sawyer seems so right…but Lucy's worried that once again everything's going to turn out so wrong, especially when she learns of his terrible secret. Can their newfound romance survive?

I can't tell you how much I've enjoyed being a part of Harlequin's officially licensed NASCAR romance series and working with such a talented group of authors. Like Lucy, NASCAR is my favorite sport, and it's been fun to create this fictional world and bring my characters to life against such a fun and exciting backdrop.

I hope you enjoy *Out of Line* and my other upcoming NASCAR book, *Tailspin*. Thanks for being with me as Lucy and Sawyer discover true love, and as always, feel free to drop me an e-mail through the link at my Web site, www.micheledunaway.com.

Enjoy the romance,

Michele Dunaway

//////NASCAR®

OUT OF LINE

Michele Dunaway

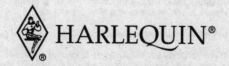

HARLEQUIN®

TORONTO • NEW YORK • LONDON
AMSTERDAM • PARIS • SYDNEY • HAMBURG
STOCKHOLM • ATHENS • TOKYO • MILAN • MADRID
PRAGUE • WARSAW • BUDAPEST • AUCKLAND

ISBN-13: 978-0-373-21790-8
ISBN-10:   0-373-21790-0

OUT OF LINE

Copyright © 2008 by Harlequin Books S.A.

Michele Dunaway is acknowledged as the author of this work.

NASCAR® and the NASCAR Library Collection are registered trademarks of the National Association for Stock Car Auto Racing, Inc.

www.eHarlequin.com

Printed in U.S.A.

MICHELE DUNAWAY

In first grade Michele Dunaway knew she wanted to be a teacher when she grew up, and by second grade she wanted to be an author. By third grade she determined to be both, and as an adult, she succeeded. In addition to writing romance, Michele is a nationally recognized journalism educator who sponsors the yearbook and newspaper at the school where she teaches.

Born and raised in St. Louis (hometown of several NASCAR drivers), Michele has traveled extensively, with the cities and places she's visited often becoming settings for her stories. Described as a woman who does too much but doesn't know how to stop, Michele gardens five acres in her spare time and shares her Missouri River townhome with two young daughters, five lazy house cats and one crazy kitten. Michele loves to hear from readers. You can reach her through her Web site at www.micheledunaway.com.

For Marsha Zinberg and Tina Colombo for letting me be a part of this fantastic series, and to all the other authors writing Harlequin NASCAR books who have since become my good friends. This one's for you.

REARVIEW MIRROR:

The Murphy family once again made headlines when Rachel Murphy took over as engine builder for Fulcrum Racing, the team her brother Justin drives for—and when she became engaged to sportscaster Payton Reese. Meanwhile, the investigation into the disappearance of Hilton Branch—father of NASCAR drivers Bart and Will Branch—and the millions of dollars stolen from his bank, his customers and even his family continues.

CHAPTER ONE

"HI, RACE FANS. I'M Guy Edwards and, along with Malcolm French, we'd like to welcome you to Friday's edition of 'NASCAR A.M.,' live from Richmond. Today teams are busy preparing for tonight's NASCAR Nationwide Series race and tomorrow's NASCAR Sprint Cup Series race under the lights."

Malcolm smiled. "One of the main concerns for some teams is how their drivers are doing after four months of racing."

"Dean and Kent Grosso and Justin Murphy are off to a rocky start, especially after all three did not finish in Las Vegas and Murphy took forty-first in California," Guy agreed.

"But the season's still young when it comes to Chase points. Another story continues to be the Branch twins," Malcolm said.

Guy nodded. "Imagine having your own father embezzle tons of money from the family business, leaving you virtually penniless and without a sponsor."

"And if that's not bad enough, every passing week brings you one day closer to publication of your father's mistress's tell-all autobiography," Malcolm added.

"I can't imagine driving with that cloud over my head,"

Guy continued. "Will, who's usually the more erratic of the twins, has been doing better than Bart, who placed fourth at Martinsville and sixth at Texas but hasn't placed higher than twentieth since."

"With predictions on how the Branch brothers will run in Richmond, we turn to Payton Reese with the story."

The camera panned to Payton. "Thanks, Malcolm. I'm here outside Bart Branch's hauler, where he'll be joining us shortly to comment on his performance...."

AS PAYTON REESE BEGAN speaking, Lucy Gunter gave herself a little shake and turned away from the television set in the pediatric-cancer ward visitors' lounge. The TV broadcast to no one in particular—except for Lucy, the room was empty. Tonight, though, the space would be filled as family members of young patients camped out for the night.

The television was on twenty-four-seven.

Not that Lucy cared.

Okay, perhaps that was a big white lie. Despite her recent resolve, she had to admit she was still more than a little interested. NASCAR remained her favorite sport, even before Carolina Panthers football. Give her a Sunday where she had to choose between the two, stock car racing won every time.

She'd been an avid fan ever since her father had taken her to her first race at age eight. That very first autograph from one of her favorite drivers was now preserved in her scrapbook. She'd remembered the awe when he'd signed the photo…just last year she'd met that driver again. Now a racing legend, he'd been equally as kind and his wife equally as sweet when Lucy had spoken with them in the garage area.

At that time Lucy had belonged. She'd been an insider, a race car driver's girlfriend.

But this past February she'd put that lifestyle behind her. She'd broken up with Justin Murphy, driver of the No. 448 NASCAR Sprint Cup Series car for Fulcrum Racing.

She'd tried everything to make their relationship work, but, like trying to manufacture diamonds from coal, her efforts had been futile. Justin had been a round hole to her square peg. They'd had some great times, but long-term they weren't right for each other. Deep down, that eternal love and commitment Lucy wanted hadn't been there.

In her case, that fantasy of marrying a driver and living happily ever after was not meant to be.

So, as for being up close and personal, being in the garage area and smelling the car exhaust, listening to the shouts of crew members and feeling the vibrations of forty-three engines as they roared to life, she'd been there, done that.

Her friend Tanya may have won a driver's heart, but Lucy's reality would be much different.

No matter how much she missed it.

She was trying to put Justin Murphy and NASCAR behind her. She'd limited her involvement to watching races on TV, but sitting at home was a far cry from experiencing the real thing from the pits.

She jutted her chin and fed her dollar into the soda machine, the real reason she'd entered the lounge. She'd always been a survivor. She'd earned a pretty good promotion this past March. She now supervised the entire hospital computer network. She was a problem solver. So while she loved NASCAR and would never give up watching, she was trying to leave her personal involvement where it belonged—the past. Determined, she changed the channel to a game show and strode from the room, cola in hand.

"SO THAT'S YOUR BROTHER, huh?" Johnny Blankenship asked.

Sawyer Branch glanced at the TV, where Payton Reese was interviewing Bart Branch. "Hard to believe, is it?"

Johnny nodded, his body pressed back against the white hospital bed. "He doesn't look a thing like you."

Sawyer laughed. He'd heard that before, possibly more times than he could count. Unlike his brothers and sister with their blond hair, Sawyer's physical attributes were a throwback to his Greek paternal grandmother. Thus he had black hair, black eyes and a permanently tanned complexion. He stood five eleven; his older twin brothers were six two.

"So you never wanted to race?" Johnny asked.

"Nah." Sawyer shook his head. That had always been his brothers' thing.

"Not even a little?" Johnny pressed. For a fifteen-year-old, he was pretty wise. Sawyer figured having cancer did that to a person—made you grow up fast.

"Maybe a little," Sawyer admitted. "But I wasn't any good at it. Now, Will and Bart, they're naturals."

"And you don't mind?"

At thirty, his brothers were working in their careers. Two years younger, Sawyer had flitted from college to college and had recently finally figured out what he wanted to do for the rest of his life. But he didn't tell Johnny that. "I think all brothers are a little envious of one another at times. That's normal. And I'm better at math."

"Yeah. My brother gets to play baseball and I don't. It bugs me sometimes. It sucks that life's not fair."

"I agree," Sawyer said, wishing Johnny hadn't been shorted in the life department. Instead of playing baseball or casting fishing lines, Johnny made frequent visits to the hospital. Over the past year Sawyer had been visiting the pediatric ward as part of his doctoral research, and he'd gotten to know the teen well.

"Hey, Johnny!"

"Hi, Brice," Johnny greeted the orderly as he came in with a food tray. Sawyer rose to leave. Usually Johnny's mom arrived during lunch.

"I'll catch you later," Sawyer said before walking out into the hall.

As he walked through the cancer ward, a few nurses and orderlies glanced his way and some greeted him. Sawyer smiled back or gave a quick wave. Since his Ph.D. dissertation involved creating mathematical formulas to predict and manage cancer remission rates, he was a familiar face on the floor.

He rounded a corner and came across Lucy Gunter. He slowed his footsteps as he surveyed the unfolding scene.

"That should finish your upgrade, eliminating your problem," Lucy said to the woman seated at the cancer ward's reception desk. "We'll give it another minute to check everything before I go."

"Thanks. I know you don't usually do this yourself," the nurse said, her expression one of gratitude that her computer had been fixed.

"Oh, it's no problem," Lucy said with a warm smile. "Kyle's on vacation this week so I'm filling in everywhere that's needed. It gets me out of the office. I rather like the change."

As neither woman had seen him, Sawyer inched back

slightly. He'd always admired Lucy, and not just physically. Sure, she was about five six, slender and had the most beautiful shade of strawberry-blond hair, but Sawyer also knew she had brains. She worked at the hospital as a network administrator and he'd heard she had a master's degree in computer application or something like that.

In essence, the few times they'd spoken both at the hospital and at the race track, he'd found her to be articulate and able to hold her own against him. That impressed him a great deal.

However, one of his cardinal rules was that you didn't poach another man's woman, so until recently Lucy had been off-limits.

But now that fate had provided him this perfect opportunity, Sawyer approached the desk at the same moment Lucy straightened. Her blue eyes widened slightly in surprise and then relaxed in greeting. "Hi, Sawyer. Been visiting the kids?"

He nodded and found his voice. For a brief second, he'd thought the cat had his tongue. "Yes. Even though I'm just about finished with my research and have begun putting my dissertation together, I'm admittedly attached to quite a few of them. I was visiting Johnny. So, do you have a minute?" he asked Lucy, nerves suddenly tight. He wanted her to say yes.

"Sure," she said, stepping around the reception desk counter. "What do you need?"

"Here, I'll walk with you," Sawyer said, pushing the button that opened the door that led out of the ward. Just in case she said no and turned down his advance, he certainly didn't want to ask her out in front of everyone. They stepped out about ten feet into the floor's lobby area, which was thankfully deserted of hospital employees.

He found himself nervous, an unfamiliar state. Sure, he knew he was attractive—in that classical Mediterranean sense that women seemed to like. He was one hundred seventy pounds of lean muscle that came from running, biking and swimming. Women found him sexy, and the more aggressive ones had no problem telling him so.

But that didn't mean he couldn't be rejected, and that had been happening a lot lately, including by his own father. There had to be something Freudian in that somewhere. He inhaled a breath. They stopped and Lucy smiled tentatively as she waited for Sawyer to explain.

In for a penny…

"Do you want to go get some lunch?"

"LUNCH?" LUCY PARROTED. She hadn't been anticipating his question and he'd taken her totally by surprise.

"Yes, lunch," Sawyer repeated. He laughed. "That meal around midday. I thought we could get some pizza?"

She blinked. She had to be standing there like the world's biggest idiot. He waited expectantly. "You mean now?" she clarified, glancing at her watch. She must appear a fool. She hadn't dated since Justin.

"If now works," Sawyer said, and she could read relief in his expression. "I know we don't really know each other and this may seem kind of awkward and out of the blue but…"

Lucy shook her head. Stranger things had happened in her world and the word *pizza* had made her stomach grumble. She'd skipped breakfast.

"I was thinking Sleeter's," he said, and the peanut-butter-and-jelly sandwich Lucy had packed for the second day in a row paled in comparison. She could eat that for dinner instead.

"I haven't had their pizza in ages. Their deep-dish is the best."

As if on cue, her stomach rumbled and his grin widened. "You sound hungry and we're in agreement on that deep-dish. Just tell me you'll eat more than pepperoni or sausage."

She laughed a little. The few times she'd met Sawyer briefly at the track she'd found him charming. A year ago she'd met one of his dates in the infield restroom at Charlotte. The woman, a local model, had confided that Sawyer was difficult, often getting caught up in his research. Lucy had found herself siding with Sawyer, even though she'd heard later through the NASCAR grapevine that Sawyer had gotten wrapped up in math equations, forgotten to call the woman and that had been that. Lucy hadn't been too impressed with her, anyway.

"So, Sleeter's?" he asked.

Maybe it was the way his black eyes twinkled. Lucy had just determined to stay away from NASCAR. But he wasn't a driver, just his brothers. And a good deep-dish pizza never hurt anyone. Her stomach growled louder. "I don't think there's a pizza topping I've ever disliked. Okay, maybe anchovies. I'll go."

"Great. I'll drive."

His smile widened and Lucy's heart gave a tiny flip. She calmed herself. Down, girl. Nothing but lunch. No big deal. Life post Justin had begun.

CHAPTER TWO

SLEETER'S WAS ONE OF THOSE places you went when you were broke in college and loved even years later. The place always felt like home and the menu never changed.

Sawyer pulled up in the parking lot, marveling a bit at his good fortune. She'd said yes. For a moment there he'd had doubts.

After all, his life was a bit of a mess. Aside from a ride in a current-year Corvette, the case could be made that he didn't have a lot to offer.

Some scandal, maybe. A date with a soon-to-be math professor.

He pushed those thoughts out of his mind as he and Lucy ordered a Sleeter's deluxe pizza.

"I like your car," Lucy said.

"My father's guilt gift," Sawyer volunteered.

Her expression sympathized but didn't pity. He appreciated that. He'd also appreciated that the car had given him a nice view of her calves as she'd climbed in, the floral skirt she was wearing hiding everything above the knee.

"So your dad really did run off with everything?" Lucy asked. She covered her mouth with her hand and he noticed she wore pink nail polish. "Sorry. It's rude of me to bring that up. You don't even know me so scratch that I asked."

He shook his head. He'd been pretty tight-lipped, but today he felt like talking. If nothing else, he'd find out very quickly if Lucy went running for the hills.

"No, it's okay," he told her. "Everyone asks. Fact is, yes, he pretty much embezzled everything. I get a quarterly allowance, and next installment's not coming."

Her eyes widened. "I'm sorry."

He shrugged. "Don't be. I'm graduating the last week of July, and once my dissertation's presented in June, I'll be officially hired for the State U. teaching job I applied for."

"So you're doing okay, then. As well as you can," Lucy pressed, and Sawyer could tell her curiosity came from genuine concern for people, not just so that she could relay his sad story to others as many wanted to do.

In fact, for the first week after the scandal, several women had hit on him, their concern a front as they probed for information. He'd sent them packing with little to show for their efforts.

"I'm doing fine," he reassured her, fibbing slightly. He refused to doom himself before he got past the starting gate. Besides, he'd have his personal financial matters all cleared up soon, making everything his family worried about a nonissue. All it would take were a few more trips to Vegas and some rendezvous with Lady Luck at the blackjack table.

"Tell me a little more about your Ph.D. project," Lucy asked, switching the subject. "I think you mentioned it to me before. Something about predicting cancer remission rates?"

"Yes." Sawyer hesitated in telling her the rest, reaching for the sweetened iced tea he'd ordered. He'd been declared a math geek too many times over.

"Is there more to it than that?"

He stared at her, trying to see if she were serious or just making polite conversation. "You really want to hear it? Most people's eyes tend to glaze over when I start to explain everything."

"I'm not most people," Lucy declared forcefully.

"No, you're not," Sawyer said aloud, realizing the full truth of his statement later after he'd explained everything. She'd even asked pertinent follow-up questions, which proved she'd not only listened but also understood. "I'm sorry if I misjudged you."

She nodded, satisfied. "You have to remember that computer programming involves math. Administering a network, especially one the size of State Hospital's, requires quite a few calculations. I took math classes to boost my GPA."

"So you don't mind hanging out with a math geek?" Sawyer asked, liking Lucy more and more as the waiter brought her pizza.

She frowned at him, the remnants of any lipstick long having vanished. Her lips were perfect without and absolutely kissable, Sawyer decided. "Is that what you think you are?" she asked.

He tilted his head. "That's what I've been told."

She came to his defense. "I don't think so. I love math. Math's cool."

He grinned slightly. "Thank you."

She gave a short, proud nod. "You're welcome."

He sobered and gestured that she should take the first slice of pizza. "My dad once asked me what you'd do with a Ph.D. in math. He wasn't too thrilled that my answers were to teach college and continue to do research. He told me there wasn't enough money in that."

"Teaching is a noble profession, and this situation with your dad has to be so awkward," Lucy said in a small burst of anger. She reached out her hand and touched his in a show of support. "I can't imagine what you've been through."

"You made the local stage for a while," he pointed out, enjoying her touch. He then winced. The last thing he wanted to do was bring up the ex-boyfriend.

Lucy removed her hand and contemplated his statement. He was discovering that Lucy thought first, spoke second. She didn't rush. When she was ready she said, "Yes, but my breakup with Justin was old news within a week. No one cares about the ex-girlfriend if there's no money involved or any scandal. I'm just labeled as one of the girls who revolve through a single driver's life. Sort of the nature of the beast, I guess. Easily forgotten and replaced."

"I shouldn't have brought it up. I apologize."

She shrugged and paused, the piece of pizza she'd just picked up suspended in midair. "Like you told me earlier, it's okay. Everyone knows there are some drivers who change girlfriends like they change their helmets. A new one every race. Then there are others who have the most devoted marriages. I wanted the latter and wasn't afraid to admit it. I'm still not. I've got a great job, but I wouldn't be opposed to meeting the right guy and settling down. Justin just wasn't that guy. He may never have been, but I wanted him to be. Maybe my Mr. Right isn't a race car driver at all."

She sat a moment reflecting before she took a bite.

Sawyer put a slice on his own plate and laughed to break the tension. "Okay, we've already committed just about every dating-guide no-no. I don't think we're supposed to talk about the exes until the third date."

She arched an eyebrow. "Is this a date?" He didn't answer and the corner of her lip inched upward. "Okay, let me add it up. You drove and I'm assuming you're paying. So I guess we can call this a date."

"I agree with that definition so we probably shouldn't discuss our wacky family members, either," Sawyer said, watching as amusement lit Lucy's blue eyes.

"Probably not. Dangerous territory for a date. Speaking of which, though, did I tell you already this was a great choice of lunch venue? I never get this way much." She took another piece and this time turned it around, so she could devour the crust first. "I often eat it backward. I'm strange that way. You're originally from Texas, right?" Lucy asked.

"Dallas," Sawyer confirmed.

She washed down her food with the strawberry lemonade she'd ordered. "How did you get this direction? Drawn by NASCAR like everyone else?"

He grinned. "That's my brothers."

"Good, because I'm giving it up." Lucy gave a resigned sigh.

"What? NASCAR?"

He seemed a tad shocked and she nodded. "I love it, but I can't spend any more of my life at the track. It's time to move on."

"I can understand that. This is the longest I've been in one place, aside from growing up in Dallas. I often had a lot of wanderlust. Didn't want to let the grass grow under my feet once I left home."

"Really? I've lived here all my life. Never left Charlotte."

"Not me. I went to Stanford for my undergraduate degree and decided I didn't like California. So I transferred my credits to Columbia University in New York City, changed my degree plan to journalism and then decided that big-city living or writing for a newspaper wasn't for me. My real love has always been numbers. By this time my family was a bit fed up with what they called my lack of direction. My brothers had decided they wanted to race on NASCAR's Sprint Cup level and were committed to that path. My sister, Penny, had her modeling career. I was the permanent student. My father called it Peter Pan wanderlust."

"Ouch," Lucy emphasized.

"Yeah. I prefer the term *nomadic,* but reality is I took a while to find my calling. I transferred to State University about four years ago because of their combined master's/doctorate program in applied mathematics. I've been hooked and satisfied ever since. I think that's what's important. You should do what you love."

"I agree wholeheartedly," Lucy said as she took another sip of her lemonade. "You have to be happy with yourself and your career choice. My job is one area of my life I'm satisfied with. I guess my wanderlust came later. I've never moved far."

"That's not a bad thing."

"No, but I thought it was. I think that's something that appealed to me about Justin. I always wanted to travel and dating Justin provided me with the opportunity to travel to a different city every weekend. That's not a good reason to stay in a relationship. We said we weren't going to talk about this, and here I am violating that. Okay, I fail."

"Maybe we should just get it out of the way early," Sawyer laughed. "So where would you really love to go, given the chance?"

Her answer was instantaneous. "Alaska and Hawaii."

"I've been to the Big Island," Sawyer said. "Great place to visit, but expensive."

"I've got to finish paying for my college before I travel anywhere. One year left on my loans."

"Well, despite my dad's actions, he paid for all my course work."

"That's one good thing."

Sawyer chuckled. "I think he was thrilled I was no longer just some aimless slacker trying out colleges like my sister tries on shoes. As for State, you know what they say about its mathematics program."

Lucy smiled. "Yep. John Nash would have done his graduate work here in his early years had he not attended Princeton. Heard it a few times from guys trying to pick me up."

Sawyer leaned forward, his tone light and teasing. "Did it work?"

"What do you think?" Lucy attempted to keep her face straight and then she burst out laughing. "Heck, no. If you'd used that line on me, not even Sleeter's would have tempted me to say yes."

"Then I'm lucky I didn't." Sawyer chuckled.

"See, I knew there was something different about you that set you apart from the rest of the pack hanging out at the race track," Lucy said.

"Nah. It's only because I can't change a tire or build a car," he said.

"You're funny," Lucy said, and Sawyer took her words

as a compliment. He could tell she was enjoying lunch and they made small talk and jokes until Lucy finally glanced at her watch and groaned a little. "I guess we should get back soon. I can only play hooky for so long."

"Not me. Today's my day off. I serve as one of Larry Grosso's teaching assistants. He's also my Ph.D. mentor, and so I teach study sessions and have other commitments throughout the week. Friday I'm free."

"Is your professor related to the Grosso racing family?"

Sawyer nodded. The Grosso racing family was well established in Charlotte, having been there since the very beginning when Milo Grosso chased gangsters for the FBI and raced stock cars on the weekends. "Larry's Milo's grandson. He's also Steve's dad and Kent's uncle."

Kent Grosso was the reigning NASCAR Sprint Cup Series champion and drove the No. 427 Dodge for Maximus Motorsports.

"Steve works as Kent's spotter," Lucy said, showing her knowledge of Kent's racing team.

"Right," Sawyer confirmed. "You sure you're not going to miss NASCAR if you give it up?"

"Oh, I'll still watch. I'm still friends with Tanya Wells, Kent's fiancée. Tanya and I went to high school together, although we weren't friends back then."

Sawyer took the bill from the waiter. "I have to admit, I'm what you'd probably call a fair-weather fan. I enjoy being at the race track more than watching on TV, which means that I don't see many races unless I'm there. It might be the next day before I find out who's won."

"I'm weaning myself from checking the Internet immediately," Lucy said.

Sawyer removed a wad of cash from his pocket. He

peeled off enough for the bill and a twenty-percent tip and placed the money on the table. He stood. "Shall we?"

"Thank you for lunch," she said as they walked back to his car. "I enjoyed it."

"Me, too. I hope I haven't made you late."

"It's fine," she reassured him, giving him a smile that warmed his insides. "I'm the boss."

They talked about various miscellaneous things until they reached the hospital lot. Sawyer drove up to the main doors but left the car idling.

"So are you coming back inside?" Lucy asked.

He shook his head, a lock of dark-black hair falling over his right eyebrow. "No. I should be back sometime next week. I'll stop by. Maybe we could do lunch again."

"That might work," Lucy said. "Thanks again."

"I'd say I'd call but I've got a lot of work to do. I don't want to promise something I can't deliver. I can disappear for days when working out a problem."

"I saw other guys like that. Math gave them one-track minds." Lucy opened her door and placed one high-heeled pump on the pavement before Sawyer could get out and assist her.

Probably for the best, Sawyer thought as he drove away a few minutes later. If he had done the chivalrous thing and held her door, she'd have been within kissing range and that might make for an awkward moment.

Already he had a light-headed feeling traveling through his bloodstream. Sure, today had been laid back and casual, two people eating lunch and enjoying each other's company. Yeah, they'd broken the rules and discussed things best left for later dates.

But, like long ago when he'd first seen her, he'd felt

something beyond the flicker of interest a guy gets when viewing a pretty girl. She was a woman he seriously wanted to get to know. She understood his career and liked math. How perfect was that?

His cell phone rang and Sawyer reached over to where the device rested in its hands-free cradle. He pressed the button, sending the call to speakerphone. "Sawyer Branch."

"Sawyer, hey, glad I caught you. It's Craig."

"Hi," Sawyer said hesitantly. While Craig Lockhart was married to his sister, Penny, Sawyer's gut told him this wasn't a social call.

"Look, I told you when we discussed your situation in private after the family meeting that I'd get back with you. It's been long enough. Did you get my messages? The federal regulators have definitely cut off your quarterly allowance from Hilton. All Branch family assets in any Branch bank are frozen until this is all over. Hilton siphoned off a lot of money to pay for Alyssa."

Alyssa Ritchie. His father's mistress of twenty years. Just hearing her name was like tasting tin foil. He cringed and had a bad taste in his mouth.

"So how much is there?" Sawyer asked.

"What's left isn't enough to buy the tip of an iceberg."

"Great," Sawyer said, concentrating on driving back to his condo. The early May day was bright and sunny, perfect for bike riding. He'd already passed several cyclists and planned to partake himself in about an hour.

"Listen, what are you planning to do?" Craig asked. "I'd like to know. You've been putting this off for too long."

"Don't worry about it," Sawyer replied, tension tightening his hands and causing his knuckles to whiten where he gripped the steering wheel. "I've got the situation handled. You don't need to worry about me or my finances."

"Sawyer, you've got a *one-hundred-thousand-dollar* unsecured signature loan at BMT." Craig named the family's banking conglomerate. An accountant by education, Craig had been the one to discover the financial irregularities in the accounts. He'd brought the information to Hilton, who had subsequently taken off, spurring the federal investigation into the family's holdings.

"So what?" Sawyer asked.

"That's highly irregular," Craig said. "I've told you, the bank can call in that note at any time, and with the feds involved, they'd be fools not to do so. There's tons of money missing and the trouble keeps getting bigger and bigger."

"The FDIC insures everyone's accounts up to one hundred thousand," Sawyer stated flatly. His father didn't only have a mistress; no, to make matters even worse he had to go and bankrupt the family as well. "No one's lost any money by having an account in the bank, other than my family and anyone else foolish enough not to diversify."

"You have to pay this loan back," Craig urged.

"And I've already said I will." Sawyer parked in his assigned place. Another gift from his father, the two-bedroom town house he lived in was near campus. Thankfully both the car and the town house were in Sawyer's name free and clear. He turned off the engine and retrieved the phone. He held the device to his ear as he went inside. Up until recently, he'd always liked the condo. While narrow in width, the condo had vaulted ceilings and second-floor balconies. The overall effect was of bright-ness and space. The downer—he'd learned from the tabloids Alyssa had played a role in picking it out.

"Listen, Craig, if Dad's quarterly draft had come through then it would have paid off a quarter of what I owe. I've got a little money saved up and I can get the rest."

"How, by gambling? That's how you got yourself into this mess in the first place." Craig's words had Sawyer tightening his grip on the phone.

"The family knows you have a gambling problem and that your dad bailed you out," Craig continued, his voice edging up a notch as he tried to again make his point.

"I do not have a problem, and even if I did, it's none of your business," Sawyer snapped, losing a little control.

"It's everyone's business. Your brothers have just gotten new sponsors. Alyssa's publishing a memoir and she's out for any negative dirt she can get on the Branches. If your debt becomes public…" Craig's voice trailed off.

"It won't. I won't hurt my mother like my father did," Sawyer declared. He was not like-father, like-son. For one, Sawyer was completely faithful to whatever woman he was dating. He didn't keep a mistress. He never planned on doing so.

"Good. Your mother already has had enough stress. The feds are still after her to explain where the money is, although they're beginning to back down now that Alyssa's come forward with her exposé. They're hopefully starting to believe your mother had nothing to do with Hilton's em-bezzlement."

"I'm glad. I'll call her later. Give Penny my love and don't worry about me. It's handled."

"Sawyer, you have a problem," Craig said, but Sawyer's

patience had exhausted itself and he hung up. When Craig called him right back, Sawyer let the call go to voice mail.

The hell with Craig. Sawyer let his anger temporarily find a convenient target—his brother-in-law. His digging around had started the ball rolling on this whole mess. Finding out your father didn't love your mother, well, at least not enough to be faithful, was enough of a blow. Add that Hilton had been cheating on everyone, including the bank he'd owned and all of its clients, had been another whammy.

Sawyer loved his father. He loved his mother. These things weren't supposed to happen, and without his father being present to explain his actions and his side of the story, Sawyer had had to believe the worst. Of course, the evidence was insurmountable. Every tenet he'd ever held true for his life had, in one moment, been blown to smithereens.

His family, although perhaps a tad dysfunctional—whose family wasn't?—had worked until Hilton's defection had upset the checks and balances of Branch dynamics. Now everyone was in uncharted waters as they reassessed and questioned their relationships with one another.

He exhaled, releasing the tension as he changed into some bike shorts and his riding shirt. It wasn't Craig's fault, and he was simply trying to make things right for everyone. But Sawyer didn't need Gamblers Anonymous. He was a mathematician, not an addict. They were so busy accusing him that he didn't bother explaining.

Sawyer grabbed his racing bike, determined that he wouldn't let the rest of his day go downhill. He'd had a great lunch with Lucy.

As for his debt, it wasn't insurmountable, not for a man of his stature and abilities. No one in his family understood how Sawyer's mind worked, except maybe his father, and that really wasn't a good reference at this juncture.

As for the money, he just needed to win it back, that was all. He planned on starting this weekend.

CHAPTER THREE

"I THOUGHT YOU WERE GIVING up NASCAR," Tanya Wells said as she spooned more of Luigi's fettuccine Alfredo on her friend Lucy's plate. With the intention of sharing, the two women had each ordered something different off the menu.

"It's *Sawyer* Branch, not Bart or Will. He's not at the track every weekend. He's a mathematician," Lucy replied.

The warm breeze blew, lightly lifting her hair. She'd been wearing it loose around her shoulders lately. She told herself it wasn't because she hoped she'd run into Sawyer, but honestly, who was she trying to kid?

He'd been all she'd been able to think about this past weekend, even with the visit to her sister's house in Asheville to keep her mind off things.

"You don't even need six degrees of separation. That's only one degree away," Tanya said.

Lucy finished giving Tanya some of her lasagna and handed her plate back. They were sitting outside in the restaurant's courtyard on the Wednesday following Lucy's Friday lunch date with Sawyer.

Tanya had been the one to suggest lunch, and needing to confide in someone besides family about Sawyer, Lucy had quickly agreed when Tanya had phoned that morning.

"Although, I'm only one degree, too. You could always come to the track with me, you know," Tanya continued.

"I know," Lucy conceded.

"Giving up racing is like you giving up chocolate. Lucy, you're not going to be able to do it. You should just give up. And just because Sawyer is related to Will and Bart shouldn't make him off-limits."

"I wasn't thinking that," Lucy said.

"I know you. You were," Tanya said. "You're forgetting that we used to hang out all the time while Kent and Justin were racing."

"Oh, I remember." Tanya had provided a welcome ear many times.

"Then you should know I know when you're lying," Tanya said. "Even if I haven't seen you for a few months. It's not like you had to lie low."

Lucy sighed. "True. But Justin started dating Sophia and for a while there I felt awkward. I mean, she'll be your sister-in-law."

"I do understand why you did it," Tanya said. Kent's sister, Sophia, was now engaged to Justin.

"You also seemed to need some time alone with just Kent. You didn't need my problems distracting you," Lucy pointed out.

"It was a bit of a rough go there for a while," Tanya admitted. She and Kent had endured a few personal trials over the past few months, including his revelation that he'd been kicked out of State University for cheating in his freshman year. The public disclosure, made during an interview before the Vegas race, had shocked many.

Still, as Tanya had told Lucy, it had been his ability to tell the truth that had finally convinced Tanya that Kent was a man to be trusted and that there would never again be any secrets between them. Things had been great between the couple since. They'd even bought a house, falling in love with the first one they'd seen. The deal had been so good, Tanya and Kent had taken the plunge and closed within weeks.

"Mmm, this is good," Lucy said, letting the cheesy flavor of Luigi's lasagna roll over her tongue. "If I don't watch out, I'm going to spoil myself and start packing on the pounds. I ate two extra slices of deep-dish when I was at Sleeter's with Sawyer. I definitely indulged."

"You've got room to spare. I'm only five three and if I don't work out I pack it on." Tanya lifted a forkful of lasagna to her lips and took a bite. "Oh, this is good. You're right."

"Told you," Lucy said, eating more. The fettuccine Alfredo could wait. Sleeter's had whetted her appetite for red sauce and cheese.

"I haven't been to Sleeter's in forever. And with Sawyer, too. That man is hot. He's like one of those guys you read about in those romance novels. You know, the Greek tycoon coming in to sweep you off your feet. Put him in Armani, add a five o'clock shadow, and ooh la la. Lucky you. I may be engaged to the most wonderful man on the planet but as a photographer, I can appreciate beauty."

Lucy laughed. "Me, too. And I admit, I'm a bit excited that this might be the start of something new. I've replayed our lunch date multiple times, analyzing every minute."

"Don't you love how women do that?" Tanya asked. "We females microscope everything."

"We do," Lucy agreed. "It was a good date. Casual yet…I don't know. I sensed something. I liked that he was so open and honest with me. Guys as good-looking as Sawyer are often players, but he was the polar opposite."

"So, has he asked you out again?" Tanya interrupted.

Lucy sobered slightly as Tanya's words burst her bubble. "Therein is the problem. He didn't ask for my phone number. He said he had a math project this weekend. He said he'd run into me at work and maybe we'd do lunch again. I don't think it was a brush-off but I haven't seen him, either."

"I'm sure it wasn't," Tanya reassured, polishing off the lasagna. "Guys are strange like that. They're secretive without even trying. It's like there's some rule book they follow that no one but them is privy to. If we had a copy, we'd know what was going on inside their heads. I swear it's usually nothing, but what do I know?"

Lucy laughed a little at that. "Yeah, a rule book would be something, wouldn't it? If I'd had one of those maybe I'd have saved myself some grief had I realized long before February that Justin and I were not compatible for the long haul. We'd been having some problems, but I chose simply to ignore them. I think I enjoyed my position more than the relationship. I mean, Justin Murphy was my boyfriend. How many other women would have killed to be in my shoes?"

"Speaking of Justin." Tanya's tone turned hesitant. "There's something I wanted to ask you."

Lucy thought she had an inkling of where this was going. "If it's to be nice to Kent's sister, that's fine. I'm not getting in the way of his and Sophia's happiness. I realize now that Justin and I would have made each other miserable if we'd continued dating. They seem happy together and I'm glad for them."

Tanya appeared relieved. "Well, it does involve Sophia but not in the way you think. Kent's worried about her."

Lucy's brow creased. "Why? Justin's not that bad of a guy. He'll treat her with respect, especially if he really loves her. He's not the philandering kind. He's actually a great guy. He was never disrespectful."

Tanya shook her head. "That's not it at all." She hesitated and glanced around. No one was seated near them. "Promise me that you won't repeat what I'm about to tell you."

"This sounds serious," Lucy said, her fork hovering over her plate.

"I don't even know where to start," Tanya said honestly. She took a drink of the iced tea she'd ordered. "The whole thing sounds like a bad B-movie plot, but it's all true. Whatever you do, you can't repeat what I'm about to say. Please. There are too many lives at stake and I don't want to see Kent worry anymore."

Lucy set her fork down. "You're starting to worry me. Of course I promise. You know I'd never do anything to hurt either of you. And I'm not a gossip."

Tanya nodded. "I know that. It's not that I don't trust you. I do, or I wouldn't be revealing this or be asking for your help."

"You need my help?" Lucy had no clue where this was going.

"Yes. Let me start at the beginning. It makes more sense that way, although really, it's all a nightmare. It began with an e-mail Kent received. Actually, he got two. The first one's subject line read 'Y U left State U.' It was really strange. I mean the subject line contained the letters *Y* and

U. Not even spelled out. That's usually how spammers write. Here, I brought copies."

Tanya dug in her purse and withdrew two crumpled sheets of paper. She passed over the first one. "If you read that you'll see that it refers to the cheating scandal."

"Which Kent owned up to to the press in Vegas," Lucy said.

Tanya's lower lips quivered slightly. She was definitely uneasy about something. "The trouble is that this e-mail arrived before *Daytona.* This was one of the reasons he had to come forward. I wish it ended there, but it didn't. Another e-mail arrived before the California race. This one was worse."

Tanya slid the next sheet over and Lucy began to read. The header read U Know Who Killed Troy Murphy and then the contents of the e-mail claimed that Patsy Grosso, Kent's mother, had been the one to run Troy down. The e-mail also contained a grainy photo of Patsy behind the wheel of a pickup truck. Worse, in the foreground of the photo was the rural bar where Troy died, a few cars in the lot, and a shadowy figure, presumably Troy, coming out the door. Troy was Justin's father and he'd also been a race car driver, although not a successful one.

"This is horrible," Lucy said, reading the last line. From dating Justin, Lucy knew how much the Murphy and the Grosso families hated each other. Both had been in NASCAR since the beginning and their feud went back almost as many years. The Murphy family still maintained that Dean Grosso had been the one to kill Troy even though he had a solid alibi.

"I can't believe anyone would do something like this!" Lucy exclaimed, trying to make sense of it all.

Tanya's lip quivered. "Neither can I. I mean, who would doctor a photo and then demand $100,000? I found the original photo the blackmailer used. It came from an old magazine article. None of this is real. It's all faked."

The sender had done a decent job. Lucy's first impression had been that the photo was genuine. "So what did Kent do?"

"Kent never responded. He let the blackmail deadline pass and nothing further ever came out of it. We were thinking that it might be some kind of a sick joke, you know, something to blow his concentration before a big race."

That made sense. Lucy returned the sheets of paper to Tanya. "So why worry about these e-mails now? It's been more than three months since they arrived. It's May and this first one was in February?"

"Yeah. Kent and I didn't want to make too much of it, but the problem is, the more time marches on, the more we both believe that Justin might be the person who sent the e-mails."

From the torn expression crossing Tanya's face, Lucy knew how much this whole situation pained her friend.

Tanya continued, "Could there have been others to come? I don't know. Justin's now dating Sophia. She's besotted with him and it's serious. If he sent those e-mails to Kent to shake his concentration, and if he's the culprit…"

Her voice trailed off and she looked away, studying some of the tiles embedded in the courtyard wall. Then she reconnected her gaze to Lucy's. "I think we need to know the truth, especially since we just put a chunk of change down on the house. I don't want to get blackmailed next month or next year. Everyone knows the Grosso and the Murphy families have been enemies and rivals for years. If it *is* Justin who's done this, it could break Sophia's heart. She's going to be my sister-in-law. And before I go further, let me tell you how awkward this is. I'm here, asking one of my good friends to see if she can help investigate her ex-boyfriend."

"It is a bit disconcerting," Lucy admitted. "But I'm okay with it. As I said earlier, I know Justin wasn't the one for me. I'm not a petty person who holds grudges."

"Of course you're not," Tanya said quickly. "I never meant to insinuate…"

"I know you didn't," Lucy reassured. "I might be a little bitter, but it's not at Justin. I'm mad at fate for dealing me a bad hand. By now, I wanted to be married with kids, and be happy like my parents and my sisters. I don't want to give up hope, but I'm not getting younger. I'm sounding desperate and I hate that, but I also hate to think that marriage isn't in the cards for my life."

"Maybe Sawyer's that guy," Tanya offered with a lifting of her shoulders. "You never know."

"No, which is why I'll get back out there on the dating circuit, starting with Sawyer," Lucy admitted. "It'd be much easier to be a hermit than to suffer any more rejection. But like all things, finding the love of my life is going to take work. I refuse to be afraid of that, no matter how painful dating can be at times."

"So do you think Kent and I are wrong in pursuing this? Besides protecting ourselves, we only want to help Sophia. Neither of us wants to see her hurt," Tanya pressed.

"If it *is* Justin, I'd prefer he doesn't hurt anyone, either," Lucy said. As for Justin being the blackmailer, Lucy couldn't rule out that possibility. She wouldn't put something like this past him, especially if it might help him get ahead in the points. "So Kent is in agreement with you? You told him you were talking to me?"

Tanya nodded and waved off the approaching waiter. "Yes. We don't keep secrets anymore. We both talked this over and thought that you might be someone who could help us, but we wanted to wait until you were over Justin. So can you help?" Tanya asked, her tone pleading.

Lucy's chin moved up and down, signaling her acceptance of the challenge. She loved to problem-solve, and this one intrigued her. "I think I want to know the truth myself. Sending those e-mails is something he might do, especially if he thought it would give him some sort of mental advantage out on the race track. While he's for the most part an honest guy, Justin's not afraid to play a little dirty when his career's on the line. But this second e-mail, I admit, it does feel a little off."

Lucy gestured and Tanya again passed over the printout. Lucy studied it. Something bothered her about the whole tone of the e-mail.

"What is your instinct saying?" Tanya asked.

"I don't mean to insult the man, but Justin's not clever enough to doctor a photo like this. He's about grease and engines, not Photoshop. However, given the contents and the fact that he is a Murphy, who knows? Maybe he had help. Justin uses Web mail for all his correspondence because he travels so much. I set Outlook Express up for him on his desktop, but he never bothered to use it."

Tanya frowned. "I'm not following you."

"Justin uses Web mail exclusively. That means Justin doesn't download any e-mails onto his personal computer.

He logs onto the Internet and goes from there. Unless he's changed everything, which I doubt, I still have all his passwords. I can do a little digging into his Sent folder without him being the wiser. I'll let you know what I find."

"Thank you. You don't know how relieved this makes me," Tanya said, thankful she had secured Lucy's help.

"I'm just glad you and Kent are in agreement that I do this," Lucy said, passing the e-mail printout back over.

Tanya bobbed her head vigorously to emphasize her point. "Oh, we are. Don't worry, things have never been better between us. That's why we decided not to ignore the matter any longer. Even though the e-mails stopped, we'd like to know who sent them, if only to put the matter behind us once and for all."

"What will you do if I find out it was Justin?" Lucy asked.

Tanya tapped her fingers on the table in rapid staccato. "I don't know. Kent and I discussed that. I mean, what do we do? Do we confront him? Do we continue to ignore the e-mails unless another one arrives? We really didn't come up with an answer so we agreed we'd cross that bridge when we came to it."

"And if it isn't Justin?" Lucy probed.

"That's even more scary," Tanya admitted. "As I said earlier, this is like some cut-rate spy thriller, only it's my life. Heck, I've given up trying to understand why this happened. The whole thing has been driving me crazy and I want to just concentrate on Kent, our careers and on getting married."

"I'll do whatever I can," Lucy promised, sensing that her words gave her friend some solace. She empathized with Tanya although she couldn't imagine being in the situation herself. And it would be easy enough to check Justin's e-mails. Of course, the header said Bob Smith. But e-mail headers and addresses could be faked pretty easily. All one had to do was look at the spam sent daily to know how common bogus addresses were.

"So Sawyer, huh?" Tanya asked, changing the subject and getting back to eating her fettuccine.

"Yeah, maybe," Lucy answered, picking up her fork so she could finish eating. "He's different from anyone I've met. Maybe it's the math thing. He didn't laugh when I told him I took extra math classes to boost my GPA."

"So it's a match made in geek heaven. Not that you're a geek. Or him," Tanya added quickly. "He's too sexy for that."

Lucy smiled as she thought of Sawyer. "Yeah, he is hot and bothersome, isn't he? No man should be that good-looking. But he doesn't wear his sexiness on his sleeve or have any type of egotistical attitude about his appearance. He hardly noticed the women looking at him, and let me tell you, there were plenty giving him a double take."

"Blinders on, that's a good sign in a man. A guy should only have eyes for you," Tanya confirmed. "Or his race car."

"I'm done with race cars."

"Then he'll only be looking at you," Tanya said, and they both laughed and continued to talk until the bill arrived. Tanya snagged it first. "I've got it. My treat for helping me out. It's the least I can do. Remember, I'm around all weekend."

"Photography gig?" Tanya was a very sought-after wedding photographer.

"Yes. Normally I'd fly out to see Kent, but the wedding

I'm doing has a brunch that they want photographed. Seems the nuptials don't end until the bride and groom leave early Sunday evening for a two-week Hawaiian cruise."

"That sounds nice," Lucy said, remembering her conversation with Sawyer.

"Yeah, it does, and I guess it'll give me time to work on the house. The people from whom we bought it were relocating to France so they left most of the furniture. But the place still requires those personal touches. Oh, and while I'm thinking about it, Kent and I are considering a Christmas wedding. I'd like you to be one of my bridesmaids."

"Really?" The offer flattered. "Me?"

"Yes, you," Tanya said, her smile wide and infectious. "I promise not to put you in a hideous dress. Believe me, in my line of work I see enough of those."

"I'd be honored," Lucy said. She'd been in both of her sisters' weddings and in a few of her sorority sisters'.

"Great. If you're lucky, you'll still be with Sawyer and I'll toss the bouquet your way."

"We've only had one date, and it was lunch," Lucy protested.

"So?" Tanya said. "I've photographed people who have gotten married after less."

"They're crazy," Lucy said.

"Perhaps, but they pay well." Tanya giggled at that, and while Lucy tried to put the whole matter out of her head after lunch ended, she found herself contemplating weddings as she drove back to her office.

One day it would be her turn to marry. Just not to Justin, as she'd often fantasized while dating him. Like Kent and

Tanya, she and Justin would have had to get married in the off-season if they wanted a real honeymoon. While NASCAR took an occasional weekend off here and there, for the most part drivers had little free time from February to November.

Then again, testing filled the off-season as race shops worked to perfect the next season's vehicle setups. Teams also tested during the week; in fact, so long as it didn't rain, NASCAR was hosting sanctioned testing in Charlotte today and tomorrow.

So was Justin Murphy responsible for the e-mails?

Lucy found herself unsettled as she parked her car. Maybe her easy acceptance of Tanya's request was rooted in a desire for revenge. Even though Lucy was happy for Justin and Sophia, part of her wished Justin hadn't found someone so fast. He'd wounded her pride by not mourning their breakup. Nope, he'd immediately fallen in love with someone from his family's enemy camp, while Lucy was still alone.

Lucy entered her office and glanced around. With her recent promotion she'd moved to a room with a view, albeit the parking lot.

"Hey, Lucy, while you were at lunch you had a visitor." Marcie, the department's administrative assistant, stood in Lucy's doorway.

"Who was it?" Lucy asked, figuring it was someone from the hospital's administration wing. They always needed something, and for some reason, even with getting new computers installed within the past six months, they seemed to have the most problems.

"He didn't give his name, but he did leave you a note." Marcie came forward and handed over a pink message slip.

The contact information had been left blank, but Lucy knew instantly. Sawyer. Who else would have written in a bold scrawl, "Came by to see if you wanted to go to Sleeter's. Will try again."

A warm, fuzzy feeling settled over her. He hadn't blown her off.

"Thanks," she said, ignoring Marcie's curious expression. Lucy read the note again, then clutched it to her chest as if it was gold.

She shouldn't be so giddy that he'd stopped by, but she was. Heck, she hadn't had this type of a tingle since…high school. Oh, God. She was acting like a silly schoolgirl. That was a bad sign, right?

Lucy entered her password, unlocked her computer and regrouped by checking her e-mail. She'd had enough heartbreak in the past few months that she certainly didn't need to go gaga over some sexy man who'd simply taken her to lunch. That would be foolish.

She finished the reports she had due and at 5:00 p.m. pressed the button to turn off her computer.

The standby/restart/turn off menu appeared and, after a moment's hesitation, Lucy clicked on the fourth choice, a small horizontal cancel button in the lower-right corner. Her screen brightened and Lucy hit the Internet Explorer shortcut.

Within minutes she'd logged into Justin Murphy's e-mail account. She tried to ignore reading anything in his in-box, but couldn't help but noticing the massive number of e-mails from sender Sophia Grosso. The subject headings were such simple things as Love You and Last Night Was Good. He had a few e-mails from friends whose names she recognized and several from his crew chief.

Slightly creeped out by what she was doing, Lucy didn't scroll down to see if any of her messages were still in his folder.

Instead she double-clicked on his sent messages icon. She ignored the bazillion e-mails to Sophia and scrolled lower, watching the dates. There were a few to her. Happier times, Lucy thought with a small, sad smile. She recognized a subject line and remembered that particular e-mail from Justin, sent early on when she'd been naive and believing that they could work things out.

She swallowed hard, forced herself to go on and studied every e-mail subject header and to whom Justin had sent that message.

She went as far back as December but found nothing. If Justin was the blackmailer, he hadn't sent the e-mails from this account.

She logged out, erased her history and her computer cookies and shut the machine down. Then she used her cell phone and called Tanya from the car on her way home.

"Justin didn't send it from his own Web mail," she told her friend when she answered.

"No?" A crackle of thunder caused a bit of static. Rain was moving into the area.

"No, he didn't." Lucy navigated the late-afternoon traffic and headed the fifteen miles toward her condo, which was located in a newer part of town. She'd forgotten her yoga gear, and if this stoplight didn't change, she was going to be about five minutes late to the YMCA where she took her classes. Worse, if the sky opened up, she was going to get drenched.

"So could he have used another e-mail?" Tanya asked.

Lucy braked as a car cut her off, glad she had the phone

in its hands-free unit. "Yes. He could have used another e-mail. If I'm going to figure out where these things come from, I need to take a look at the e-mail properties."

"What are those?"

Lucy tried to explain in layman's terms. "Where and when the e-mail came from, and how it traveled. It's part of the actual e-mail itself. Do you think Kent would let me use his computer? I'd like to see the originals if he hasn't deleted them, not just printouts."

"I'll ask him. He's testing today so he's at the track. I wouldn't want to say yes without talking to him first."

"Why don't you speak with him and let me know a good time when I can come over. He can be there or not, it doesn't matter. It's whatever you and Kent are more comfortable with. I'm unfortunately very free over the next few days, so I can be at your disposal."

"You could come hang out with me at the wedding I'm working this weekend if you want. I'm allowed to bring a guest," Tanya offered.

The idea appealed, for about a second. While hanging out with Tanya would give Lucy an excuse to get out of her house, it wasn't necessarily fun to go to someone's wedding you didn't know and sit by yourself while Tanya did her photography thing. "I think I'm going to pass, but thanks for the offer. Since I'm not traveling much anymore, I'm thinking about getting a kitten. Probably not this weekend, but it's on my radar. I should probably clean house, do some research into pet ownership. Maybe visit a shelter."

"Once you find one, there are plenty of pet-sitters and pet-boarding places around here that cater to the NASCAR teams," Tanya said.

Yeah, but those all probably cost an exorbitant amount of money, Lucy thought. She pulled into her assigned parking space. "Hey, Tanya, I'm home. I have to get inside and grab my yoga gear. How about you call me when you know something?"

"Will do. Hey, Lucy." Tanya's voice stopped Lucy from disconnecting. "You've been around the track and know everyone. If it's not Justin, who do you think it could be that would do this?"

That was the part that really bothered her, the information Lucy now wanted to learn for herself. She grabbed her purse and gave Tanya the only answer she had. "I have absolutely no idea."

THE SKIES HAD DARKENED considerably by the time Sawyer Branch strolled through the garage area. NASCAR was hosting testing today, and he'd wanted to see his brothers, offer a show of solidarity and support, which he hadn't given in the last few months. Whereas driving wasn't for him, Sawyer loved the track. So many numbers. So much applied mathematics.

The garage was full of cars, some painted and others simply primer-gray metal. All around crew members for the various race teams worked on perfecting setups. NASCAR officials hovered, recording data for their own purposes.

Sawyer knew NASCAR tracked loads of data, on everything from lap times to fuel economy, making for a mathematician's dream. If he didn't teach college, Sawyer could envision himself working for NASCAR doing something with numbers and race statistics.

He passed the empty stall of Justin Murphy, who was currently out on the track. This afternoon Sawyer had found himself needing a break from writing his dissertation. His visit to the hospital had been unproductive—Lucy had been out to lunch with a friend. So he decided to visit his brothers.

He had to admit that he'd never thought his older brothers would stick with driving. Will and Bart had started racing in high school and their father had bought them midgets. They'd begun more as a lark; they'd heard that aside from playing guitar being a race car driver was the ultimate way to meet women.

Their father had taken to auto racing like a duck to water. He'd hired Will and Bart coaches so they could compete in the NASCAR Whelen All-American Series. Hilton had embraced the suite life and had two divisions of BMT sponsor his boys so they could work their way up. At the track in Texas, he'd held great parties in the fabulous private enclosed seating above Turn One.

Lightning flashed and thunder boomed as the storm moved in. The cars roared off the track and into the garage area, making it to safety before the skies opened up and dumped a hard rain. Bart took off his helmet, slid out of the car and spoke for a few minutes to Philip Whalen, his crew chief. Then Bart saw Sawyer and ambled over, his uniform now unzipped to the waist.

At six two, Bart was three inches taller and he weighed thirty-five pounds more than his brother. Compared to most drivers, Bart was a large man. "Hey," he said in greeting. "What's up?"

"Not much," Sawyer said, falling in step as Bart made his way to his hauler. "Thought I'd come by, see how things were going. I offered to do some calculations, but Phil said they'd gotten the data they needed."

"We're lucky. The car's good. We're trying a new setup. We need a break. I gotta get in the top ten a lot more. I owe it to Richard, my car owner. So how's everything with you? Handling that matter?"

Sawyer knew his brother meant the hundred-thousand-dollar debt Craig had exposed. They dodged the fat rain-drops as they ran the short distance to the hauler. "I'm about halfway there."

Bart seemed pleased. "Good. Anita's really worried this will hit the press. Last thing I need is bad P.R. I'm not driving well enough as it is."

"I told everyone I'd take care of it. You know I'll make good," Sawyer insisted. They stepped into the lounge area of the hauler and Bart began taking off his uniform, starting with the shoes.

"I guess no one believes you," Bart said. He saw Sawyer's expression. "Hey, don't get mad at me. Look at all your various career plans and not one of them came to fruition. Now you're wasting your life away gambling under the guise of mathematics."

Sawyer had been wrong to come. "It's not like that. I told you before. It's a card-counting ring and—"

Bart cut him off. "Sawyer, I've been to Vegas several times. I saw the security cameras. I just can't buy that ex-planation. Card counters get caught. You get made."

"I told you Jake—" Sawyer began to describe his friend's dissertation, but Bart waved his hand and inter-rupted.

"Yeah, another permanent student. Damn, Sawyer, I know this sounds selfish, but what you're doing affects me. I've already lost everything. Richard is on my case. Anita's worried. Heck, I've taken up personal training with Terri,

Philip's daughter, just to ease the stress. Like my cars, I don't want to hear reasons. I just want results. I need results or everything's going to explode, starting with my head. There better be some acetaminophen in here." Bart began opening cabinet doors.

Sawyer recognized the toll everything had taken on Bart. Anita, Bart's P.R. rep, had helped him find new sponsors. Richard Latimer, his car owner, had stood by him through Hilton's defection. But all of them, including Phil Whalen, Bart's car chief, needed Bart to win. "I'll get the results."

"Good. Do it soon and then quit, okay?" Bart found the headache medicine and washed it down with bottled water. "Now, what else is going on? Dating anyone new? You always were one who could attract the ladies. Will and I used to joke that we had to wear our racing uniform when we stood next to you. If not, we faded into the woodwork."

His brothers had never had a problem attracting women, though, and although he'd planned to tell Bart about Lucy, Sawyer changed his mind. Doing so might doom the relationship, make things public before they had gotten beyond one lunch date. "Nothing new," Sawyer replied.

"We should all go out one night, have a beer. You, me and Will. We haven't done that in ages," Bart said.

"Yeah, that'd be great," Sawyer said, knowing the probability of all their schedules matching to be extremely low.

"Hey, Bart, you in here?"

The voice belonged to Anita, and she came into the front of the hauler. "The media would like to talk to you if you're available."

Bart glanced at himself in the mirror. He'd stripped out of the uniform and wore jeans and a tight T-shirt. He raked his hand through his curly blond hair and touched the cleft in his square jaw. "I guess I'm ready," he told Sawyer. "Yeah, I can be there in a second. You need to get me an EZ-Plus Software hat," he told Anita.

"Will do." She headed back outside.

Bart glanced at Sawyer. "Let's do that beer. Will and I promise no practical jokes."

Sawyer arched an eyebrow. "And I'll believe that when I see it."

Although not as gifted in math as his younger brother, Bart was still highly intelligent. His eyes narrowed as Sawyer threw Bart's earlier words back at him.

"How about you get out of that situation we discussed and Will and I promise we'll never pull another practical joke on you again. Deal?"

Sawyer cracked a smile. "Now, that's some motivation. You have a deal."

Sawyer followed Bart to the tail end of the hauler. Anita's eyes glared when she saw him, but she only said, "Sawyer," to which he replied, "Anita." The media had gathered under the overhang provided by the hauler's gate lift and Bart slipped on his sponsor's ball cap and began taking questions. Sawyer squeezed his way through the crowd, but not before noting the wide-eyed appreciation on some young female reporter's face.

He nodded at her and stepped out into the storm. The rain came down in sheets, pelting him as he strode through the garage area. He stopped for a moment, staring at the No. 427 car belonging to Kent Grosso, who was nowhere in sight. Then he moved on, passing Will's empty garage as well as the cars of Hart Hampton, Ronnie McDougal, Dean Grosso and Justin Murphy.

By now Sawyer was so wet the rain didn't bother him. It plastered his T-shirt tightly across his chest, showing abs he worked out daily for. His tennis shoes squished and his jeans dripped water off the hem. His wet black hair fell into his eyes.

Luckily he had a towel in the Corvette. He turned around to take one last glance. Team members ran around inside the lighted garage, venturing out into the rain only when necessary. Testing was over for the day, cut short by the weather. They'd resume tomorrow once the storm passed.

But Sawyer didn't really mind the rain. He stood there, letting the downpour wash over him. The moment reminded him of those carefree childhood days in Texas when precipitation fell as liquid sunshine. With no threat from lightning or thunder, he'd run outside and played in the water, dancing in it.

Unfortunately, he was now too old to stomp through puddles. He shivered as the colder air came through. Time to go. There were no do-overs in life. As the rain washed the track clean of rubber, Sawyer realized a fundamental truth. You couldn't go back and relive the past.

CHAPTER FOUR

THE NEXT MORNING DAWNED clear and sunny, the only reminder of last night's drenching thunderstorm evident in greener grass and cleaner-smelling air. Sawyer whistled to himself as he walked out of the pediatric cancer ward.

Johnny was going home today, and Sawyer had come to say goodbye. So far Johnny's new treatment was working. Everyone was more than hopefully optimistic, even Johnny himself. Sawyer had left the hospital room in great spirits.

As Sawyer pressed the elevator button, he let the elation he'd been containing consume him. His algorithm was a success. When applied to Johnny's case, the algorithm, which was basically a set of rules for solving a problem in a finite number of steps, had worked. He'd developed not only a formula for predicting and managing remission rates, but also had programmed the computer to make the calculations. His graduate work had performed flawlessly, the data he'd predicted matching the reality of ninety-five percent of his case studies.

He had mere weeks before he went in front of the committee and presented his Ph.D. dissertation, but privately Larry had told Sawyer that he wasn't going to run into too many issues. For the first time in his life, Sawyer had done good. Real good, to slang his English. There were even whispers that once everything was final, he'd have secured in writing that faculty position he wanted, and his graduate research would mark his first publication on his step to university tenure.

He stepped into the elevator and pressed the button for the lobby. There he transferred to the other bank of elevators, the ones leading to the hospital's administrative wing.

He was working under the assumption Lucy had gotten his note and had realized he'd been thinking of her. Sure, he could have gotten her work number from the hospital directory, but he wasn't a phone person. He preferred face-to-face contact. That way he could read the other person's expressions and view the nonverbal body language.

He reached Lucy's floor and approached the reception desk. The lady behind the computer seemed to recognize him from his previous visit, when he'd thought she'd stared at him the entire time.

"I'm looking for Lucy Gunter," Sawyer said, returning her smile with one of his own.

She appeared a bit flustered as he deliberately turned on the charm. "Do you have an appointment?"

"Do I need one?" he asked, keeping his tone light and teasing. This wasn't some super-secretive executive office he was trying to reach.

"No." She laughed at her faux pas and patted the hair behind her left ear. "Let me see if she's available. Who may I tell her is asking to speak with her?"

"Sawyer."

"Just Sawyer?" The woman stared at him. Sawyer pegged her to be about thirty-seven and divorced, if her bare left hand was any indication.

"She'll know I'm not Tom," he joked, and the woman laughed at that and made the call.

"She'll be right out," she said when she put down the phone.

"Great." He glanced at her nameplate. "Thanks, Marcie."

"Oh, it's nothing," Marcie said, and Sawyer eased away, toward two plain plastic chairs pushed up against the wall. He didn't sit and instead studied a piece of generic artwork. Within about a minute, Lucy came around the corner.

"Hey," she said. Lucy glanced at Marcie, who continued to stare at Sawyer. "Come on back."

Marcie gave them a speculative once-over, which Sawyer ignored.

"So how have you been?" Lucy asked as he stopped at her office. She gestured, ushering him inside.

"Fine. Did you get my note?" he asked, surveying her domain. Nothing jumped out. She had a view of the parking lot and her diplomas hung on the walls. There was a picture of her with two other women who looked like they could be her sisters and a few Beanie Babies, which seemed to be a prerequisite for every female desk.

"Marcie gave me your message. I was out at lunch with Tanya when you came by."

She was playing it cool, aloof. Casual. "So how was your weekend?" he asked.

"Fine," she said.

Ah, the one word answer he hated most—and one he'd just used himself. How are you? Fine. Are you okay? I'm fine. *Fine* said nothing. Maybe he should have called or tried again sooner. He reflected a moment on what Bart had said. Sawyer might attract the women, but his brothers held their interest longer.

He hoped he hadn't already lost Lucy's. He enjoyed her company and wanted to get to know her better.

"Would you like to get a cup of coffee? Get out of the office for a bit? Today is actually my last visit. I came in for Johnny's going-home party and I wanted to see you before I left. I probably won't be back."

"Oh." She seemed a bit surprised. She flushed slightly, her face turning a delightful pink shade that contrasted with her green silk shirt. She also wore a long, matching floral skirt, giving him only a peek at those nice, toned legs hidden underneath.

He'd learned enough of fashion from his sister Penny's modeling career to recognize when clothes were designer label, and hers weren't. She was a normal, average American middle-class working girl who immediately rose in his esteem. He'd dated a few of his sister's friends and found them too high-strung. They worried too much about their weight and their clothes to be any fun. The last thing he wanted was to date someone like that again.

He pressed her for an answer. "So, does the cafeteria sound okay? I know that you have your cell phone so work can reach you." He grinned then, trying to charm her. Quite a few women had described his smile as one of his best assets, but he hadn't cared until now—when he wanted Lucy to say yes.

She gave in and the corners of her mouth inched upward. "Yeah, I can take a break. Let's go celebrate your newfound freedom."

"It's a tad bittersweet," he admitted as they went through the cafeteria line. "I'm ready to graduate and finally be out in the real world, but I've made a lot of friends here."

They sat down and he watched as she took a bite of cake, wrapping her lips around the tines of the fork as she drew the chocolate inside her mouth. She had no idea the rote movement was making parts of him a tad uncomfortable.

She took a drink to wash the food down and said, "You seem like the type to keep in touch."

"I'll find out," Sawyer said. He'd watched her eat pizza backward and now the cake. "I don't want to lose touch with you, that's for sure."

She looked up and blinked.

"Seriously," he added.

She leaned back in the red plastic cafeteria chair and studied him to see if he was serious. "Are you asking me out again?"

"Yeah," he nodded. "A date." Heck, he'd thought of little else, and it hadn't helped his concentration much this past weekend. Jake had commented on his lack of attention during a round of blackjack. Still, Sawyer had come out on the plus side, so that had to say something, right? He hadn't won as much as he would have preferred, but he hadn't lost. He suddenly had an idea.

"Look, I have some business to attend to this weekend, but next weekend the NASCAR Sprint Cup Series race is here in Charlotte. I know you said you're giving up NASCAR, but would you like to go to the track with me? I've been invited to watch from Richard Latimer's suite and I can bring a guest. I'd like it if you'd join me."

She stared at him, and when she didn't answer right away he began to get nervous. Maybe the track reminded her too much of Justin. She'd indicated…he'd thought…

"I'm sorry. My offer was probably insensitive especially since you indicated…." He let his words trail off lest he make the situation worse.

Her lips thinned. "I liked racing before Justin. I don't want to lose that, even if I said I was giving it up. Racing's like chocolate cake. I like it too much."

He waited as she took another second to contemplate his offer. Her blue eyes blinked when she reached her decision and Sawyer found himself on the edge of his seat.

"I think I'd like to go with you. Besides, it might do me good. You know, that 'once you fall off a horse you've got to get right back on' type of thing."

Sawyer's outward composure didn't reflect the pent-up tension he'd experienced while he waited for her answer. "Bart got me a hard card. I'll get you a pass."

"I still have mine from Justin's team, which is valid for the season. No one told me I couldn't use it so I think it's still good."

He nodded. "Should be. This'll be fun."

She brushed a hair away from her face and took another bite of cake. "I think so."

He reached out then, covered her free hand with his. The touch lasted only a brief second, but it was enough to convey his message. "Good. I'd like to take you out a few times. I've thought of little else since our lunch."

At that moment her cell phone began ringing. She glanced at the number. "Hold on a moment," she told Sawyer before she answered the call. "Hey, Tanya, can I call you back? I'm having coffee with Sawyer. Let me get back to my desk and we'll gab." She clicked off.

"Tanya Wells?" he queried, because she knew he'd overheard the conversation.

"Yes. Girl stuff."

He grinned sheepishly. "My sister used to do girl stuff. I learned to flee the house when her friends came over. You two have fun."

"We will," Lucy said.

His arms were resting on the table, and he flexed his fingers to keep the blood flowing. For a moment there he'd been afraid she'd reject him. For some reason, her saying yes had really mattered, unlike other women he'd dated.

She reached into her purse and drew out a pen and a business card. "Work's on here already, but this is my home number." She wrote on the back and passed the cream-colored card over to him.

"Thanks. I probably won't have a chance to call this weekend, but I will on Monday."

She shook her head, the hair she wore down around her shoulders swishing. "You'll call when you call," she said, her tone nonchalant.

"Monday," he insisted. "Just know, I'm a guy who keeps his word, but on occasion I get caught up in a math problem. When that happens it's like being dropped into a big black void. I don't surface until I've solved what I'm working on. But for you, I will."

"Some of those problems can take weeks," she said.

He grinned as he grabbed the napkin in front of him and began writing. "Yeah. Which is why I'm owning up to it now. It's not an ignoring game I'm playing. I get so busy or so mired down I forget to eat."

She gave a pointed glance at his clean cake plate. He laughed. "Okay, I eat in spurts."

Her smile reassured him and he passed her the napkin with his phone number.

"Thanks. And now, I do have to get back to work. So not this, but next Sunday," she confirmed.

"We'll make a day of it," Sawyer promised. He said goodbye to her in the cafeteria, as Lucy insisted on walking back to her office alone.

He watched her exit, her skirt swishing around her legs. A moment later, his phone rang. He glanced at the number and answered. "Hey, Jake."

"Hey, Sawyer. Ready for this weekend? We've decided to hit Bennetton's. I don't think they have a line on us yet. To them, we're just regular guys out for a good time on the town."

Sawyer returned the cafeteria trays, balancing them in one hand as he held his cell in the other. "Yeah, but remember, I'm graduating soon. So are you. We need to be winding this scheme down. We've had a good run and taken in a lot of money, but my presentation is coming up and…" He thought about Lucy. "I've got other things on my mind, like moving back into the real world at some point."

If he didn't, he'd probably lose any shot at Lucy. She wasn't the type to put up with nonsense, which was one of the things he liked about her.

Jake's tone was scornful. "Yeah, but it's not as if any of us fit in that real world. I just need a few more big scores and then I'm going to be all set."

Having grown up with money, Sawyer couldn't relate to the desperation of those who'd lived without. Even with his father's debacle, Sawyer knew he was fortunate. He'd insulated himself by not spending foolishly. He had thirty thousand sitting in his personal account, something the feds investigating his father couldn't touch as it wasn't located in a Branch bank but rather at one of their competitors here in Charlotte.

Sure, Sawyer had that huge loan hanging over his head. But he had a plan. One that benefited everyone. He only needed time. For a moment he wondered what Lucy would think about his *hobby*. He had a feeling that like his family, she wouldn't understand. Better not to even bring it up.

"I'll be on the five o'clock flight. You'll see me late tonight. You know the drill," he told Jake as he disconnected.

Sawyer walked to his car and drove the short distance to his condo so he could pack. He hadn't lied earlier when talking to Lucy. He had business to take care of this weekend. He was headed to the City of Lights to indulge in a little pastime called blackjack. He was headed back to Vegas.

The card-counting ring was ready to play again.

CHAPTER FIVE

LUCY RETURNED TANYA'S phone call as soon as she reached her office. "So what's up?"

Tanya giggled. "You tell me. Coffee with Sawyer. That's a pretty good sign. What is this, informal date number two?"

"Perhaps." Lucy twisted the phone cord between her fingers, not wanting to make the situation into more than it was. "He stopped by. Today was his last day at the hospital and he dropped in to say goodbye to one of the young patients he's been working with. The boy was discharged today."

"And…?" Tanya prompted.

Lucy caved. She was a little excited. It was nice to be pursued and the news was much too good to keep to herself. "He asked me out. To the race next weekend. We're going to watch it from Richard Latimer's suite."

"Enjoy that AC. I'll be out on the pit box."

Lucy recognized Tanya's jest. While many wives and significant others often watched the races from their motor homes and then made their way to Victory Lane if necessary, Tanya loved being on the top of the war wagon. Lucy had sat atop Justin's once or twice, but as she was only a "girlfriend," she hadn't felt part of the team but rather in the way. More often than not, she'd watched the race by herself in his motor home, the Manor.

"So you and Sawyer have another date, that's awesome," Tanya continued. "Will you see him before that?"

"He said he has business to take care of this weekend but that he'd call me on Monday."

"I'm glad. That sounds like a plan."

"Yeah, but now I'm not sure what part of relationships is the worst. The beginning, middle or end," Lucy said with a sigh. She swiveled and stared at the parking lot, locating her car in its usual spot. "You know when things are too good to be true they often are."

"I used to believe that, especially when Kent was keeping secrets from me. But we worked through our trust issues and we're stronger and more in love than before. So maybe this won't end. Maybe he's the one. You never know."

"It's far too soon to tell," Lucy said hastily.

She heard Tanya scoff. "Oh, come on. Admit that every woman judges every man immediately as to his potential to be *the one*. We size them up and have them rated within the first half hour of saying hello."

Lucy smiled despite herself. "Yeah, we do. But my size-o-meter's off since I've run through a string of bad ones."

"Practice makes perfect," Tanya quipped. "So since you're free this weekend, how about coming over Sunday afternoon to access the computer? I have that wedding Saturday and Kent's racing Saturday night in the All-Star Challenge, but Sunday we're both open with no plans. He offered to grill steaks out on our new deck. Let me tell you, the man can cook and he's in heaven having an outdoor grilling space. Maybe we should have bought a house sooner. He likes to relax by mowing the grass. Who would have thought?"

"I heard some of the drivers like to do that."

"They do and Kent's one of them," Tanya said. "There's even one who mows the lawn at the race shop he owns with his wife. I guess I should be grateful I don't have a dirt go-kart track out in the backyard like one of the wives I know. So, say about four?"

"Sounds perfect," Lucy confirmed.

"Great. Kent's looking forward to seeing you again."

Sunday afternoon about four-fifteen, Lucy drove up into the circular driveway of Kent and Tanya's new house on Lake Norman. Tanya ushered Lucy toward the back sunporch where Kent was reading the local newspaper. He stood up and gave her a quick hug. "Hi, Lucy. Great to see you again."

Lucy had always gotten along well with Kent Grosso, last year's NASCAR Sprint Cup Series champion. Despite her dating Justin, his family's "enemy," Kent had always had a kind word for Lucy, especially when she and Tanya had begun their friendship.

"Can I get you anything to drink?" Tanya asked.

"Water is fine," Lucy replied. She sat down on a brown wicker chair covered with matching floral fabric. The vaulted sunporch offered a fantastic view of the lake, which was quite busy with people out skiing or fishing as the spring temperatures were ten degrees warmer than normal. The sunlight glinted off the rippling water, washing up against the dock where a runabout was hoisted up on its lift.

"The boat came with the house. We got really lucky," Tanya said before disappearing inside to get Lucy some water.

"So Tanya tells me Justin didn't send the e-mails," Kent said, putting down his paper.

"Not from his Web mail," Lucy replied, pulling her gaze back from the million-dollar view. Her condo had a twenty-by-thirty-foot backyard, enough for a small table, chairs and a few flowers along the privacy fence that divided her abode from the neighbors'. Kent's perfectly manicured yard stretched to the water's edge, and to enjoy the outdoors, the previous owner had built a deck, swimming pool and smaller pool house.

"How will accessing my e-mail help?" Kent asked, drawing her attention back to the real reason she was here.

"I want to see the source. I'll be able to start tracing the message backward by looking at the e-mail properties. There's a button on your computer that will allow me to do that."

Tanya returned with a tall glass of ice water. "Do what?"

"Access the source of Kent's e-mails. Now, it can get complicated. You'd be amazed at how many layers there can be. It's like passing a note. Each time a different hand touches it, that additional fingerprint blurs the original."

"But there's a way to do it?" Kent asked.

"Maybe. It just might not be simple," Lucy admitted. "It's a process of decoding the code the sender used. If your black-mailer has any common sense, he's not going to send the thing directly from point A to point B. Now, maybe he's just a novice, sending this as a joke. If he's computer illiterate, he might have left a pretty easy trail. If he's an expert, he's going to cover his tracks and have multiple trails for me to trace."

"Then we'd be back to square one," Kent observed.

She knew they'd like things to be simple. The stress he'd endured had almost done their relationship in. "Perhaps. I won't know until I look at your e-mail."

"The computer is in the office."

Lucy and Tanya followed Kent out of the sunporch, through the great room and down a short hall. Kent's domain was done in dark wood tones. One wall of his office had built-in display cases and here he'd showcased some of his racing memorabilia.

"Those are the trophies and mementos I can't bear to have anywhere else. I have to admit, this room sold me on the house." He pointed to an empty shelf. "That's where I plan to put this year's championship trophy. I'm leaving it empty for motivational purposes."

Kent sat down behind his desk, a huge oversize cherry piece that would have been at home in any corporate executive's office. Tanya sunk into the wing chair in front and promptly rearranged her limbs so that one leg was dangling over the side, her heel sliding out of the flip-flop sandal that Lucy knew came from one of the pricier stores in town, not Concord's outlet mall.

Lucy strode around the desk and Kent moved slightly. He'd logged in and accessed his e-mail account. "Open the first message," Lucy asked.

Kent doubled-clicked on the first message, titled "Y U Left State U," and the e-mail popped open. As she'd read on the hard copy, the sender's name was Bob Smith. "Do you mind?" Lucy asked, and Kent, seeing her intention, scooted his chair out of the way. Lucy right-clicked on the sender's name and saw that the return e-mail address was from a Hotmail account.

She sighed. Hotmail was a free e-mail service often maligned. Spammers faked Hotmail addresses with annoying frequency and most of the e-mail didn't ever originate from a genuine Hotmail address. Lucy then clicked on the button marked Message Source. She read the information, confirming that the message didn't come from any legitimate Hotmail server. She also wasn't surprised to see how many servers the e-mail had traveled through, each one adding a layer of complexity. The blackmailer wasn't a novice. He or she knew exactly what he was doing.

Kent peered over her shoulder. "Found anything yet?"

"Only that this person's an expert," Lucy replied honestly. "He understands computers. This will take me a little while, but I think I can handle it."

"That's good," Tanya replied, relief evident in her voice.

Lucy hated to dissuade her friend but knew she must. "Don't get your hopes up. I still have a way to go before I get close to finding out who sent this."

"Here, take my chair," Kent said, rising. "I'm going to fire up the grill and get ready to start cooking. Do strip steaks sound good? I've had them marinating in my special recipe since last night. You're our first houseguest who isn't family."

As she'd skipped lunch, Lucy's mouth had started to water the moment he mentioned steaks. "Sounds delicious," she replied, her brow creasing as she sat in Kent's oversize leather chair and stared at the e-mail. She made herself comfortable and got to work.

"HEY, HOW'S IT GOING?" Tanya asked about an hour and a half later. "Kent pushed dinner back a little. His mom called, so he talked to her for a bit."

"It's going," Lucy said with a resigned sigh. She'd lost

all track of time and she pushed back from the desk and stood. While Kent's chair had been cushy, her body needed a good stretch.

"Are you at a point where you want to stop and eat?"

"Yeah. I'm actually famished and I'm finished here." Lucy kneaded the back of her neck to work out a kink.

Tanya's eyes lit up. "So you know who the black-mailer is?"

Lucy shook her head and rubbed her eyes. "No. I hit a dead end. The only thing I can tell you is that the e-mail came from a public computer at State University. It appears to be in the math department somewhere, but I can't be sure. I don't have a computer schematic of the place."

"Kent's uncle works in their math department," Tanya confided.

"Yeah, but is there a correlation?" Lucy asked. Having taken so many math classes, she knew that often things that seemed random had an underlying pattern.

"Larry helped Kent hide what he did by making it appear that Kent dropped out of State. The truth was he'd cheated and got kicked out, but at that time only Larry and Kent knew the truth. I mean, we all do stupid things when we're in college, don't we? Larry thought he was protecting his nephew."

Lucy suddenly thought about one of her college boy-friends. "Uh, yeah, we all make dumb mistakes at some point," she admitted. "And we all know people who've cheated at one time or another. It's pretty common to use notes and released tests to study from."

"Kent's crime was a little worse. It was college algebra and some money changed hands. So can we find out what computer the e-mail came from?"

Lucy tilted her head, stretching out her neck. "Even if we did, the probability of tracking down the culprit at this point is very low. Kent left years ago. Why would someone care now? The only person there who knows him is his uncle."

"Oh, it couldn't be Larry," Tanya insisted immediately. "He's a bit bookish, but the guy's a genius. He's received quite a few grants. Some really big bucks for the university."

Lucy played devil's advocate. "Still, what do you know about him personally? Maybe he's had a falling-out with the family or something. Maybe he was tired of keeping the secret and this was a way to prod Kent into revealing it."

Tanya thought for a moment. "Yeah, that makes sense, if you only consider the first e-mail. But it doesn't fit the second one, which was much more vicious. Threatening to reveal that Patsy was responsible for Troy Murphy's death and doctoring a picture is just evil. Why would Larry want to do that?"

"I agree with you, which is why we're at a dead end." Lucy closed Kent's e-mail program and stepped away from the machine. She massaged her temples. Something about this whole blackmail situation was simply off. She couldn't put her finger on what was bothering her.

She knew the math building well. She'd taken classes there. Sawyer took classes there now. Could he be involved? His brothers competed against Kent. This whole thing had given her a small headache.

"Maybe it's for the best if we don't know," Tanya replied. "Larry's wife died suddenly a few years ago and losing her affected him deeply. He doesn't date or get out much. I think the fact he can quote just about every sports statistic scares people off. He also has no sense of style. Not like Sawyer. That man always dresses fine."

Lucy agreed that everything looked good on Sawyer. The other day his shirt had showcased a chest that simply begged to be touched.

"He does." Lucy paced for a moment. Maybe she could pick Sawyer's brain. See if he knew anything. She winced. He hadn't even been at State when Kent was there. This was all silly. "Maybe I'll have Sawyer give me a tour of the math department or something. See what the computer labs look like."

"What a good idea. You can kill two birds with one stone. You'll get information about where the e-mail came from and get to spend time with your guy."

"He's not my guy," Lucy answered automatically.

"Yet," Tanya teased as she and Lucy walked out onto the back deck. "I have a feeling you'll solve that problem with Sawyer in no time flat. How are the steaks coming?" she called to Kent.

"About done," Kent replied, smiling at his fiancée. He dropped a light kiss onto Tanya's lips and Lucy felt a momentary pang of jealousy. Natural under the circumstances, she reassured herself. She was twenty-seven and very single. She fully admitted to wanting a love like the one Tanya and Kent seemed to share.

Could Sawyer be her future? Tanya was correct that women sized up a guy to his potential. Sawyer had passed the first test, but it was far too soon to be serious.

And now he was a suspect. She felt a bit guilty about using him to help Tanya and Kent. This clandestine stuff wasn't her.

She brushed off her slight feeling of unease. Logically, seeing State University was part of getting to know Sawyer better.

However, the conundrum bothered her when she arrived home later that night. She stared out at her tiny backyard, which was at least shaded in the summer as it had a good-size tree on the other side of the fence. She debated for a moment, and then picked up her phone. She'd learned to confront her problems head-on, and before she lost her nerve, she dialed Sawyer's number.

SAWYER GLANCED DOWN AT the ten of spades in his hand and frowned as his cell phone vibrated in his pants pocket. He ignored the device, placed the card facedown on the table and announced flatly, "I'm good."

The dealer nodded, moved to the person on Sawyer's left and gave him a card. The man groaned and flipped up his cards, revealing he'd busted.

The dealer finished and drew a card for himself. Sawyer's expression didn't change and his eyes didn't flicker. He'd long mastered the poker face and air of aloofness he carried with him on these trips. If Jake's formula remained correct, the next card would be a four or five. The dealer turned it over, revealing the five of hearts. He stood at nineteen and all around him, Sawyer's tablemates flipped over their cards, some losing, a few others winning.

Sawyer turned his card over, revealing that he had a total of twenty. The dealer slid Sawyer his chips, at which point Sawyer announced he was ready to cash out. He stood, leaving the table with thirty thousand.

He'd been careful while playing tonight, attempting to not make himself too obvious by winning every hand.

Casinos were sophisticated operations that took everyone's photo, watched you through multiple cameras that caught all the angles and doubted that Lady Luck was real. Sawyer had had one visit to a casino security office before, where he'd been frisked and harassed before being cleared and released without apology.

However, he was now part of the casino's profile, which was shared with others around the country. That meant that everywhere he went, he'd be watched.

Sawyer cashed out his chips. Probably one of the only reasons he hadn't been harassed further and labeled a card counter was that there was no physical evidence to tie him to any organized group of casino scammers.

All Sawyer's winnings were first deposited into a non-Branch bank in Dallas. He used his real name when at the casino and provided his parents' address, which was still the one he used for his taxes, although he didn't stop and visit his mom when he flew through. He'd never had a yearbook picture taken; he didn't think State University even had a college annual, one of the ways the MIT gang had been caught.

Still, in the casinos' view, he was a cheater. He was part of a card scam, as that early 1990s Massachusetts Institute of Technology blackjack team had been labeled. The gamblers' link had been their college campus and they had used a card-counting system rooted in statistics and mathematical theory. They'd traveled as complete strangers under aliases and had relied on investors to pay their bills until they could win.

Sawyer took the casino's check, filled out the requisite IRS tax form and headed for the hotel lobby. He'd pick up his carry-on bag from the bell captain and depart.

He'd won enough to bring his debt down to sixty thousand after repaying the ten thousand seed money he'd taken from his account. Coupled with what he'd won last weekend, fifty thousand and he'd be clear.

Sawyer hailed a cab to the airport, checked in using a self-service kiosk and soon settled into one of those uncomfortable plastic airline waiting area chairs until he boarded his flight to Dallas.

Jake had come up with the idea to try the MIT card scam again, more than fourteen years later. He'd researched both the mathematical theory and the way the casinos had used the MIT group's own technology against them. Jake had theorized that any new group would have to master the inner workings of the casinos themselves, in addition to creating new ways to play. So far, the six-member State University team had flown under casino security radar. The Select Six, as they'd dubbed themselves, never tried to win more than mid–five figures.

They didn't play under aliases or fake IDs and used their real tax addresses, which were all around the country. They kept all their winnings in banks in their hometowns, which they could access and transfer via the Internet. The biggest thing was to not let the playing and the perks go to anyone's head. They quit before they reached the level of being offered free meals and complimentary rooms, enticements casinos used to get high rollers to keep playing.

The system Jake had set up worked, and he'd incorporated the gambling ring into a Ph.D. project. Eventually he planned to either sell his system to the casinos themselves or write a book. He hadn't yet decided which.

Sawyer had willingly participated in Jake's brainchild. Now he was tired of the game. The thrill of the challenge had worn off; perhaps it had happened when his mother had looked at him with such sorrowful eyes the last time he'd seen her. Yeah, Bart and Will could have their thrill of racing, but Sawyer's sport was somehow "tainted."

He'd tried to explain, but with the weight of Hilton's own defection coloring his family's viewpoint, Sawyer hadn't stood a chance in making anyone truly understand he wasn't an addict deluding himself.

He pulled out his cell phone and glanced at the missed call. A Charlotte number. It would be a little after 10:00 p.m. on the East Coast. He pressed the button for his voice mail.

"Hi, Sawyer. It's Lucy. I know we're getting together next weekend, but…" He heard her hesitate. "How about lunch this week as well? Say Wednesday? I'll meet you in the math lounge at noon. I remember where that is. Call me if that won't work. If not, I'll see you there and we can go over to the Underground."

The Underground was the campus's best food court, often serving locally grown produce from the agricultural students' farm. He frowned. He'd never brought a date to the university. Women found the math department "geeky." A few he'd dated hadn't wanted a wanna-be math professor.

But this was Lucy. He didn't want to alienate her by saying no, and soon he'd be that math professor. He had to trust his instinct that she really was different from the others, as she'd so far been.

The loudspeaker announced his flight, and, as he rose to board his plane, a tremor shot through him. He recognized the sensation as one he hadn't experienced in quite a while.

Hope. Promise. Lucy was the direct cause—this time she'd asked him out.

The cloud of melancholy he'd been living under seemed to dissipate slightly, letting a sliver of welcome light through.

He slept the entire way to Dallas.

CHAPTER SIX

LUCY DROVE ONTO THE State University campus about ten minutes early for lunch with Sawyer. If she remembered the layout correctly, visitor parking was scarce around the math building. Luck was with her, though, and she found a space close to the west entrance. Her one-inch pumps traveled over the fresh asphalt, her floral skirt lifting a bit in the light wind that toyed with her hem. She tugged on the glass doors and stepped inside.

The math lounge was on the third floor of the Edison Building. The size of two average classrooms, the lounge consisted of some couches that had seen better days, round tables with nondescript plastic chairs, an ancient color television tuned to CNN and a couple of vending machines. People were sprawled out around the beige-painted room. Four were playing cards at one of the tables, a few were fascinated by things on their laptops and one was stretched out on a couch, his arm over his eyes as he caught a few Zs in between classes.

She didn't see Sawyer anywhere. She glanced at her watch. Having found parking quickly, which had never happened when she'd been a student, she'd arrived before the designated time.

"Can I help you?" one of the guys playing cards asked. He paused in the middle of shuffling and all the guys at the table eyed her as she entered the room.

Even during her time at State, the number of guys taking high-level math classes outweighed the girls four to one. Thus, girls were a rarity in the math lounge.

"I'm looking for Sawyer Branch. He's meeting me here. Have any of you seen him?" Lucy asked.

"He's got class until 11:50. Should be done any minute," the dealer said.

"Then I'll wait," Lucy said.

"Jake, you finally going to deal that?" one of the players asked.

"What game are you playing?" Lucy asked, curious. In her day everyone had played spades and she'd gotten quite good, even when playing partners with people she didn't know well.

"We're playing blackjack." Jake cut the cards himself and set half the pile on the table. Lucy noticed a cut on his thumb and that he bit his nails to the quick. "You play?"

"No. I don't gamble."

He shrugged. "No money involved. Just some probability. You can sit in a hand while you wait. It'll change the odds a bit," he offered.

"Okay, I guess," Lucy said, taking the empty chair to Jake's left.

"I'm Jake," he said.

"Lucy."

"So you're waiting for Sawyer," he stated, dealing out the cards.

"Yes."

"Ah," Jake said, his concentration more on the cards

as he set the remaining ones on the pile. "You do know how to play?"

"A little," Lucy said. Like poker, blackjack had a bunch of rules and terms, things like doubling down. She had no idea what that meant.

"House stands on seventeen. You play the house." Jake began to deal and Lucy studied him. He wasn't as attractive as Sawyer, fitting more of the stereotypical nerd image. Still, he seemed nice.

"I remember this part," she said, lifting her facedown card.

"Well, you're up first. Hit?"

She had an ace and a five. Either sixteen or six. The idea was not to go over twenty-one. "Hit," she said.

Her next card was a two, putting her at eighteen. "I'm good," she said.

"So have you been on campus before?" Jake asked.

"A few years ago, I took advanced math classes when I got my master's."

"Not much has changed," Jake answered, moving to the next guy, who was studying his cards with way too much concentration. "Hey, Jason. You gotta be ready. Confidence, remember?"

"Yeah," Jason said. "Hit me."

He immediately busted, and the third guy passed on taking a card. Jake turned over his card, revealing a ten and a queen. The house had twenty, and everyone but Jake lost.

"Luckily this wasn't for any money," Lucy said.

"The advantage always belongs with the house," Jake said, dealing the next round.

"You sound like you've done your research," she said.

He shrugged. "It's math. It interests me. Blackjack is all about card counting."

Lucy glanced down at her face-up card. Two of spades. She reached for the facedown card and lifted up the edge.

"Jake! What are you doing?"

The fury in Sawyer's voice surprised Lucy so much that she almost tossed the card, the ten of hearts.

"Hi, Sawyer," Jake said, his eyes widening as he absorbed Sawyer's reaction to the card game. "I was only entertaining Lucy until you got here."

"Don't," Sawyer said. He pulled Lucy's chair out and immediately schooled his handsome features into neutral. As quickly as the anger had come, Sawyer dissipated the emotion, making it seem like a trick of the light that his displeasure had been there at all. He gave her a smile that would melt icebergs. "Hi, Lucy. Glad you could make it. I'm sorry I'm running late."

"Oh, I was early," she said, pushing her cards toward Jake and standing.

"Are you ready to go?" he asked.

"Yes." She gave a parting glance at the guys at the table, uncertain as to why the dynamic had shifted so quickly. Jake didn't even look up as she said, "It's nice to have met you."

With that, Sawyer cupped her elbow and guided her out into the hall. "Sorry about that," he said easily. "Jake's a card shark. He didn't try to get you to bet any money, did he?"

"No, we weren't playing with any money. I wouldn't have played otherwise. I don't gamble. The idea of going to Vegas and risking my money has absolutely no appeal to me whatsoever."

"Have you ever been there?" he queried.

"Only once, with Justin when the Cup Series was there

last year. He at least was wise enough to quit before he lost any big money. A few other drivers weren't so lucky."

"The casino really does hold all the cards," Sawyer quipped.

"That's what Jake just said. I can't understand why people play. The saddest thing I saw was some of the senior citizens. They'd be in wheelchairs and oxygen tanks forking money into the slot machines. Pathetic, really. I want nothing to do with it. It's like the lottery. You have a better chance of being hit by lightning."

A sign caught her eye and she paused outside a doorway. The placard outside read 315 Lab. "So is this the math department's new computer lab?" She glanced in, noting row after row of PCs. Only a few had people at them.

"This is it," Sawyer said.

"It got upgraded from when I attended," Lucy commented, stepping inside.

"They installed all the new machines over Christmas break," Sawyer said.

"Are there other computers, as well, like in the professors' offices?"

He blinked as if he found her question strange. "I guess. Most professors have laptops they bring to class and hook up into the LCD projector. Since some like chalk instead of the new white marker boards, all the boards slide up and down and all the classrooms and lecture halls have both types."

"I hate chalk. I would always end up walking around with a yellow smear on the back of my pants."

She walked down one of the aisles, glancing over the shoulder of one of the computer users. He was checking his e-mail.

"So shall we go?" Sawyer prodded from where he stood in the doorway. "I'm due to assist with a class at two."

"Oh, yes, sorry. The network administrator in me likes to know how things are set up. Are all these attached to a single server?"

"I think so," Sawyer said.

"What about e-mail?"

"We can log in on any machine and access our files. Our e-mail's accessed via the Web. Why?"

"Just curious. The hospital's setup is similar in some ways. A friend of mine got some spam from someone in the math department."

He shrugged. "I wouldn't know anything about that. Computers and programming aren't really my thing. They're more Jake's. I can design the algorithms and the flowchart, but I need help with the actual computer inputting. I'm not nearly as efficient as Jake and often use too many steps. Not that I want you to have anything to do with Jake," he added quickly. "His dissertation involves using card-counting strategies to beat the house at blackjack. That's why you saw him practicing. The guy's a player in every sense of the word."

Hmm. That explained a lot. "Sort of like that MIT card-counting club?"

"You've heard of it?" he asked.

She nodded. "Yeah. Saw a show on A&E."

"Sort of like that," Sawyer said. "Nothing you should worry about."

Lucy reached for Sawyer's hand and squeezed it once before letting it go. "I won't, since I do not have any interest in Jake," she said. "Just you."

She followed Sawyer from the room, giving the area

behind her one last glance. Unless she hacked into the main server or got on every computer and tried each machine, she wasn't going to be able to track the e-mail Kent received. More than likely, only the State University server held the answer, and she'd given up after one more attempt to penetrate it.

These computer guys were the best at maintaining security; a few years back a student from State University had hacked into the Pentagon. He'd managed to talk himself out of jail time and now worked as a security consultant for the federal government.

No, if Larry Grosso had sent the e-mails, he'd have used his own laptop, not one of these lab machines that advertised that their history and anything left on the hard drive would be automatically wiped at 12:01 a.m. The only record of the e-mail would be the server.

She'd hit a dead end.

Unless Sawyer was involved… She dismissed that thought. No, he'd just said he wasn't a computer guy and had to have someone else help him with his programming. Whoever had sent the e-mails knew what he was doing.

They'd reached the parking lot, but they bypassed their cars and walked through the campus quadrangle to the Underground. They took the stairs down two levels. The Underground was unique. While technically the basement of the Newton Building, the Underground soared two-stories high so the area was quite spacious. From the outside the windows were at ground level, but inside they were just below the ceiling. Lore maintained that this had once been an old gym, but sometime in the seventies had been converted into food-service use.

They went through the line, selected their food and sat

at a table far away from where a large-screen television broadcast a soap opera, the same one that was showing during Lucy's tenure.

"So tell me more about your family," Lucy suggested before taking a bite of the chicken salad sandwich she'd ordered. "Just Bart, Will and Penny?"

Sawyer unfolded a paper napkin and placed it in his lap. "Yep. I'm the youngest. My sister Penny's the oldest. Will and Bart are the middle children. They were handfuls growing up. They're practical jokers *extraordinaire.* You've read the Harry Potter series, haven't you? Think of the Weasley twins, Fred and George. That's Will and Bart, just without magic and blond hair instead of red. They go way beyond short-sheeting people's beds and make Ashton Kutcher on *Punk'd* look tame."

"That doesn't sound good," Lucy remarked, noting her food was pretty tasty, more than it had been when she'd been in attendance years ago. Boy, you leave and everything gets better.

"Bart and Will's pranks are never good. They once put plastic snakes in the punch bowl during one of my mother's garden parties. The mayor's wife shrieked and ended up with a big red stain on her new white Ralph Lauren dress."

"Ouch." Still, Lucy had to smile because it was rather funny picturing two boys, punch and plastic snakes, especially if you weren't the one wearing the stained dress.

"Racing gave them an outlet for their excess energy, and once he got over the fact that they weren't going to be linebackers for the Dallas Cowboys, my dad began to support the idea. He gave them everything from midgets to NASCAR Sprint Cup cars if it made what they wanted to do easier. I guess I was the disappointing one."

So she could give him her full attention, she'd stopped eating. "I can understand. My older sister was into dance. There was a dance competition every single weekend. My dad called her his precious ballerina. I was the one he came to when he wanted his checkbook balanced. In high school, I was a math-lete, not a cheerleader. He only came to one competition, when we made it to the state finals my senior year. I don't know. He got a big promotion in the police ranks about that time as well, so maybe that was it. He was always working."

"My dad gave me money. Like he was trying to buy my affection."

"Maybe that's the only way he knew how to tell you he loved you?" Lucy offered.

"Yeah, maybe." Sawyer paused, took a bite of food. The silence lasted about two minutes and Lucy ate half of her sandwich.

"You know, maybe it's just that my dad is really messed up," Sawyer said suddenly. "Look at him. He keeps a mistress for twenty years. I still can't comprehend it. That means I was eight when he started seeing her!"

He pounded his fist on the table suddenly and a few curiosity seekers glanced their way.

Sawyer steadied himself. "Sorry. I didn't mean to lose control."

Lucy had instinctively moved her hand to cover his. He didn't pull away. "Were you and your father close?"

He blinked once. "I don't know. Now that I know the truth, it's like dawn chased away the darkness, but the picture I can see isn't pretty. My father used my mother for her society connections early in her marriage, and then, since divorce isn't cheap and would have ruined his social status, simply replaced her with the younger, prettier model on the side. That's the only explanation I can come up with."

"Sex at one place, children at the other," Lucy added.

"I've got fifteen hours in psychology when I thought I might want to major in the field." Sawyer gave a harsh laugh. "And my dad told me I was the one who couldn't find myself. Maybe he should have looked in the mirror or taken some classes himself."

"I'm sorry," Lucy said.

His tone sharpened. "I don't want your pity. Heck, I'm telling you things I shouldn't be. You'll never want to go out with me again. You'll think I'm off my rocker."

Lucy shook her head and tightened her grip on Sawyer's hands. "Never. In fact, I'm glad you're opening up to me. It lets me know who you really are. I don't like secrets. I've seen the harm they do to relationships."

"Yeah. Just look at my family. Okay, no secrets between us."

She'd been thinking of Tanya and Kent. "We have to be so strong and tough but everyone has vulnerabilities. It's the man who can admit his weaknesses that impresses me, not Mr. Invincible whom I know is only putting on a brave front."

"I don't want you in the role of a therapist," Sawyer said. "I'd like to date you, not unload on you."

She could appreciate his concern. That would create an unhealthy relationship. "Don't worry. That's not going to happen. My listening when you have a problem is what friends do."

"I don't want to stop at friends," Sawyer said. "You're very special." He used his free hand to cover their joined hands, giving Lucy that warm-and-fuzzy feeling deep inside.

"Thanks." They stayed like that for a moment before reluctantly breaking contact so they could finish eating.

Lucy relaxed as lunch went on. One thing had become clear. Her connection with Sawyer went further than just a surface, physical link.

"Hi, Sawyer," a group of students called as they went by. He waved and Lucy watched as they departed.

"You fit here, don't you?" she observed.

He paused, his sandwich almost to his mouth. "I like to think so. I'm finally happier than I've been in years."

He chewed, the movement of his lips making Lucy wonder what it would be like to kiss him. She'd noticed the appreciative glances of several young collegiate girls as they'd walked by. Yet Sawyer wanted her.

"You'll get past this thing with your father," she encouraged.

He nodded. "I know. My sister and her husband had separated for a while, but they're back together. Bart and Will have new sponsors. I'm worried about my mother. I haven't seen her in a while and I don't have a free weekend until June."

"I can't imagine what she's going through."

"Neither can I. Bart told me he's trying to hook her up with his financial manager. If my mom says yes, hopefully the guy will be able to do some good and help my mom out."

"I hope so," Lucy said, not offering advice. Instead she let Sawyer talk.

"It would have been so much simpler if my father had been killed. You know, just died. Does that sound horrible of me? If he'd died, the scandal wouldn't have been half as juicy. Instead, he's a fugitive for white-collar crime, only my mother's true friends have stayed by her, our lives have made the tabloids and we've been publicly humiliated by Alyssa Ritchie and we'll have to endure more when she publishes that memoir this August. I know you aren't supposed to hit girls, but if I came across that woman I don't know if I'd be able to hold myself back. I mean, what was she thinking, breaking up my family? She even tried to become Will's sponsor. She's a menace."

Lucy didn't have an answer to that. "Twenty years is a long time."

"I will never do that to my wife or my family," Sawyer declared forcefully. He reached out and grabbed her hands. His black eyes seemed like pools of liquid obsidian as he held her gaze. "Never."

She nodded, seeing the truth there in his eyes. Sawyer was a one-woman man. He'd never be anything but. "I believe you won't."

"Good." They sat perpendicular to each other, and Sawyer leaned over the corner of the table and brought his face closer to hers. He dropped the lightest of kisses onto her lips before easing back into his own space.

That feather touch shattered her. The promise in the kiss and in his eyes had been genuine. The kiss, while brief, shook her to the core with the sensations it evoked. Her toes had actually curled. Sure she'd dated, but she'd never experienced anything like this before.

He didn't apologize for the public display of affection, for the light touch that had branded her as his. She found herself not minding in the slightest.

"Shall we go for a walk before you need to get back?" he asked. "It's nice weather. We could go out by the pond."

The university had a small asphalt walking path around a nice-size pond. Often people would spend their entire lunch hours outside on warm days.

"Sounds great," she replied, a little overwhelmed by the emotions she was experiencing. She'd like nothing more than to take him back to her apartment and rip his T-shirt and jeans off. Yet at the same time, he'd caught her up in the romance. He'd shared his deepest feelings and he'd treated her with respect. As an equal.

This was new ground. Unfamiliar, exciting territory. Could he be the right man? Only time would tell, but as he carried her tray to the cafeteria return, the possibilities suddenly seemed endless.

CHAPTER SEVEN

THE DAY OF THE LONGEST RACE of the year dawned sunny and bright, perfect weather for racing. Neither too hot nor too cold, the track conditions would make for some exciting side-by-side action.

Lucy knew all these details from dating Justin, but he wasn't her concern anymore. Today she planned to focus on the new man in her life, Sawyer.

After their latest lunch and time spent walking and talking, she was becoming more at ease with the idea of a relationship. Never the type to jump from one guy to the next, Lucy was one of those who often questioned herself endlessly. She wasn't one who believed something until she'd seen it. Her history with men had her a bit of a cynic.

She'd learned that the start of any relationship was new and exciting. The attention received was flattering and could make you giddy, giving you a false sense of security. Then the first bubble burst and let disappointment enter.

But so far nothing with Sawyer seemed ordinary. He'd kissed her briefly at her car after their lunch in the Underground and Lucy hadn't wanted the moment to end. She'd wanted to take him off into a dark corner and let passion reign.

That was scary considering they were only several dates

in. Too many of her relationships had fizzled once the sex started. Either that, or the sex had dominated the relationship so much that she and the guy didn't have much else in common when they weren't in bed.

So, while she sensed potential in this relationship with Sawyer, she was hesitant about taking any next step. Not that any type of physical contact with Sawyer wasn't guaranteed to make her melt. If he lived up to his dark Mediterranean looks and those sensual kisses, bedding him would be nothing less than phenomenal.

However, she wasn't a girl to loosely climb into the sack with just any man. With all the men she'd ever been with, who weren't that many, she'd wanted to have a connection, that emotional substance that maybe she was the one. Gratuitous sex wasn't for her. Never had been.

They'd arrived at the track a couple of hours before the race. The last practice had been the day before, so most teams were doing final preparations. A lot of the drivers had gone home and wouldn't show up until they had to.

Lucy called Tanya and got her voice mail, which wasn't surprising when Lucy heard the news. It was all over the garage that earlier that morning animal rights activists had thrown paint all over Kent Grosso's race car, ruining the finish and the sponsor—Vittle Farms—decals. The activists had carried the paint using opaque water bottles.

As she and Sawyer had hot passes they were in the garage long after the protesters had been evicted. Yet, the damage had been done and Kent would have to drive his backup car. His team, lucky it wasn't an impound race, was still trying to get it set up.

Lucy frowned and wondered if the two incidents, Kent's

blackmail and the vandalism, could be related. She made a mental note to ask Tanya the next time they spoke.

"Ready," Sawyer asked. They were outside Bart's hauler. Inside, Bart was receiving one final pep talk from his crew chief now that the driver/crew chief meeting had ended and the prerace introductory activities were about to start. People filled the stands, ready for the green flag to fly in less than forty minutes.

"Richard said we could catch a ride with him in his golf cart. He'll be out in a minute," Sawyer told her as they sat in the director's chairs placed under the gate lift that provided shade.

Richard Latimer was Bart's car owner and he was also inside the hauler, as was Anita Wolcott, Bart's P.R. manager from Motor Media Group. The mirrored doors opened and Anita stepped out.

Lucy had always envied Anita. Lucy had strawberry-blond hair and pale blue eyes, and while she'd only met Anita in passing, the P.R. rep had deeper-red hair and green eyes. Lucy had even tried colored contacts once to get Anita's look, but those hadn't worked very well. She consoled herself with the fact that, because of her skin coloring, Anita tended to freckle; something Lucy luckily had avoided all her life.

"Are you guys ready to go over to the suite?" Anita asked, gesturing to the empty four-seater golf cart.

Richard Latimer stepped out at that moment, and Lucy frowned as she took her seat in the back of the cart and waited. She'd seen Richard around the track while dating Justin, and he'd always had an upbeat smile and warm hello for her. Today, his gait seemed uncertain, as if all of his seventy-three years were beginning to catch up with him. Not that his thinning hair hadn't turned white years ago. He folded his five-ten frame into the cart and turned around slightly.

"Sawyer, glad you could make it. Bart assures me he's bringing home a victory today," Richard said in his trademark southern drawl.

"I hope so," Sawyer said. It was no secret his brother hadn't been performing very well lately. Coupled with the fiasco of Bart's family and sponsorship, maybe that was the reason Richard's normally rosy cheeks seemed paler today, as if he were overtired from months of stress.

"Lucy, nice to see you again," Richard finished.

"You, too," she replied.

Anita put the golf cart into gear and drove through the infield and toward the tunnel that would take them outside and give them access to the suites high above the track. Unlike many team owners who had condominiums on Turn One, PDQ Racing leased a suite high above the start-finish line.

Lucy had brought an oversize purse with her just for this purpose. Each of the suites had glass walls that allowed views into the suites on either side. Unlike the race goers in the grandstands wearing shorts and T-shirts with their favorite driver's picture, people in the suites usually dressed to the nines, as if attending a high-end cocktail party. In her leather tote, Lucy had a pair of high heels, a slinky black sheath that could be folded without wrinkling, and a strand of black pearls. She'd head to the restroom and change the moment they arrived.

As for Sawyer, he was dressed appropriately already in black dress slacks and a white shirt that accented his olive coloring and wavy dark hair. The man was simply gorgeous and easily could have been a model.

When she stepped out of the restroom, her infield khaki pants, polo shirt and flat shoes were stuffed in the bottom of her handbag.

The suite fit sixty-eight, and from Lucy's estimation, the place had reached capacity. She'd told Sawyer she wasn't ready for a cocktail and so he handed her a glass of water before they moved to sit in the plush stadium-style seating that gave a bird's-eye view of the entire track. Hung high up in each corner of the suite so they didn't obstruct the view, plasma screen televisions tuned to the race broadcast showed live feed. About six stories below, drivers crossed the stage, where they were introduced to the crowd. Then they were driven around the track in convertibles. The broadcast focused on Kent Grosso as the media asked him questions about the protestors.

"I really have no idea why this happened, but I'm not going to let it affect how I race," Kent was saying.

"They say it has to do with your sponsor buying Vitality, the cosmetics manufacturer, and the accusations of animal testing," the interviewer representing the broadcast channel prodded.

Kent handled the probe in stride. "I can't comment on that except to say we had a really great car and my team has worked hard to get the secondary car into the same setup. All I'm concentrating on today is to try to bring home a victory."

Realizing they weren't going to get much more out of Kent, the media panned to someone else and moved on to interview the next driver.

Sawyer turned to Lucy. "Can I get you anything else to eat or drink? You're almost out of water."

"I was parched." The suite would host a full buffet dinner

at some point during the race and it had a wait staff that would also bring food to their seats. However, the appetizers a guest had in the row below her did look pretty delicious.

Being thirsty and having come from being outside in the garage, Lucy had drained her water almost immediately. "I think I do want something else to drink. I can go get it."

She shoved her purse under the seat and stood. Sawyer rose with her, and together they climbed the few steps back to the main area of the suite. Here people lounged in various leather seating areas, the action on the track audible only on the plasma-screen TVs.

They waited in a short line for the full, open bar, and as it was still early afternoon, both she and Sawyer opted for soft drinks. Back in their seats, they could feel the vibration from the five–fighter plane flyover but hardly hear the roar.

"Some would say this isn't real racing," Sawyer said about the lack of noise.

"I know. When I first started attending races, I was down low. I liked to feel the wind off the cars as they flew by, and I liked the smell the burning rubber and the sound of squealing brakes. I have to admit, though, from up here you can see all the action. Without a race scanner, it's hard to know what's going on out on the track. However, I never liked having to wear headphones. They're heavy. But you don't get any information unless you're listening to a scanner. So it's a catch-22," Lucy said.

"My favorite sport to play is billiards. Golf's another one. I can watch both as well. I like the mathematical equations behind those sports. Even though I tried racing when I was young, I admit I didn't really appreciate it until I started crunching the numbers. NASCAR's a wealth of statistical data. That's the part I like."

"My mother's a football widow every Monday night during the season. I guess that's my second-favorite sport. I'm a Panthers fan," Lucy admitted.

"I'll watch it on occasion. Football's really big in Texas."

His collar had gaped a little, giving her a peek at the smooth skin underneath. "As for racing, I do enjoy it. Like the physics behind a roller coaster, the mathematical elements were what hooked me in. I found it impressive that Bart has such a short distance to drop almost fifty miles per hour or more to hit the proper pit road speed, and that it's done using a tachometer and not a speedometer. Even more interesting is how teams determine whether they have enough fuel to finish the race. I've seen races won and lost on that, and the time of their pit road stops. I like the numbers part of NASCAR, like the fact that a lot of the time the person who leads the most laps or who is the fastest doesn't always win."

She considered that for a moment. NASCAR allowed fans access to tons of data via the Web site. "So do you think you would have gotten into racing if it hadn't been for your brothers or the math?"

Sawyer tapped his fingers on the arm of his chair. "I think so. I don't know how you live in the greater Charlotte area without becoming some sort of a fan. It permeates the culture in this part of the country. Even if Bart and Will hadn't been racing when I arrived, I think I would have picked up on it just because I go to State University. Some of the fraternities are intensely one-driver or one-owner oriented."

"That's true. They are, aren't they?" Lucy said, enjoying

the fact that, like at lunch, Sawyer wasn't afraid to share his opinions. She'd dated guys who'd been closed and guarded, as if they had far too many secrets and would never let you in. Another thing she liked about Sawyer was that he didn't have some underlying need to dominate a conversation.

Movement in the aisle to Lucy's right caught her attention as a woman Lucy recognized from the track, but really didn't know, approached. She gestured to the open seat next to Lucy. "Mind if I join both of you?"

A small twinge of irrational jealousy flared through Lucy as Sawyer smiled and said, "Feel free. We'd be happy to have you sit with us. There's an empty seat."

He stood, and Lucy shifted so that the woman moved past and sat on the left, into the middle seat. The rest of the seats in all the rows quickly filled as people prepared to watch the green flag fly. Lucy sighed. She'd wanted Sawyer to herself; although, she chided herself, that was a little unrealistic given they were watching a race with more than one hundred thousand other people. As for her momentary jealousy, she'd been silly, but it did prove one thing—how interested she'd become in Sawyer.

Below, pit road had become a flurry of frantic activity now that the official "gentlemen, start your engines" command had ceremoniously blared through the loud-speakers. At the command, the cars had roared to life and were slowly moving off pit road and following the pace cars.

The cars traveled around in two lines, with the pole winner, Hart Hampton, occupying the inside first spot. On his right, outside, was the No. 427 car driven by Kent Grosso.

"It's too bad he'll be moving to the back of the field,"

the girl next to Lucy said. She held out her hand and Lucy shook it. "I'm Terri Whalen. You might know my father, Philip Whalen. He's Bart's crew chief."

"That's why you look so familiar." Lucy had heard of Terri. She'd become a personal fitness trainer for many of the drivers, including Bart. No wonder she was so thin and fit. She worked out constantly. "I'm Lucy Gunter."

"Oh, you used to date Justin," Terri said cautiously.

Lucy managed to keep her smile in place. "I did, but that's ancient history. I'm sure you know Bart's brother, Sawyer."

Sawyer turned and gave Terri a brief salute before turning his attention to the action on the track below.

"So were you in the garage when they dumped the paint?" Terri asked.

Lucy shook her head. "I wasn't. We arrived later."

"I was." Terri leaned closer, her reddish-brown hair swishing around her shoulders. She smiled, eager to impart the scoop. "Kent's garage stall is directly across from Bart's. Kent's team tried to clean the paint off but the damage was pretty intensive. I don't think I've ever seen Kent's boss, Dawson Ritter, so mad."

"I saw the interview Kent did. The media wanted to know if Steve's girlfriend was involved because Heidi's business partner is a well-known animal rights activist," Lucy said.

"And Heidi is a vet, too. Dawson sure blames her—and Steve," Terri said. "Steve better not mess up spotting today."

Steve was Kent's cousin and spotter. Lucy frowned as she watched the first pack of cars, those in the front of the field, pass the start-finish line. There seemed to be an awful lot of drama going on lately in the Grosso family. So could the vandalism and the blackmail be related? It was a possibility she had to consider, especially since she hadn't had time to discover any more information despite her visit to the math department.

The cars below entered Turn One and Lucy's frown deepened as the No. 448 car driven by her ex, Justin Murphy, moved out of line and decelerated to let the others pass by. "Is Justin in the back, too?" Lucy asked.

"He changed engines." Terri was a wealth of information. "He had problems during the final practice and they didn't want to risk engine failure. My dad certainly wasn't too sorry to see those two head to the back. At least Bart's starting in better position than he has been lately."

Bart was starting in the twenty-third spot, but because of Kent and Justin, he would be twenty-first when the race started. He'd struggled during qualifying but had managed to pull out a mid-field position.

"Hopefully he can place in the top ten at least," Sawyer said, entering the conversation as the two packs of cars came together and the second pace car entered pit road. As the front pace car passed the flag stand, the official gave the one-to-go sign. The cars lined up, each as close to the one in front's bumper as possible without wrecking until they were one big mass of forty-three machines, in two lines, ready to start the race the next time around.

Terri leaned forward so she could see Sawyer. "You and me both on that top ten. My dad needs a solid finish. My mother wants him to retire at the end of the season and he's trying to convince her that he's not ready to go yet. But if he can't get Bart doing better, he might just find himself without a job, anyway."

"I know Bart would like to have a good run tonight. He's had a lot on his plate," Sawyer said, his attention on the cars as they entered the back stretch.

Terri glanced around as if seeing who sat nearby. "Richard Latimer's much more tolerant of the team's struggles than many other owners would be. He understands that sometimes drivers have ups and downs. Now his nephew Jim loves the sport, but he's not as…" Terri's voice trailed off as if she'd thought twice about the gossip she'd been about to impart or perhaps Terri's sudden speechlessness was because the race had begun.

"Would you like anything?" A waitress stopped at the end of the aisle next to Sawyer.

"I'd love another diet cola," Lucy said, holding up her empty glass. She might have a glass of wine with dinner.

"And you, sir?" the waitress asked, her gaze on Sawyer.

Sawyer seemed oblivious to her appreciative stare and requested a soda for himself and an order of potato skins.

Lucy exhaled the breath she'd been unaware she'd been holding. She really had to get over this inferiority complex she'd gotten after Justin. Just because Justin had gotten engaged shortly after they broke up didn't mean anything. They were both at fault for their breakup. But dating Sawyer felt different. Maybe it was because their other dates had been so private. But here they were out as a couple and it still felt the same.

"I hope you like potato skins," Sawyer said.

The buffet had all sorts of appetizers, including some she couldn't pronounce. Out of all of them, Sawyer had picked one of her favorites.

"What?" he said with a grin as he caught her pleased expression. "I'm not a mushroom person and I don't do snails even if you dress them with butter and a fancy French name. I like plain food. I think there were some mini tacos up there. We can share some of those instead if you'd like."

Lucy laughed a little. Unlike baseball stadiums, where you often had nary a cup holder, these seats had a thin, six-inch metal shelf in front of them to hold food. "I do like Mexican food and I love potato skins. Those were a perfect choice."

"See, I'm that good and, baby, don't you forget it," Sawyer said, raising his almost-empty glass to her in a toast.

"I heard that dinner's going to be steak, shrimp and a baked chicken dish that's one of Richard's absolute favorites. The caterers make it only for this suite," Terri said, inserting herself into the conversation.

Suddenly there was a roar from the crowd surrounding them as, fifteen laps into the race, already one driver had hit the wall high above Turn Three.

"Wow, look how loose he was," someone said, watching the replay on the monitors.

"Caution's out," someone else commented, and directly below the suite, trackside, the official waved the yellow flag and the field lined up behind the pace car that had emerged from pit road.

"Everyone's going to come in," Terri predicted, and sure enough, the moment pit road opened, the majority of the drivers exited for new tires and fuel.

"Darn it," someone a few rows lower groaned. "Bart overshot his pit box. He's in there now."

Beside her, Lucy saw Terri cringe and then turn around to see if she could see Richard Latimer's reaction. Even Sawyer had tensed, as if he had a personal stake in the race aside from Bart being his brother.

"That's already cost him valuable seconds," Terri said about Bart's mistake, and she turned her attention to the monitor, which had a close-up view of the pit box and Bart's pit crew. He finally raced off. "Seventeen seconds in the pit. Ouch."

Even worse, Bart was black-flagged for speeding during his exit from pit road, meaning he had to take a pass through penalty, which immediately put him a lap down. The overall atmosphere in the suite sobered.

"It's not that bad," someone called out, trying to rally everyone. "There are more than 350 laps to go."

Knowing there was still time cheered up the guests in the suite. The average length of this particular race was a little over five hours and they weren't that far in. Track conditions would change dramatically when the sun dipped below the horizon and the drivers went from driving in the afternoon May heat to the cooler temperatures created by driving under the lighted night sky.

As the evening wore on, Sawyer and Lucy left their seats and socialized with the various people in the suite, who included friends and sponsors of PDQ Racing.

"It was nice meeting you," Lucy said, leaving the conversation she'd been engaged in with a sponsor's representative. She wanted to freshen up a little, and when she exited the restroom her gaze immediately located Sawyer over by the bar, a little ways away from everyone else as he was in deep conversation with Anita. Even with heels, Anita remained several inches shorter than Sawyer, and he'd bent his head so he could hear her.

Lucy glanced around the room. She could join in somewhere else, return to her seat or…she drew herself up slightly. This was silly. Sawyer had asked her to attend this event. She'd come here with him. Dating wasn't supposed to be this hard. She forced her feet to move.

"SAWYER, YOU REALLY HAVE to deal with this," Anita repeated.

"Not you, too," Sawyer said, attempting to keep his expression one of benign disinterest. "I've already heard enough from Bart and Will. And Craig."

"Then you should be doing something about it," Anita insisted. "The prepublication publicity that Alyssa Ritchie is getting is starting to explode—and the book isn't out until August! The public is lapping up stuff like 'I was a hidden mistress for twenty years.'"

"Trust me, I'm well aware of what's going on with the tramp," Sawyer said.

Anita crossed her arms and then just as quickly let them drop to her sides, as if realizing the effect on her body language. "Which is why the fact that you continue to do what you shouldn't and your cavalier attitude are putting everyone in danger. The last thing the media needs is to become aware of your situation."

"I don't have a cavalier attitude and I'm sick of everyone trying to rush me. The only people who are going to expose this are you and my overactive family who can't give it a rest. Bart and I talk, and then he has you get on my case. I'm not going to respond to your double-team. I'm handling everything."

"But not fast enough," Anita pressed.

"If he wants it handled so darn fast then tell him to come up with the money," Sawyer said.

"He doesn't have that kind of cash lying around. Both his and Will's allowances got cut off, too!" Anita pointed out while trying to keep her voice down.

"So there you have it," Sawyer said, irritated that Anita had approached him here. "I'll mind my business and he can mind his. I thought I'd made that clear at testing. I have everything under control. Just let me do what I do and trust me."

"Sawyer, you have a big problem and it's getting worse...."

"Not now, Anita," Sawyer commanded, using the same harsh tone he'd used with Jake in the math lounge. Lucy was within earshot, and from the curious expression crossing her face, he had no doubt she'd overheard a little of the exchange. Of course she'd have no idea it was about his debt, and while they'd said "no secrets," he wasn't about to reveal this one. In a few weeks the debt would be paid in full, the loan closed, and it would be a nonissue. He refused to damn himself with Lucy this early in their relationship. Not when things were going so well and held such promise.

Anita fell silent as Lucy approached. Lucy smiled tentatively. "Did I miss anything?"

"Not really," Sawyer told her, sliding his arm easily around her waist as if it belonged there. She felt great next to him. "Nothing's changed on the track and they're about to serve dinner."

"Good," Lucy said.

"I'll catch up with you two later. If Bart wins this, are you going to Victory Lane?" Anita asked.

"Sure," Sawyer said, although at this moment Bart was in no position to win the race, as he was still a lap down. "Is that okay with you?" he asked Lucy.

"Fine," she said, watching Anita walk away. Then she faced Sawyer, the movement dislodging his arm from her waist. "You two seemed a bit put out. Is everything okay?"

"It's fine. Anita's just doing her job meddling in Bart's life. I was telling her perhaps she could back off a little," Sawyer said, spinning a version of the truth. "It's nothing to worry about."

"Okay," Lucy said, not seemingly convinced.

A small chime sounded, indicating that Richard wanted to make a brief speech. "I just wanted to thank you all for joining me today. Words cannot express my appreciation for your support of PDQ Racing, so I'm going to keep this speech short and sweet. Dinner is served."

"Best news I've had," Sawyer said, thinking it couldn't have come at a more welcome time, either. Having been literally saved by the bell, he eased Lucy into line.

CHAPTER EIGHT

"YOU'VE GOTTEN QUIET."

Lucy glanced up. How to answer that? She'd been thinking about the conversation she'd overheard since dinner. The fact that Anita had described Sawyer as having a major problem, something to do with money, was weighing heavily on Lucy. For someone who'd insisted on keeping no secrets, it seemed like Sawyer had a big one. A black cloud had descended on the day and the earlier joy she'd felt vanished.

"I'm just concentrating on watching the race," she told him, which wasn't an outright lie.

The race was in the final twenty laps and all around her people had returned to their seats. Lucy looked at the scoring pylon and then turned her attention to the television high in the corner. Hart Hampton, the pole sitter, had regained the lead, but not by much as Kyle Doolittle was hard on his bumper. Owing to several earlier accidents, only nineteen cars remained on the lead lap, and Hampton was about to enter a pack of lap-down traffic that showed no intention of doing the proper thing by moving out of the race leader's way.

"Something's gonna give. There are too many rookies in that group for Hampton to get through if they don't give him room," Terri predicted, and sure enough, within seconds, one of the drivers making his first appearance in a NASCAR Sprint Cup Series race drifted up the banking in Turn Four, clipped Hart Hampton and sent him spinning.

Hampton's green No. 413 Chevy hit the wall with his back left quarter panel, the impact ricocheting him back into traffic where it was like watching bumper cars at an amusement park, only with smoke and crunching metal.

The cameras would later show who hit who first, but like a big chain reaction, several drivers ended up in the infield grass near the start-finish line, Hampton and Doolittle ended up in the garage unable to continue, and five of the cars on the lead lap found themselves in the horrible position of needing major repairs with ten laps to go.

The official waved the caution flag and the field fell in line behind the pace car.

"Bart's the lucky dog again," Anita announced. Lucy turned around to glance at the P.R. rep, who seemed much happier now that Bart Branch returned to the lead lap in twelfth position.

"Are they going to pit?" someone nearby asked.

"He should have enough gas to stay out," Terri answered. "Stay out," she commanded, as if her father could somehow hear her on pit road.

The minute pit road opened, many of the new front-runners headed in.

"He's staying out!" Terri said. "Yes!" She glanced at Lucy. "It's a risk, but he needs to take it."

Lucy glanced at Richard Latimer, who was sitting nearby. He didn't seem tense at all with this development.

"This sure changes things," Sawyer noted. Also choosing not to pit were Dean Grosso, Justin Murphy and

Kent Grosso. Will was in the pits for two right-side tires and fuel.

The official gave the one-to-go sign, and soon the cars readied for the restart, with Bart still in the lead. Lucy gripped her seat tighter.

With ten laps left in the race there was one more caution and crash, with Justin Murphy and Kent Grosso the victims. Lucy felt a pang of remorse for Kent, who had to return to his pit for repairs. From her vantage point, it had seemed as if Justin had cut Kent off in Turn Two.

"Bart's going to win this thing if he doesn't run out of fuel," Terri said. Her excitement had permeated the room, where everyone seemed to hold their collective breaths as the official gave the one-to-go sign before the race resumed. Too afraid to lose any track position, not one car had pitted under the last caution.

As for Bart's lead, he needed an excellent restart or either Dean or the former NASCAR Sprint Cup Series champion Ronnie McDougal was going to pass him by. The crowd in and outside of the suite was on its feet.

The cars hit the start-finish line, accelerating. The average race speed for the event had been one hundred twenty miles per hour. These last few laps would be much faster as everyone really pushed himself for final scoring position. Hart Hampton had won the pole with a speed of 192, but the track couldn't handle racing all forty-three cars on the track at that speed without putting all the drivers in serious danger.

The white flag waved, indicating this was the last lap. Ronnie McDougal showed why he was a champion as he eased past Bart Branch on the inside groove coming off Turn Three.

The group gathered in the suite groaned. "No way! Come on!" Terri yelled. "Do not let Ronnie McDougal win this race."

The cars entered Turn Four.

"Second's not so bad," Lucy consoled her. Bart and Ronnie were five car lengths ahead of the field, where cars battled for third through sixth spots.

But as McDougal rounded out Turn Four and expanded his lead, his car suddenly decelerated and fell back.

"He's out of gas! Oh, my God! I don't believe this!" Terri turned and hugged Lucy as Bart Branch, with plenty of fuel, passed McDougal for the checkered flag and the win.

Lucy had enough composure about her that she was able to keep an eye on the rest of the race. Dean Grosso managed to eke out third place.

"We're going to Victory Lane, people!" Anita shouted.

They had about five minutes tops to make it to the infield as Bart did his celebratory backward lap and burnout. The rest of the cars had begun to enter pit road. The top three finishers would be inspected. The rest would load up and go home.

"I can't believe this! We should have gone down earlier. We'll need to hurry," Anita said as she ushered Richard, Sawyer and Lucy into the golf cart.

Victory Lane buzzed with nonstop action by the time Sawyer and Lucy arrived. Anita ushered them through Security. Bart had already taken off his helmet and exited the car. As was protocol, the network doing the race broadcast had first interview and Bart grinned as he answered the reporter's questions. Bart stopped for a minute as his twin, Will, entered Victory Lane.

Lucy watched as Will, who'd placed eighteenth, hugged his twin and gave him a quick pat on the back. The two exchanged a few quick words, the media filming the congrats. Then Will left the party for his hauler, where he'd strip out of his uniform before heading home.

"This way," Anita said, moving Lucy and Sawyer closer to Bart before deserting them altogether. NASCAR had a set order of who could interview when, and the media personality next in line stepped up to Bart. Next would come the presentation of the trophy, which would be followed by the hat dance, a tradition where the entire team took multiple pictures, each time wearing a different sponsor's hat.

"I guess we're on our own," Sawyer observed.

"That's fine," Lucy replied. She'd been in Victory Lane when Justin had won. While the media had assigned spots on risers, she and Sawyer would be free to move around, so long as they stayed out of everyone's way.

"You going to congratulate him?" she asked.

"Trying," Sawyer said. He eased toward the fray. Bart had lifted the trophy above his head and flashbulbs flashed. The Victory Lane celebration would be quick, with the top three finishers due in the media center. Then Bart would have a few sponsor obligations. Luckily the race was in Charlotte, meaning he was less than an hour from home instead of a plane ride away. In fact, many drivers simply took a helicopter ride back, and all around various choppers were rising into the night sky.

As Anita brought a box of hats forward, there was a break in the action and Sawyer walked up to Bart. Lucy lagged behind. While both brothers smiled and hugged, the conversation between them was brief, and within seconds Sawyer was back by her side.

"Okay, let's get out of here," he said.

"That was quick. You don't have to do anything else?" Lucy asked.

He shook his head. "Nope. I'll talk to Bart next week. He's got too much to do right now. And Will is already on his way home. Come on, the car's this way."

She trotted after him, her high heels working to keep up. Sawyer noticed her wobble and slowed down. They made their way through the garage area, where all around team members loaded up the haulers. Terri had arrived and she waved at them as she made her way toward the celebration Lucy and Sawyer were leaving behind.

Anita had provided VIP parking passes so they didn't have far to walk once they got through the infield and back through the tunnel. Now that Sawyer's pace had slowed, they took their time. Traffic would be an issue for about another half hour.

"So what's next?" Lucy asked.

He smiled, his sexy grin causing butterflies to take flight in her stomach. He reached for her hand, his strong fingers intertwining with hers. The friendly gesture indicated a new level of intimacy, and those butterflies flew a little faster. She'd never experienced such a sensation before, not even with Justin.

"I was thinking we could go out. Maybe get a drink? Or some coffee?"

"Coffee would be perfect," Lucy said. She'd had one glass of wine with dinner and the desserts in the suite had been positively decadent. His offer was welcome. She didn't want the night to end yet.

"Perfect," Sawyer said. He lifted their joined hands to his lips and kissed her skin.

A tingle traveled through her and had her momentarily clenching her toes inside the heels she wore. She balanced her oversize purse containing the clothes she'd worn earlier. She'd look a little overdressed for a coffee house, but that was okay.

But as they left the race track behind, Sawyer didn't take her to one of the area's late-night spots. Instead he drove away from the business district and into a more upscale residential area.

They were going to his place.

Unlike many condo complexes that looked like apartments stacked on top of one another, Sawyer's neighborhood had mature trees and each unit, while architecturally different, worked to create one building that blended seamlessly into something eye-pleasing. The garage door slid open and Sawyer drove the Corvette inside.

She turned to him, questioning his intentions. "Your place?"

"If you don't mind. I have a professional machine inside and a bunch of different varieties. I figured it would give us someplace quiet to talk. I promise I'm a gentleman."

He hadn't opened the driver-side door and she could see his profile in the light attached to the garage door opener. "If you're uncomfortable, I'll take you home."

She had to be honest with him. "I wish you would have asked me first. I thought we were going to a coffee shop. This took me a little by surprise."

Sawyer sighed and wrapped the fingers of his left hand around the steering wheel for support. "Sorry. I'm not necessarily the best with this stuff. I like numbers. Facts. Patterns. I find emotions erratic, chaotic—"

"Fleeting," Lucy filled in when he paused.

"Exactly. A bit disconcerting. I don't want to make a misstep. Logically my place provides less distraction. So if you're still agreeable, let's go inside and I'll make coffee. Or espresso. If not…" He didn't repeat his offer to drive her home but she knew he would.

"Coffee's fine," Lucy said. She paused behind him as Sawyer unlocked the condo door. Her fingers had a sudden urge to touch him.

Whereas he'd told her he planned on being a gentleman, which meant he probably didn't plan on seducing her, Lucy didn't find the idea objectionable. Something about Sawyer's innate sexiness made her want to sample him. She was the one wanting to rush. His touch did things to her insides. He had a body to die for and she was a red-blooded female who hadn't been close to anyone in a long time; even she and Justin stopped making love near the end of their relationship. Any kisses had been perfunctory, quick required things that had left little lasting impression. She'd written off both of their disinterests to the pressures of the upcoming season.

As Sawyer ushered her inside, she wondered what kissing him would be like. His lips were full and perfectly shaped. For a second she imagined his front teeth sliding over the top of her tongue and she shivered.

"Cold? I've got the AC on. Pollen count's high right now."

"I'm fine," she said, surveying her surroundings.

The condo had vaulted ceilings and skylights and Lucy sat at the breakfast bar located between the great room and the kitchen.

"My office is up in the loft and my bedroom beyond that," Sawyer said. "There's another bedroom and bath down on this floor and a small foyer and eating area. The place isn't very big."

"Yes, but it feels spacious," she said.

"My dad bought it for me. I'm thinking about selling. I read in the tabloids that Alyssa picked it out on one of those many business trips."

"That sort of taints things, doesn't it?" Lucy murmured.

Sawyer nodded, a frown crossing his face. "Yeah. The opportunistic gold-digging…" His voice fell off as he checked the expletive. "Sorry. I keep coming back to that. I'm starting to sound like a drag and a broken record."

"I can't imagine what you're going through," Lucy said. He'd moved to the other side of the counter, nearer to her, and she slid her hand forward even though she couldn't reach him.

"It's certainly complicated," Sawyer agreed.

"That's probably the understatement of the year."

"Yeah." The coffeemaker was doing its thing and made a hissing sound. He ran a hand through his dark hair. "It's been stressful. Nasty, really. My mom's the one suffering the most."

"They say tragedy brings people closer," Lucy said, deciding that statement sounded inane the minute she voiced it.

"Not in this situation," Sawyer disagreed. "Depending on the day, this situation can have us all at one another's throats. I'm worried that all my family drama will push you away before I've even gotten a chance to really get to know you."

"Your family is part of what makes you who you are," Lucy said. "Even though I'm close to my sisters, this past February was really hard on me once Justin and I broke up. I mean, they have husbands and kids. I thought I'd be there by now. You know all of us swapping baby stories. But that hasn't happened."

"Your situation is a little different from mine," Sawyer said.

"Yes. It is. But parts of it are the same. You've been trying to find yourself. I thought I had what I wanted, but didn't. Have you not at times been thinking, is this as good as it gets?"

He tilted his head. "Yeah. I envy my brothers and sister at times. They all knew what they wanted and went for it. They made it to the show. I'm finally reaching my dream, which isn't anywhere near as exciting."

"No, but it fits you and who you are. It took breaking up with Justin to realize that I was trying to make something happen that wasn't."

"You sure you didn't take any psychology classes of your own?" Sawyer teased. The coffeemaker finished brewing, but both he and Lucy ignored it. He sobered his tone. "I know what you mean. I think your twenties are this great exploratory time where you find yourself. Some of us just take longer than others."

"Maybe it's about contentment," Lucy added. "I wasn't married. I had Justin and things weren't working. I wasn't happy or satisfied. I wasn't content."

Sawyer propped his elbow on the table and leaned his head on his fist. "I finally am with some things. It's my family who isn't. I think I've exhausted their patience having them wait on me this long."

He straightened and rose to his feet. "I'm going to get us some coffee before it gets cold. Do you want any cream or sugar?"

"Both please," Lucy said. Sawyer poured her a cup of coffee and brought back some sugar packets and a small carton of milk.

"I'm not here enough to buy real groceries. It's simply easier to eat out," he explained, handing her a spoon.

Lucy automatically checked the expiration date, something she'd learned to do the hard way while dating Justin. The milk was fine and she poured some into the mug.

As she stirred she remembered the conversation Sawyer had had with Anita. Could Sawyer be in trouble? She could picture the headlines: Father Deserts Family; Son Stands to Lose It All.

She wanted to pry but knew that despite how close she and Sawyer had become in talking tonight, she should show him respect and wait until he was ready. So far he'd been open and upfront with her. He'd already stated he was afraid his family drama might drive her away. Better not to press.

"You've grown quiet again," Sawyer said.

"It's just late and I'm starting to get tired. It's not the company at all," Lucy insisted.

"It has been a long day," Sawyer agreed with an understanding nod. "I should get you home. At least you can sleep in tomorrow. It's Memorial Day."

"So can you. No classes."

He gave a wry grin. "Nope, no rest for the weary. Even though it's a holiday, I'm meeting with Larry Grosso, and I don't have everything ready so I have to get up early and finish a few things. I'm presenting my dissertation in two weeks."

"That's great! I remember my master's. I was nervous."

"Larry says I shouldn't have any problems, but there's

a lot riding on this. If I pass, I'm on track for a summer graduation and a fall teaching assignment. We're going over everything tomorrow afternoon so that there aren't any big holes."

"I understand. They grilled me unmercifully on my thesis. I thought I'd failed until the results came out. I can't begin to fathom the pressures of doing a doctoral dissertation," Lucy said.

She placed her half-empty cup of coffee on the counter and rose to her feet. Sawyer stood as well and soon they were in the Corvette on their way home to her place. When they arrived, Sawyer walked her to her front door.

"I had a great time," he said. He reached forward and gently touched her cheek with the backs of his fingertips. "May I kiss you?"

She found herself delighted and impressed that he'd asked. Most guys simply assumed, but Lucy was fast discovering that Sawyer wasn't like most guys. He had class. Charisma. Tenderness. Couth. The list could go on. He was a gentleman in the first degree.

"I'd like that," she said.

His lips came down on hers, soft at first then more and more insistent. His hands slid behind her neck and into her hair, and she let his touch sweep her away until the magic ended and his lips left hers. She could have kissed him forever. Maybe he should stay and…

"Since I'm busy tomorrow, shall we do dinner Tuesday?" Sawyer asked as he broke off the kiss.

He ran his thumb over her lower lip and Lucy nodded, wanting to be with this man more than she had any other. "Yes."

"I'll call you in the afternoon after my meeting," he said,

and then he kissed her one more time before he was gone, disappearing into the night. She could hear the Corvette long after she lost sight of it. She touched her lips once before going inside, a satisfied smile on her face.

CHAPTER NINE

"So?" TANYA DEMANDED TUESDAY morning when she called Lucy at 11:00 a.m. "What happened? I saw that you called but it's been crazy dealing with Kent and the paint fallout. So tell me, how was your weekend with Sawyer?"

"Great," Lucy said. She reached forward and touched the petal of one of the dozen red roses sitting in a vase on the end of her desk. They'd arrived about fifteen minutes ago with a card that had simply read, *I'm enjoying getting to know you. Sawyer.* "He sent me flowers."

"Justin never sent you flowers," Tanya said.

"I know. I don't think I've ever gotten them from a man on a nonholiday." Which was why all she could do was sit back and enjoy the warm, fuzzy feeling consuming her.

The florist had arranged the blooms tastefully, complete with stalks of baby's breath and a red-and-white striped ribbon.

"So what kind did you get?" Tanya asked.

"A dozen red roses."

"Wow," Tanya breathed. "Did you sleep with him?"

"No!" Lucy protested.

"Well, darn. I mean…that's impressive. He's smitten."

"I am, too. He's amazing." Unable to resist, Lucy fingered a soft petal again.

"Wow," Tanya repeated, as if lost for words. "And you were worried about how this thing was going to begin. I'd say you started off with a bang."

"But what if it fizzles? Or if life gets in the way?" Lucy asked, self-doubt suddenly rearing its ugly head. Unfortunately relationships didn't come with a guarantee you wouldn't get hurt. She'd already had plenty of personal experience with that.

"Surely that won't happen," Tanya reassured.

"I hope not. But I'm a bit skittish. His life is crazy with all the scandal surrounding his family. He's already getting pulled in multiple directions and his family members are demanding things from him. He's also been working weekends. Today he's working on his thesis, although we're meeting up for dinner tonight."

"Just relax," Tanya commanded. Lucy inhaled a deep breath. "That's better. I heard that. You worry too much so just stop. A guy doesn't send flowers unless he's really interested. If Sawyer's all you think he is, then just let things progress naturally."

"What if things are moving far too fast?" Lucy asked. She'd never been irrational in her fears, but the idea that if she jumped into bed with Sawyer, and then he found her lacking or too serious scared her.

"Sex is like a bike," Tanya said with a reassuring laugh. "You go for a ride and enjoy yourself. Besides, he's so hunky it's just gotta be good."

"Yeah, but I've had other relationships where the fantasy didn't live up to the reality. Worse, what if he thinks that means I want everything right away. I already told him I wanted to be married someday. I don't want to scare him off this soon."

"You'll only give yourself a headache stressing about this. Just enjoy yourself and let tomorrow take care of itself," Tanya suggested. Lucy heard a small beep. "Oh, that's Kent calling. He's at the engine shop and I'm supposed to meet him later. Something might have come up. I've got to go. I'll call you again soon. I want the details. Well, not all. You know what I mean."

"Yeah, I do," Lucy said, hanging up. She stroked one of the red petals one more time before getting back to work.

"SO YOU LIKED THEM?" Sawyer asked later that night long after Lucy had thanked him for the flowers. He'd taken her to one of downtown Charlotte's premier dining establishments. Located in the top of one of the city's tallest buildings, the restaurant boasted a five-star menu and prices to match.

"I loved them. I've never gotten flowers outside of Valentine's Day and those weren't as fancy."

"I saw them and thought of you," he said, a bit of relief filling him. He'd been in the local supermarket and wandered past the floral department. Unlike the grab-and-go bouquets, this place was full service and the red roses had caught his eye. The gesture had been impulsive, and after he'd made it, he'd worried all day that it might have been too much, too soon.

He'd never been on eggshells in a relationship before. Just looking at Lucy made him worry. She was beautiful. She wore a green silk dress that emphasized every curve. He swallowed. In every other relationship, something had gone wrong. He'd made some sort of misstep, whether intentional or not. He'd gotten bored with women who'd not matched his intellect. He'd had women dump him when they discovered his goal was to be a math professor and not something more exciting or glamorous like his brothers.

Lucy was different. Yet, he had that small issue of one hundred thousand dollars hanging over his head and a woman who didn't like gambling. He'd told her he'd be open and honest with her, but on this matter…

He smiled at her as their wine steward brought over the vintage he'd ordered. Candlelight always made everything better, and the glow accented the way Lucy's lips glistened as they wrapped themselves around the edge of the wine-glass.

He wanted her. It was that plain and simple. Yet, there was something deeper to his need, something intangible. As they talked, Sawyer realized he felt comfortable around her. He could open up, be judged on something aside from his appearance or his wealthy family.

Before he'd always kept part of himself back, kept himself more aloof. He'd learned early in life that women could hurt you pretty bad when they left. He'd learned to insulate himself, create buffers so that when a relationship ended, he just didn't care.

With Lucy, he already cared too much. He'd been the one to suggest tonight's dinner. He already hated being away from her, found himself distracted thinking about her instead of the dissertation he had to finish. That had never happened before.

They were kindred spirits. He had more in common with her than he did with his brothers. He realized that, for the first time in his life, if the other shoe dropped, he'd be losing a piece of him. His heart.

THREE HOURS LATER, the waiter discreetly dropped the check on the corner of the table. The place had thinned out except for about five tables. Lucy blinked. She hadn't realized so much time had elapsed. This had been one of the best nights of her life.

"We'll have to come back here another time," Sawyer said. He slid a credit card into the holder.

"That would be nice," she agreed. Her watch read a little after nine.

"We're just beginning," Sawyer said, noticing her actions.

"With the night?" she asked, anticipation heightening.

"With everything," Sawyer responded. The waiter snagged the credit card holder and within minutes after its return, Sawyer helped Lucy to her feet. "Shall we go? I have a little dancing place all picked out."

The drive to the venue took about ten minutes. Unlike modern dance clubs, Sawyer had chosen a place playing more classical music, and styles ranged from swing to ballroom. Even though it was a weeknight, the dance floor was crowded and Lucy found herself lost in the moment as Sawyer pressed her body next to his. She looked into his eyes. Those dark black pools held promise and suddenly Lucy didn't care about taking things slow. She wanted him now, wanted to be as close as two people could get. "I'm ready to leave," she said.

"We just got here. Are you sure everything is okay?"

She stood on her tiptoes and pressed a needy kiss to his lips. "I'm fine. No, I'm not. Please. Take me home."

He stared at her but wordlessly grabbed her hand and led her to the car.

The car ride seemed to dampen some of the emotional intensity she'd had at the club. Sawyer walked her to her front door and she trembled slightly, waiting. How did you just blurt out that you wanted a man to make love to you?

And she wanted that contact. She was ready for more than a few kisses on her doorstep. She wanted the rest of the romance. She wanted to touch him, to feel his skin next to hers.

"Come in for a while," she whispered.

He leaned closer, scrutinizing her expression. "Are you sure?"

"Yes. Positive."

She heard him groan and then his lips were on hers. He kissed her hungrily and her body reacted. She touched his biceps, feeling hard muscles beneath the suit coat he wore. She threaded her hands into his hair, her fingers memorizing the texture of his silky locks. This was her man. She wanted him: body, mind, spirit and soul.

"We're not inside," she whispered.

"If we go in, I'm not going to be able to leave," Sawyer said, dragging her close to him so she could tell exactly what he meant.

"Good," she replied, kissing him and undoing one of the top buttons on his shirt.

"I've never felt like this before. I want you to know that," he told her.

"Me, neither," she said against his mouth. Tonight held nothing but endless promise and…

Magic was her last thought as she led him inside.

CHAPTER TEN

THE NEXT MORNING WHEN Lucy woke up, she was satiated and well loved. She could hear Sawyer moving about her bathroom, freshening up. Unfortunately, both of them had to go to work. Lucy actually had a meeting with her staff or she'd play hooky. She hadn't gotten much sleep. Not that she minded.

Sawyer stepped out of the bathroom, his shirttails hanging out and covering the dress pants he'd worn to dinner. His suit jacket and tie remained crumpled on the floor and he leaned down to pick them up.

As he straightened he caught her eye. "Hey. Finally awake?"

"Yeah," she said. He came over and sat beside her. The sheet slipped a little, but she remained covered.

"So, still planning on giving up NASCAR races?"

That was out of the blue and Lucy frowned. "Why?"

He dropped a kiss on her forehead. "Well, Bart and Will want me to go to Dover this weekend and watch the race. I'd like you to join me. We can catch a ride up with some PDQ Racing employees on Saturday morning and enjoy the Nationwide Series race once we get there."

"I think I'd like that," she said.

"Good. I'll call Anita and have her arrange everything."

He kissed her again, this time on the lips. He lingered a while, teasing her lower lip with his tongue until he groaned and pulled back. "You're going to be late and so am I. Can I see you tonight or is that too much, too soon?"

She shook her head. Already her body longed for his touch. If neither of them had a meeting… "Tonight's fine," she said.

"Then I'll call you later."

IT WAS ON THE PLANE RIDE to Dover, Delaware, that Lucy realized she was falling for Sawyer Branch. By Saturday morning, when they boarded the plane with a variety of PDQ Racing employees and guests, Lucy had seen Sawyer every night that week.

They'd become almost inseparable. She wasn't sure exactly how it had happened. After their date Tuesday night and some spectacular lovemaking, neither had wanted to be apart from the other.

He'd kept his promise to call. They'd been like silly fools all week. He called her several times a day and they spent every night together. Wednesday night he'd even barbecued, the one meal he laughingly said he could cook. He'd done exceptionally well.

"I'm from Texas—we're raised on the grill since birth," he'd told her, and she smiled at the memory. He'd cooked everything over charcoal: steaks, baked potatoes and corn on the cob. He'd even bought a prebuttered, prewrapped French bread that he'd tossed on. They'd eaten and made love.

Thursday they'd found another excuse to be together. This time they'd ordered pizza and rented sappy black-and-white classic movies. Friday they'd attended an outdoor concert after she'd called him and invited him over for spaghetti and salad.

Now here they were, seated next to each other on the PDQ Racing charter, heading toward their overnight adventure in Dover.

The plane landed smoothly and they joined a load of people in a Suburban heading first for the hotel and then the race track. The mile-long oval wasn't too far from the hotel and they arrived in plenty of time to catch practice.

The intense roar of the cars rushing out onto the track, racing a few laps and then coming in for adjustments greeted Sawyer and Lucy. NASCAR assigned the garages by driver points. Thus the current leader was in the first spot and the last-place driver in garage forty-three. They found Bart and Will's spaces. Will drove in and after about five minutes of team work, sped back out for more laps.

"So who are we hanging out with this time?" Lucy asked.

"Bart. His new sponsor rented a suite so we'll be up there for the race."

"Do you ever hang out with just Will?" she asked.

Sawyer shook his head and a strand of black hair drooped over his eye, reminding her of how Sawyer appeared during lovemaking. "Not usually. It's either the three of us or just me and Bart. I'm a bit closer to Bart than I am Will. Not sure why. Just the way things are, I guess."

"Even though I'm close to both of my sisters, I'm closer to my older sister than my middle sister, who's more my age," Lucy said.

They moved to Bart's garage area at about the same second he drove in. He remained in the car and within two minutes he was back out on the mile-long oval.

Once practice ended, Lucy and Sawyer joined Bart's team for lunch.

"Hey, Sawyer," Bart said, greeting his brother when he entered the hauler. His eyebrow arched in silent query at Lucy's appearance.

"Bart, this is Lucy."

"Nice to meet you," Bart replied. He'd stripped out of his helmet and uniform and wore jeans and a T-shirt. He gestured to the woman at his left. "You guys know Terri?"

"We met last weekend," Terri Whalen added helpfully, giving Lucy and Sawyer a smile. "Good to see you both again. This is my dad, Philip Whalen."

"Hi," Lucy said. There were only five people eating inside the air-conditioned hauler, the rest of the team outside under the overhang. She and Sawyer took their seats. "Isn't Anita joining us? She flew up with us."

Bart shook his head. "I've got some jittery sponsors and she's gone to calm them. You heard about Richard's stroke?"

Lucy nodded. PDQ tried to keep quiet for as long as possible the fact that Richard Latimer had had a stroke a few hours following Bart's trip to Victory Lane last weekend, but it had been all over the local news and covered by the specialty racing shows for the past two days. They'd reported that Richard's nephew Jim had taken over PDQ.

"I imagine this has been hard," Lucy said.

"Yeah," Bart admitted. "While everyone's trying to remain positive, things aren't the same."

"So, Terri, are you here for work?" Lucy asked.

She nodded. "I am. I coach Bart and a few other drivers. Not only do I do physical fitness, but also mental exercises to help the drivers manage sports-related stress."

Lucy took a bite of her chicken sandwich. The caterer had served green salad, grilled chicken breasts, roast beef and mashed potatoes and even brownies for dessert.

"Terri graduated from State with a degree in healthcare management," her father said proudly. "She has a small studio in Concord."

"She's also got a studio set up in her motor home, which is in the Drivers' and Owners' lot," Bart added. He patted his stomach. "She's been working with me to get the weight turned into pure muscle."

"Bart's my best client. He always follows my directions." She eyed his plate and the amount of food he'd piled on it. "I'm going to have you on the treadmill an extra mile come Monday," she warned him.

"I'll sweat it off tomorrow. It's supposed to be really hot then," Bart said.

"The average driver loses eight pounds per race. Most of it's water weight. The average person has five to ten pounds of it depending on how much sodium he consumes," Terri said with a nod. She'd pulled her hair up into a ponytail and it bounced beneath the PDQ Racing cap she wore.

"So Lucy, I take it you're seeing my brother?" The question from Bart came out of the blue.

Lucy glanced at Sawyer, but before she could answer, Sawyer said, "Yep."

Bart looked from one to the other, his blue eyes taking in everything. "Good," he said simply, forking another bite of mashed potatoes into his mouth. "Never was very impressed with Justin. I think you've got the better man here, Lucy."

"Thank you," Lucy said. "I'm prone to think so, too."

"You know, Sawyer, you settling down would make Mom happy."

"She'd like to see all of us settle down, including you and Will," Sawyer pointed out.

"Probably even more so me and Will," Bart added with a laugh. He glanced at Terri, who had shuddered. "What?"

"You all can have your settling down," she said with another exaggerated shudder. "I am not willing to give up my freedom. Knowing my luck, any man I meet probably wouldn't like racing. I've got my career to build. I'm at the track every weekend."

Her father looked pained and she patted his hand. "Oh, it's fine, Dad. No more racing guys for me. I have enough trouble managing Bart and he's just my client."

"Crew chiefs. Now, they're the really loyal ones," Bart said.

"Been married to my wife for thirty years this November," Philip said proudly.

"And you have three grandchildren from my brother to play with when you need your grandkid fix," Terri insisted. "You don't need more from me."

"Your mother would like more," her father pointed out. "Even though your brother's only an hour away, we don't get over there much."

"No?" Sawyer asked.

Philip shook his head before adjusting the cap that covered his gray hair. At fifty, he'd been a crew chief for more than fifteen years, having worked his way up from doing body fabrication. "Zack owns a sporting goods store. He does really well but he's always busy and our schedules don't match."

"He's the practical, nine-to-five one in the family," Terri

said with a smile that didn't quite reach her hazel-green eyes. Lucy got the sense that there might be some tension between Terri and her brother.

Lucy also noticed the slight tension between Bart and Sawyer even though they both tried to pretend it wasn't there. The conversation had changed to their childhood in Texas and Bart's first midget race. "Sawyer's a genius. Back when I first started racing, he analyzed my fuel usage and figured out a way to make my car more efficient while still getting more power to the engine."

"It was nothing," Sawyer said modestly.

Bart smacked his brother on the back, a jovial gesture. "The heck with that. Because of your help I beat Will for the first time. He'd been lording it over me for a year that I hadn't come close."

Lucy finished her food and put her paper plate in the trash receptacle. "So what's the schedule for the rest of the weekend?" she asked.

"I'm hosting racing tonight," Bart said. "Remote-controlled cars," he filled in for those who weren't in the know. "We set up a course out by the motor homes and have at it. I'm second in points. You should come by. Cheer me on."

"I'm sure we can at least drop by for a little while," Lucy said quickly.

Sawyer shrugged, giving in. "Sounds fine."

Philip glanced at his watch. "The NASCAR Nationwide Series race will be starting in about an hour."

If the Dover infield was described in terms of a football field, instead of being near to each other, the NASCAR Sprint Cup and NASCAR Nationwide Series garages were located at opposite ends with the Cup garages near Turn One and the others located near Turn Three.

"That means it's my naptime," Bart announced, not interested in the NASCAR Nationwide Series race as he wasn't racing in it like several NASCAR Sport Cup Series drivers from other teams were. "When am I needed next?"

After he and Philip got the schedule confirmed, the lunch party inside the hauler lounge disbanded. Sawyer and Lucy had tickets to sit in the coveted glass bridge seating right above Turn Three and eventually they made their way in that direction after the race had started.

"I can't believe you got us in here," Lucy said as the cars raced directly underneath their feet. "I would have been happy anywhere, but this is the best."

After the race ended, they left the track for a while, catching a ride back to the hotel to freshen up and eat dinner in the hotel's restaurant before returning to the track. The Delaware day had been cooler than normal and overcast, meaning being outside was pleasant instead of unbearable as the month of May ended and turned into June.

"Nice digs," Lucy remarked as they reached Bart's motor home. The only other one she had seen was Justin's. Justin had fixed up a 1947 vintage Manor travel-trailer, and while it was nice, the thirty-five-foot-long bullet-shaped aluminum trailer was rather an oddity in the Drivers' and Owners' lot where million-dollar motor homes with multiple pullouts set the standard. Oh, there were a few smaller, family-size motor homes, like the kind you might see at a state park, but those were usually owned by the younger rookie drivers in the NASCAR Nationwide Series who hadn't reached NASCAR Sprint Cup Series-level salaries.

"Hey, Sawyer. Heard you were here." It was Will who

called out first. While Lucy had already learned to tell the brothers apart, the fact that Will wore baggy green shorts and a Taney Motorsports shirt made it easier. Will maneuvered his remote-controlled car so it stopped at Lucy's feet. "You must be Lucy."

"I am," she said, stepping gingerly around the miniature dune buggy that Will ran in tight circles around her.

"So you like my brother, huh?" Will asked.

"I do. Very much," she said.

Sawyer shot Will a warning glance and Will shrugged and moved his car back by the others.

Bart came over, shook Sawyer's hand again. "Glad you could make it. Everyone else should be arriving any minute."

Everyone else was a conglomerate of drivers and crew. Some were married, some single and dateless this weekend. Lucy noted with a bit of relief that neither Justin nor any of the Grosso family were in the group.

"We get pretty competitive," Bart warned Lucy as someone set up the small plastic cones marking out the race course.

"Yeah, like don't even dream about taking over first in the standings," one of Bart's teammembers called. "That's mine."

"Ha," Bart yelled back. "You'll have to go through me first."

"Planning on it," the guy said, revving his engine.

The first heat began five minutes later and Bart won. "Heck, Sawyer, you might be my lucky charm," Bart called.

"More than likely it's not him, it's his date," Will teased, bringing his car to the line for the next heat.

Someone called for the start of the next race and gave a three, two, one, go, and Will's competition began.

Lucy reached over and grabbed Sawyer's hand and gave it a squeeze. She leaned close to his ear and whispered, "You know, it means a lot to both of them that you're here tonight."

"Yeah, I know. Things have been really rough between us the past few months," he said, his tone not as happy as it should have been. He rubbed his thumb on the inside of her palm. "And I had other plans for tonight."

His finger teased, promised whatever she wanted. "That tickles," she said, tugging away. If he kept up the movement they'd be making a hasty exit.

"Yeah?" Sawyer said, those black eyes glittering.

"Five more minutes and we make our excuses," she promised, her breath catching a little. Even though they'd been together every night this week, she already wanted him.

He nodded, and after the next heat, where Will took third, they said their goodbyes. Unlike many tracks, Dover had no fan infield RV parking, so the journey back was pretty simple. Sawyer had phoned for a taxi, and it was waiting when they reached the specified parking lot.

"Today was good," Lucy said, holding Sawyer's hand as they rode back to the hotel.

"I thought so," he said.

"Your brothers are great," she observed.

"Maybe, but let's not talk about them tonight."

"Then what shall we talk about?" Lucy asked, giving him the opening they both wanted.

"Us," Sawyer said. He leaned over, caring little if the driver saw what happened next. "This."

The kiss lasted until the cab pulled up under the portico. A flushed Lucy stepped out. She knew her lips had to be slightly swollen from his attentions and her strawberry-blond hair had been mussed. An elderly couple entering the hotel gave her a glance, and then the woman touched her husband's hand, as if remembering.

The man glanced down at his wife and the smile the couple shared was so gentle and tender that it made Lucy almost want to cry. Would she be that happy when she was old and gray? Would she still love her husband—provided she found one, she amended—that much and without any hesitation?

She certainly hoped so. She stole a glance at Sawyer, who'd told her earlier he needed to stop by the front desk to retrieve the tickets and schedule Anita had left. Was Sawyer the man for her? Everything pointed in that direction. His touches made her simmer and just a glance made her smolder.

"Lucy? What are you doing here?"

She turned. She knew *that* voice. "Hello, Justin. I would think the question should be what are *you* doing here in a hotel?"

"I had a dinner event with one of my sponsors and their guests in the banquet room. I'm on my way back to the track now."

"Oh," she said. She could see Sawyer across the lobby, talking on his cell phone. He didn't appear too happy.

"I wanted to tell you, I'm sorry how things went down," Justin said. He shifted his weight from foot to foot and Lucy studied him. Same dark hair and soft brown eyes. Still the same height and weight. Little had changed about him. But she had.

She'd grown up. Lost her delusions. Found someone else. "Apology accepted. We've both moved on." She glanced at Sawyer, who was still on the phone, his back toward them.

"You aren't seeing him, are you?" Justin asked. "Sawyer Branch?"

She brought her chin up defiantly. "Actually, I am. We're quite happy."

"Lucy, he's got issues," Justin intoned. He glanced up at the ceiling as if that would provide him some inspiration for the proper phrasing of what he wanted to say. "A few weeks ago I was parked by Bart in the Driver's lot. Anita came by. She wasn't happy. You know Bart's had all sorts of issues."

"I know his family has problems and I'd prefer not to gossip about them with you," Lucy said. She took a step forward but Justin grabbed her arm. Amazing how his touch didn't do anything but annoy.

"Lucy, they were arguing over Sawyer. He's bad news. He's got a loan out with his father's bank or something. It's a lot of money. I heard *one hundred thousand dollars* bantered about."

"He used to receive a quarterly allowance from his father," Lucy said. Sawyer had told her about his finances a few nights ago.

"Yeah, but I'd never seen Bart so upset. I don't like the guy, but he's worried about his brother. I kept hearing Anita say 'If this gets out to the press' and stuff like that."

"So you were eavesdropping," Lucy stated, defending Sawyer although her mind had already started adding one and two and getting three. She'd overheard pretty much the same conversation last weekend.

"I couldn't help myself. They'd moved outside his motor home. I mean, anyone going by could have heard them. They weren't exactly quiet, which, if secrecy were that important, you would have thought they would have been more discreet. Anyway, when they finished, he went inside and Anita went on to do whatever she does. Look, I'm not telling you this because I'm being a jerk. I mean, just because we broke up doesn't mean I don't care about you. I don't want to see you hurt."

"Thank you," Lucy said, seeing the truth in his eyes. "Still, I'm a big girl. I can handle myself and make my own choices."

"Lucy," Justin added. "Just be careful."

"Good night, Justin," Lucy said, walking away from him and toward Sawyer, who was still on the phone. She had visions of her romantic evening going down the drain. Already the doubt had crept into her head.

No! she told herself. She had to trust her instinct, which said that whatever was going on with Sawyer wasn't that big of a deal. Sawyer had been nothing but perfect with her. Respectful. Everything between them simply felt so right.

As if sensing her, he hung up the phone, snapping it closed and turning. "Hey, sorry about that," he said with a smile designed to melt her defenses and wash away any anger. "My friend needed some information and forgot I was out of town tonight. He won't bother us again."

"Good," Lucy said. She reached out her hand, pushing her logical nature aside. Tonight she wanted to feel, to experience the entire package that was Sawyer Branch. Tonight she'd let herself go, lose herself. In the morning she could sort everything out. "Let's go upstairs."

His eyes darkened and he kissed her as they waited for the elevator. She gave him one last slip of her tongue before the doors opened and they both stepped inside. Lucy banished Justin and his warning. He was the past. Sawyer was the present. As the doors closed, she reached for him again.

"You are a greedy thing, aren't you?" he said.

"Absolutely. And don't you love it."

CHAPTER ELEVEN

SHE AWOKE THE NEXT MORNING, her body aching in all those delightful ways. The sun filtered in the closed curtains, creating a halo effect at the window. Sawyer snoozed on his side beside her, the sheet having slipped to reveal that hard, chiseled chest she'd palmed with abandon.

Who would have ever known lovemaking could have been like this? Sweet. Special. Tender. Yet at the same time mind-blowing and hot. That old cliché "it had never been like this" held true.

"You awake?" Sawyer mumbled.

"Yep," she said, sliding out of his grasp and heading into the bathroom. As much as she'd love to stay in bed all day, they'd already indulged too long. If she didn't get ready, they'd miss the start of the race. They'd made promises to people they'd be there, and those were commitments she kept.

Not that the race was that important, she realized as she showered. While she loved stock car racing, and the high-banked oval at Dover provided some of the best action, hands-down Sawyer was more important. She'd never felt so connected to a man in every way possible.

She had no regrets. That was the most important thing she discovered about herself as she shampooed her hair and rinsed. If she and Sawyer walked out of the hotel room and broke up immediately, she'd have had another night of absolute perfection. The reality had far surpassed any fantasy she'd ever woven.

Not that she expected anything to go wrong. If anything, last night had bonded them even closer, cemented them as a couple. As she stepped out of the shower she could already hear Sawyer stirring in the room beyond. He'd also have to shower and dress.

She wrapped a towel around herself and poked her head out. "I'm just about done here."

Sawyer loomed on the other side of the door. He pushed it open and entered. "I'm nowhere near done," he said, dropping a kiss on her lips and reaching for her towel.

ENERGY PERMEATED THE race track by the time Sawyer and Lucy arrived later than anticipated. The fans had arrived for the event, plastering the stands with colors from red to yellow to green, blue and black as they wore apparel supporting their favorite drivers. Since they'd be in a suite Lucy and Sawyer had dressed in slacks and shirts. However, Anita had told them that the sponsor didn't require a high-end, cocktail-party dress code.

They made their way down to the garage area. The race teams had already moved the cars out onto pit road, parked single file in the order of the starting lineup. To keep the heat out, each car displayed its sponsor's logo on a custom cover.

Team members wearing their uniforms raced up and down, making certain everything was ready: war wagons, gas cans and tires waited on the other side of the wall. The drivers and crew chiefs had gone to the media center for their mandatory prerace meeting with NASCAR officials and, when they came out, their P.R. people would move them through driver introductions, a few media interviews and then to stand by the car for the invocation and singing of the national anthem.

Unlike yesterday, when they'd been one of fifty-six lucky people to sit in the luxurious glassed-in stadium seating in the bridge over Turn Three, this time Sawyer and Lucy would watch the race from high above Turn One.

This vantage point would give them an excellent view of cars as they came out of Turn Four and down the front straightaway. The garage area was busy and teams didn't have time to talk.

"We're not going to catch up with my brothers," Sawyer told her as they passed Justin's Fulcrum Racing pit crew. "Let's head to the suite so we can get up there before the race starts."

"Sounds good," Lucy said, pivoting to follow him. As she did, she noticed Justin with his P.R. rep. If he'd seen her, he'd already glanced away.

Terri Whalen was in the suite when they arrived, as was Anita Wolcott, and both were the only two people Lucy recognized. Jim Latimer had remained in Charlotte to take care of both his uncle and PDQ Racing, although judging from the phone in Anita's hand, she seemed to be in constant contact with him.

"Hi," Terri greeted them. Lucy had to admit Terri was growing on her. Terri's carefree attitude toward life was almost the exact opposite of how Lucy approached life, so at first Lucy hadn't been sure what to make of her.

Still, Terri's knowledge of racing and her obvious lack of interest in Sawyer made her a good ally. She also had one of those infectious personalities that made people laugh.

"So how are you two today?" Terri asked.

"Doing great," Sawyer answered as they took places in the second row from the bottom of the suite's stadium seating. "What's the word from the pit?"

"Good, I hope," Terri said. "The car is running the best it ever has. As long as Bart doesn't literally drive the wheels off it or blow an engine, he should do pretty well. Dad's hoping for a minimum of a top-ten finish."

"That would help out," Lucy said.

"I'd say. Richard's stroke isn't sitting well with the sponsors. It's been too much upheaval in one season. Bart's win last weekend went a long way in calming them, but you know teams need at least ten million to field a car in every race. That's not chump change."

"Not in the slightest," Lucy said, always awed by the amount of money corporations could drop.

"There are some bigwigs in here," Terri said, leaning over so she could discreetly point them out. "Anita's been trying to reassure everyone that PDQ's not going to spin out and falter the rest of the season."

"I've been out of touch with Bart and Will this week. How's Bart handling the news about Richard?" Sawyer asked. "Richard's the reason he's at PDQ. Richard hired Bart and gave him a pretty quick promotion out of the Nationwide Series and into the Sprint Cup Series. Of course, my father's sponsorship money probably helped speed things up, but in my opinion Bart genuinely likes Richard as a person, not just as an owner. I'd think Bart wouldn't be handling this very well."

Lucy watched Terri's face. She could see the girl debate and then choose to reveal the truth.

"He and Richard are pretty close," Terri admitted.

"From what Bart told me during his training sessions, Richard's like a grandfather to him. He helped Bart personally back when news of what your father did hit the press. I think his reassurances that they'd find Bart a sponsor and he'd still get to drive kept your brother from coming unglued. Richard's a very patient car owner and he understood that Bart wasn't going to win a championship in one season."

"So Bart's not handling this well, despite trying to be jovial at lunch yesterday," Sawyer stated, wanting confirmation of his suspicions.

Terri nodded. "No one is handling this transition well. We're not sure if it's permanent and no one knows if Richard's going to pull through this or return. A lot of people are nervous—and over more than just Richard's health and welfare. He and Jim have different management styles. It's like a new sheriff has come to town, and my prediction is that it's not going to be pretty. Someone's head is going to roll as Jim makes his presence known."

The race itself wasn't pretty, either, unless you were Dean Grosso, who came in first. Rebounding from the previous week's paint job, Kent took second place.

As for Bart and Will, Bart's eighteenth-place finish was at least better than his brother's dismal twenty-fifth and Justin's twentieth.

The flight back to Charlotte on the PDQ plane was a lot less jovial than the ride up the day before. Everyone had been expecting a top-ten finish, not a top-twenty. Disappointment abounded and, coupled with Richard's health issues, made for a subdued flight.

Lucy yawned. The sun might be out for another hour, but she was tired. She hadn't gotten much sleep last night.

She smiled to herself and set the book she'd been reading in her lap. "Are you okay?" Sawyer asked.

"Going to take a much-needed short nap," Lucy said. "Someone kept me up all night. Not that I minded."

The corner of his lips lifted. "I don't think he did, either, and he certainly won't begrudge you a nap. That way you'll rest up for the night ahead."

"Good idea," Lucy said, shutting her eyes.

She wasn't sure how long she'd been asleep before she was jolted awake. Sawyer wasn't next to her, but she could hear his voice. Maybe he'd gone to the bathroom. They were seated almost at the back of the plane. Only Anita was behind them, most everyone else, including Terri, were in the seats toward the front.

"Anita, I said we'd talk about this some other time. You are beating a dead horse and making a mountain out of a molehill. If anyone's going to expose me and cause a shocking scene, it's you," Sawyer said.

"Things have changed with Richard's stroke," Anita said. Both her and Sawyer's voices were barely audible, but Lucy couldn't stop herself. After last night and Justin's warning, she strained to hear. "You have to get that one hundred thousand dollars this week."

"This isn't the best time for this conversation. Lucy has no idea."

"She's asleep."

"I said I'd handle it," Sawyer insisted.

"Look, you need to do something. I want to hear from Bart that this matter is settled by next weekend. If not, we've all got big problems. Understand?"

"Oh, I understand," Sawyer said, his tone derogatory. "Don't worry, I'll deal with it."

"You'd better. Bart's on eggshells enough. He needs to get a few more wins—especially after what happened today—under his belt, and fast."

"Fine," Sawyer said. Lucy felt him lean over her. "You awake, sleepyhead?"

She didn't respond but kept her breathing even and steady. She could swear he had to have heard her heart racing. It pounded in her ears. Justin had mentioned one hundred thousand dollars. Anita had mentioned Sawyer's big problem, and that he owed that much money. And somehow this would all affect Bart.

The coincidences to Kent's blackmail were too great. Could Bart be the one? He needed to win. Could Sawyer be involved? Had he gotten the information out of Larry Grosso? Thousands of questions swirled around in her brain and Lucy simply couldn't find any answers to any of them.

The only clear thing was that there was more to Sawyer Branch than she'd let herself believe. She'd concentrated only on the good aspects, the romance and the lovemaking. Could he have a dark side? The e-mails had come from the math lab. As Sawyer returned to the seat next to her, she just didn't know.

SAWYER BUCKLED HIMSELF in next to Lucy about a half hour before the plane landed with a gentle thump. She'd woken up a few minutes after his conversation with Anita.

Anita. Sawyer grimaced as the plane's brakes squealed. Bart's P.R. rep was becoming a nuisance. Despite Sawyer being back in Charlotte and leaving the racing world behind, his mind weighed on what Anita had said and he bristled. She and Bart were the ones becoming more and more vocal. They were the ones failing to be the souls of discretion. Lucy could have overheard everything! Luckily she'd been asleep.

She didn't need to know about his debt or his gambling. He had everything planned. Since he'd decided to present his dissertation in June, he'd officially graduate with his Ph.D. in July. He'd already discussed faculty positions with Larry Grosso, who'd pretty much secured the soon-to-be graduate one of the tenure-track undergraduate spots. Sawyer would teach three classes and continue to do mathematical research.

Besides, he was finished with gambling. He never should have gotten involved with Jake's wild ideas or his friend's dissertation, but blackjack had been a great way to make money. For the most part, Sawyer had used his winnings to help needy families who had children in the hospital. Sawyer's biggest mistake had been banking on money from his father. It was like leveraging a stock brokerage margin account right before the market dropped hundreds of points, leaving one high and dry as the account dried up. He'd planned on winning the money easily, long before anyone besides his father found out what he'd done and how much he'd risked. No, Lucy didn't need to know of Sawyer's failures or of his financial stupidity born of cockiness.

No, Lucy didn't need to know of Sawyer's mistakes. He just had to get through one more week. Like Jake, he had one more run to make before officially calling it quits. Jake's presentation followed Sawyer's, and Jake's goal of making a big score loomed. Unlike the MIT card-counting ring that had played for six figures a night, part of Jake's theory involved playing for smaller amounts over a longer period of time.

Jake's goal was to publish his findings, maybe get a job out in Vegas helping casinos. Whatever Jake did, once he went public with his scheme, Sawyer's days in any casino were numbered. While many casinos simply asked you to leave, some had security officers who played rough.

Sawyer had driven to the airstrip and he loaded his and Lucy's two carry-on bags into the Corvette's trunk, which swallowed them easily. The Corvette was fun to drive, but lately Sawyer had been considering that the car itself was impractical for daily purposes. His family had suggested he sell it when they'd learned of his debt, but Sawyer had refused to bow to that pressure. If he sold, it would be because he chose to.

"So did you have a good time?" he asked Lucy once they were on their way to her place. As for the plane ride, she'd slept most of the way home.

"I did," she said. She reached out and covered his hand with hers for a brief second. "I'm tired tonight, so I'm not going to invite you in."

"I can behave myself," Sawyer teased.

"Yes, but I don't know if I can," Lucy said. The smile she gave him didn't quite reach her eyes, and Sawyer wondered if she didn't feel well. She hadn't gotten much sleep this past week as many times after lovemaking, they'd talked until 2:00 a.m.

He'd never met anyone like Lucy. She fit him perfectly. His instincts hadn't failed him. She was beauty…and brains. The combination was deadly, and she had certainly slayed him. If all went well, he could see himself spending the rest of his life with her.

"Shall I come by tomorrow night?" he asked.

She turned her head. He'd reached her condo complex and parked in a nearby space. "Don't you have to finish your dissertation this week?"

"I'm ninety-eight-percent finished," Sawyer said. "I present next week, Thursday at noon."

"Then call me tomorrow," Lucy said.

He leaned forward and kissed her gently on the lips. "I don't know how I'm going to sleep without you."

Lucy's face colored as she remembered the night before. "You'll sleep," she said, stressing the word *sleep*, something they hadn't done much of. "The minute I close my eyes, I'm going to be out."

"I'll dream of you," Sawyer told her. The corners of Lucy's lips edged upward into a wicked smirk.

"You do that," she kidded, and then Sawyer groaned and captured her mouth with his.

He finally walked her to her door and, after setting her suitcase inside, gave her one more kiss before driving home alone, humming to himself all the way.

LUCY CARRIED HER SUITCASE into her bedroom and quickly unpacked. She sat on the end of her bed and glanced around. She was now absolutely wide awake.

She stood and went into the bedroom she'd converted into a home office and took a seat in front of her computer. Unlike Sawyer's town house with its balconies and second level, her condo was a ground-level unit with a tiny front and backyard.

Her cell phone rang, and expecting Sawyer, she grabbed for where she'd stuffed it into her pocket. Instead, it was Tanya.

"Hi, Lucy! Can you hear me? I'm on the plane home."

"I can hear you. Are you supposed to be using your phone?" Lucy asked, worried.

Tanya laughed. "That's a commercial plane. Private jet's fine. We've just left for the journey back. Kent had so many commitments. I've had champagne. Can you tell?"

"Just a little, but to me you just sound happy and excited. Tell him I said congratulations on second place. Bart's group was pretty subdued."

"I've been on flights home like that. They're not fun. Hold on."

Lucy heard a bunch of indistinct noises before Tanya returned to the line.

"I've got to go. I was calling to find out how your weekend went but that'll have to wait. Mark Wednesday night on your calendar. Kent and I are having you and Sawyer out to the house for a barbecue to celebrate. I'll call you tomorrow."

With that, Tanya disconnected and the phone in Lucy's hand displayed Call Ended.

She set the device on her desk. Her computer had loaded and it waited, ready for what she wanted to do. She hesitated. What she was about to undertake was highly illegal. Dangerous, even. While she doubted she would get caught, she was going to tap into the sophisticated e-mail server of the math department of State University. So far she'd been unable to get in, but tonight she was determined to succeed.

The lengths she would go, and all because of a man. She must be going crazy. She'd fallen for Sawyer. He treated her with kindness and respect. He cared for her. She felt like she'd known him all her life.

But Justin's warning echoed in the recesses of her mind.

She replayed the conversation Sawyer had with Anita over and over. Could her attraction to Sawyer be making her blind? She'd missed all the obvious signs with Justin, holding on to a false hope that somehow she'd be the one for him.

Was she missing the neon warning signs and acting like an ostrich and sticking her head in the sand? She'd been known to do that before.

She lost track of time as she worked, the process of hacking through protective firewalls not instantaneous. She typed and her eyes scanned the data. She looked for virtual cracks in the system, pieces of the code that would allow her to access the server. Like a secret password to a hidden passage, she just had to find the correct key.

She didn't move from her chair until she'd come close to unlocking the door to Sawyer's account. Her body was stiff and sore, but she persisted, even though she felt she was beating her head against a wall. This time the wall gave and she was through.

"Okay, Sawyer, what's going on?" she said aloud, her voice creating a slight echo in a room long silent except for the sound of her fingers clicking on the keyboard. "What have you been up to?"

And then there it was—the truth. E-mail from Craig Lockhart, Sawyer's brother-in-law, referencing the loan Sawyer owed and needed to pay back to the bank. There were several e-mails to her. She also found an upcoming flight itinerary for one person for a nonstop to Atlantic City, and with a route through Dallas on the way home.

She found an e-mail from Sawyer's sister, Penny, a plea that her brother get help—Penny had even included a link to the Web site for Gamblers Anonymous. Lucy found correspondence from Jake—the same Jake she'd met, she assumed—talking about one more run for the money and a final chance to score big bucks.

Her heart sinking, she continued to search. By the time she'd backed out, secured her own computer and erased the traces of what she'd done, her only consolation was that she hadn't found any e-mails to Kent Grosso or any mention that Sawyer had ever contacted Kent Grosso or that he knew anything of Kent or Patsy's issues.

But she'd learned enough to know that Sawyer had a problem. His "working on a math problem" had been a fancy euphemism for "going gambling." Sawyer had won and lost well into the low six figures.

The whole concept that Sawyer Branch had an addiction was astounding. But, after researching a bit on addictive personalities and gambling addictions, Lucy concluded that his family had a right to be worried.

Heck, she was worried. People lost their houses gambling. People hid everything, kept secrets from those they loved. She'd once read about a woman who gambled away her family's retirement fund, hiding her addiction from her husband and kids until men came to repossess her car.

Lucy shut down her computer and rose to her feet. Her body cracked and popped as unused limbs returned to life and her blood began to circulate. Her leg had fallen asleep, and it felt as if hundreds of tiny needles pricked the bottom of her toes and heel as she tenderly took her first steps.

The sun was starting to come up. She glanced at the clock and sighed. At this point, she might as well stay up and go into work. She headed toward her bathroom, where she washed her face and brushed her teeth. She stripped out of the clothes she'd worn to the race track and then common sense clobbered her. She made her way into her bedroom, pulled the drapes tight and let the cool darkness descend. Everything would seem better after a long sleep. She'd think more clearly, be able to put the pieces together. She'd figure out how to handle this issue with Sawyer.

At this moment, that left only one last thing to do.

She picked up her cell phone, dialed a number she knew by heart and called in sick.

CHAPTER TWELVE

THE RINGING OF LUCY'S doorbell jolted her awake with a start. The doorbell shrilled constantly and she sat up groggily and gazed at the clock. Four in the afternoon. She'd slept the day away. She tilted her neck, trying to work out the kinks.

Whoever was now pounding on her door wasn't leaving. She waited another minute, figuring one of those door-to-door people should have given up by now. The knocking stopped for a moment, only to immediately resume. With a resigned sigh, she planted both feet on the floor and stood. She stretched again and grabbed the rather staid robe she kept in her closets for just such emergencies.

She tugged it on, trudged to the front door and peered through the peephole.

Sawyer. She should have known.

She slid the feeble chain, turned the lock and opened the door. "Hey."

His expression radiated concern. "Are you okay? I've been trying to reach you all day."

"I'm fine," she replied, moving to let him in.

He leaned back, studied her to assess the depth of her lie. "I went by your office hoping to surprise you with an invitation to an early dinner. Marcie said you'd called in sick. I tried your cell and you didn't answer."

"I turned my phone off. I'm just tired."

He paused and jerked a hand though his hair, something he did whenever he was nervous. "I just wanted to make sure you were okay. See if there was anything you needed."

The fact that he was so flabbergasted and concerned touched her deeply. This was a man who cared about her. He had a core of integrity often lacking in many of the men she dated. Sometimes knowing a half truth wasn't the best thing. She'd read his e-mails, but not heard his side of the story.

"What can I get you?" Sawyer asked. "Have you eaten? Do you need food?"

"I am a little hungry," she admitted. Her mouth was dry and she made a slight face. In her rush to answer the door, she hadn't stopped to brush her teeth.

Sawyer solved that dilemma when he said, "What if I run down to the deli and grab us something to eat? Is there anything you don't like?"

She thought for a second. "Onions? Peppers? Neither of those sounds very good today."

He drew her into his arms, planted a gentle kiss on her forehead, one that had Lucy closing her eyes so that she could savor his touch. "I'll be back in a few minutes."

But even after taking twenty minutes freshening up, she was actually waiting for him in her living room when he returned.

He set three white take out bags on her coffee table and started unloading the contents. "They had fresh chicken noodle soup, and, even though it's June, I got some. I also bought roast beef sandwiches, salad and raspberry tea to drink and chocolate chip cookies."

"Sounds good," Lucy complimented, her stomach betraying her and gurgling loudly.

He heard the noise and gestured as he folded up the delivery sack. "If you haven't eaten your blood sugar's probably low," Sawyer declared. He started unwrapping the food.

"So, do you take care of everyone you know this well?"

He paused for a second. "You mean nursing them back to health? I have no clue what I'm doing. I'm improvising here."

"You visited the hospital," she pointed out.

He shrugged. "Yeah, but even there I don't do much but give the doctors predictive instruments that they can use to help their patients. I've only taken care of one person before, and that was my sister. She was about twelve and had the worst illness. My mom had some charity thing my dad had insisted she couldn't miss, especially since he would be off at the race track with Will and Bart."

"So, everyone left your sister home alone? You would have been what, eight or nine?"

Sawyer nodded. "Yeah. I guess they thought she'd sleep all day and wouldn't miss them. She woke up about ten minutes after they'd left. Penny's pretty self-sufficient, but that day I brought her all sorts of things. Our housekeeper was home but she had the same virus or she would have helped out. Gertie's always been there for us. She's staying on with my mother even though my mom can't pay her anything since all my mom's accounts are frozen."

"That's generous of her," Lucy said.

"I think they're friends. I've been gone for a while, but there's a bond between them that's more than employee-employer."

"You miss your mom, don't you?" Lucy asked.

"I wish there was more I could do to help her," Sawyer said. "I plan on seeing her Monday. I have a trip to take this weekend, to help my friend, and then I'll stop over in Dallas."

She thought for a moment about confronting him about what she knew about the money. She hated half truths. "Where are you going?"

"Not too far."

"What are you doing?" she pressed, wanting him to admit it.

"Not much," Sawyer hedged, sidestepping the question. "Nothing for you to worry about."

"Oh." She got ready to tell him what she'd overheard on the plane but Sawyer changed conversation topics abruptly.

"So would you like to attend other races this season?"

Lucy thought of Justin and then of Bart and Anita. "No. I'd like a little break for maybe a few weeks." Maybe time away from the track would loosen Sawyer up so he'd tell her what was going on. He cared about her, the proof was in his actions today. Surely he couldn't be a blackmailer. An idea formed. She knew a way to test him, see what his reaction to Kent Grosso would be.

"Are you free Wednesday night?" she asked.

"If I'm spending time with you, absolutely," he said, nodding. He held his own sandwich in his left hand and he set it on the paper wrapper. "What's going on?"

"Tanya Wells called me. She invited you and me to have dinner with her and Kent on Wednesday. Their place. She and I have been friends for a while and I think she wants to scope you out."

Sawyer grinned. "Ah. She's making sure I'm not going to cause you all sorts of bodily harm, pain or suffering."

"Exactly," Lucy said, watching him carefully for any sign of trepidation. But Sawyer didn't seem opposed to the idea. In fact, he seemed excited about it.

"I've met Kent a few times. Heard good things about him from Larry. I'd be happy to go and spend time with your friends."

"Good. I'll call her later and tell her it's a date," Lucy said, the tension leaving her. If Sawyer was the black-mailer, he certainly wouldn't want to be in the presence of the intended victim. At least, she didn't think so and hoped not. She wasn't a detective. The number of threads and speculation were starting to drive her crazy.

Dating someone should be simple. One man, one woman and a lot of caring and concern. Like this moment. Sawyer had finished his sandwich and had moved to sit next to her. His hands had moved to find her neck and he massaged gently.

This was what she wanted. A man who could anticipate her needs before she herself even knew what they were. Sawyer was perfect for her; it was as if she'd finally found the right man at the right time.

Despite all the secrecy, she refused to allow her own speculation to ruin the best thing that had ever happened to her.

"I'm feeling much better," she told him about a half hour later. The food had worked its magic and his fingers had coaxed all the tension from her shoulders. Her body trembled slightly. Her lethargy and exhaustion vanquished, she wanted him. She turned her head, bringing her lips within kissing range of his.

"Careful there." Sawyer drew back slightly. "You need your rest. None of that."

"Uh-uh," she mumbled, reaching out to thread one hand behind his neck. "You're the best medicine I need right now."

"That's a cheesy line," Sawyer teased, pleased, but not ready to give in yet.

"So it's not working?" she mumbled, moving her fingers and stroking the back of his neck. "I might have to try something else."

"I didn't say that," he said with a groan. "I'm trying to do the upstanding thing and be the perfect gentleman. You've been under the weather."

"A gentleman would have kissed me long ago," she tried.

"Liar, and lucky for you I'm in no mood to be a gentleman." Sawyer captured her mouth with his, the movement feather light.

So it was Lucy who became the aggressor, taking charge and demanding that Sawyer deepen the kiss. Tonight they were back on her turf, not some neutral-ground hotel room. They weren't in the midst of the race track and the buzzing energy it created. The excitement fusing their lips together came from inside them, not from any external sources providing mood and atmosphere.

The wrappers of the food left for later, Sawyer stood, drew Lucy to her feet and swung her up into his arms. He carried her through the condo until he placed her gently on her bed.

"Kiss me and make me all better," Lucy commanded, and, delighted that he complied, she let Sawyer sweep her away and love her all night long.

WEDNESDAY NIGHT AT SIX found Tanya admitting Lucy and Sawyer. "I'm so glad you both could make it! Kent's out back firing up the grill. I swear, he loves that thing."

She led them through the house. Lucy noticed that the place was looking a little more lived in and homey as Kent and Tanya settled in.

"Nice place," Sawyer commented.

"Thanks," Tanya said. "It's a little too big for us, but Kent and I both want to have a large family. We figured to buy large now and grow into it. I don't want to move again if I don't have to."

"Moving's such a pain," Lucy said.

"Tell me about it. Luckily this place came with some furniture. We hired a decorator to do the rest," Tanya replied.

"Oh, come on, moving's not that bad," Sawyer joked.

Tanya stared at him, eyes wide. "Are you serious?"

"He's an expert. He's moved all over the country. California. New York City. Charlotte," Lucy inserted. "Don't listen to him."

Tanya rolled her eyes. "True. You're a guy. I think it's a testosterone thing or something. You don't accumulate stuff like we do. Kent had rented all the furniture in his last apartment so he moved with next to nothing but his trophies and clothing. I had more stuff. Like, how many pairs of shoes do you have?"

Sawyer stretched out his fingers as he counted in his head. "Six? All I wear, though, are one pair of casual shoes and my tennis shoes. Oh, I do have some custom-fit running shoes that I wear only when working out."

"See? That proves my point. I have tons more shoes than

that. Shoes alone make packing impossible. I have to take a suitcase just for them when I travel for more than two days."

She opened the sliding door to the porch. A light breeze blew through the screens. "Hey, honey, they're here."

Kent stood from where he'd been sitting, watching the boats out on the water. He pointed at one. "Ronnie McDougal's out fishing tonight with his son," he said as he reached to shake Sawyer's hand. "Hi, Sawyer."

"Hi, Kent," Sawyer said, returning the handshake firmly.

Lucy watched the exchange with interest. Sawyer showed no ill ease or discomfort at meeting Kent in his own home. In fact, the two men seemed to get along famously and soon had separated themselves from the ladies. "Look at them out there, like grilling fiends," Tanya said with a laugh as she placed the salad on the kitchen table.

"They do seem to be getting along," Lucy said. Sawyer was laughing at something Kent had said.

"So have you made any progress on that matter you were working on for me and Kent?" Tanya asked, reaching into the professional-size refrigerator. She removed a garnish tray containing sliced tomatoes, pickles and lettuce. Dinner would be a variety of barbecued hamburgers, bratwursts and chicken breasts.

"I'm still working on it, but I don't have anything conclusive to tell you." Lucy busied herself with setting the table. Since Monday night she'd avoided all thought that Sawyer could be involved. Hacking into his e-mail itself was highly illegal and nothing she'd found directly linked him to Kent. The only coincidence was the one-hundred-thousand-dollar amount. That was it. Not enough evidence to convict anyone.

"Well, we think it's over. Nothing's come of it and Justin and Sophia seem to be doing pretty well. Oops."

Hearing her ex's name didn't bother Lucy at all anymore. Sawyer had completely erased Justin's presence. Now he was simply another person who'd once been in her world.

"No, it's okay. We've both moved on. I can talk about Justin. In fact, I ran into him at the lobby of the hotel in Dover and everything was civil. He actually apologized for his behavior and treatment of me at the end."

"Wow. Impressive," Tanya said.

"Tell me about it. His apology rather floored me. I also realized how happy I was with Sawyer." Lucy set the last fork down. The whole table was now ready.

"I sense a *but* coming," Tanya said.

"He does have a few secrets he hasn't told me about. I overheard Anita and Sawyer talking and…" Lucy simply couldn't say it.

"You don't have to reveal anymore." In a show of solidarity, Tanya placed her hand on Lucy's forearm. "I've been there. The wondering and the guilt of whether you should tell him what you know, it's really a pretty nasty roller-coaster ride."

"I'm certainly ready for it to stop," Lucy admitted. Her emotions had her tugging on a strand of her hair. "I have to admit, I'm afraid of losing him."

"Yes, but can you live with how you feel? I discovered that I couldn't. The weight of uncertainty got too much for me. Something had to give or I'd have gone insane."

Lucy understood what Tanya had been through. She hoped it would work out for her as well. "I agree. What's worse is that Sawyer's always said that we should be honest with each other. He's insisted that we shouldn't have secrets. Yet he's got a big one."

"Which you wouldn't have known if you hadn't over-heard him," Tanya pointed out.

"Right," Lucy said, leaving out the part about Justin's warning. "It's like a big cosmic joke that's not funny."

"You do have a dilemma."

"Yeah," Lucy said, deciding that was the understatement of the day. She and Tanya watched the guys for a moment. "I guess the key question is do I trust him? And am I a fool if I do?"

"As much as I'd like to help, you're the only one who can answer that."

Lucy exhaled a deep sigh. "I know. That makes it hard, doesn't it? He's going to be out of town this weekend."

"You should come to Pocono with me," Tanya offered. "It'll keep your mind off of everything."

"I'm not staying with you and Kent. I would feel awkward."

"You won't have to. I have a wedding Saturday night. It's June, the month everyone gets married, and I'm booked solid. So I'm not going to be flying to Pennsylvania until Sunday morning. You could come to the wedding with me, hang out here and keep me company. This place is simply too huge when Kent's gone."

"Let me think about it," Lucy said, not turning down Tanya's genuine offer outright. After all, what else did she have to do? This past week she'd spent most of her time with Sawyer. Even though she had said she didn't want to go to any races for a while, she could use a break from him and spend some quality time with her friend.

"Oh, do. I'd love to have you there. Hey, it looks like they're done."

The men were coming their way, plates of barbecued meat in hand. Soon everyone was seated at the kitchen table and enjoying both conversation and company.

"So, Kent, when did you know Tanya was the one for you?" Sawyer asked.

"The moment I saw her," Kent said.

"He was a groomsman at a wedding I was photographing," Tanya said, the bit of reminiscing making her blush slightly.

"I knew she was the one for me by the time the wedding couple said 'I do.' She took a bit more convincing, though," Kent said with a laugh.

Tanya giggled. "I did. It was love at first sight for me, too, but I was much more skeptical. I've photographed enough weddings to know that there are tons of hookups after every one. Everyone wants to experience the special joy of that weekend, if you know what I mean, but any chemistry found there rarely lasts."

"It did with us," Kent said.

"Yes it did," she concluded.

"You two are sappy," Sawyer declared with a grin.

"Yeah, ain't it great? I'm a man and not afraid to admit it," Kent said proudly. "And anyone who questions my manhood can just kiss my—"

From her place to Kent's right, Tanya playfully smacked her fiancé's hand.

"Championship trophy," Kent finished.

"Good save, honey," Tanya said, leaning over to give him a quick kiss as Sawyer and Lucy laughed.

The rest of the evening continued on in this upbeat and

fun vein. After dinner the couples paired up for a game of spades, with Lucy and Sawyer winning by only five points.

They finally left around eleven, with Lucy protesting that she had to get some shut-eye as she had to be at work by eight for an important meeting with her boss.

Sawyer walked her to her door and then hung back. She turned, surprised. "You aren't coming in?" she asked.

"It's late. I don't want to keep you up all night and you know that's what I'll be doing. You have to be on your toes for your meeting tomorrow. Can't be yawning your way through it."

It was true that they wouldn't be able to just snuggle. The man tempted her too much to allow herself to simply cuddle. They'd tried once, and she'd lasted all of five minutes before attacking him. "Alone might be best," she said.

He leaned in and kissed her lips lightly. "I'll make it up to you tomorrow night. I want to see you before I fly out. I'm not going to be home until Monday afternoon. After I finish helping my friend, I'm going to fly to Dallas and see my mom."

"Okay," she said, letting another kiss override the sense of unease his last words had created. At least he'd told her part of his itinerary. "Tomorrow. Six. Not one minute later."

"Not one," he said, sneaking a hand into her hair so he could deepen the kiss. His lips worked their magic until he pulled away before they crossed the point of no return. "I'll see you tomorrow."

And with that, he was gone, down the walk before either of them could change his or her mind. Lucy locked the door behind her. Monday night, she decided. If Sawyer didn't tell her tomorrow what was going on, they'd clear the air Monday night.

As she went to bed alone and fell into a fast, dreamless sleep, she decided she could live with that.

AS HE DROVE TOWARD HIS condo, Sawyer called his sister, Penny. Texas was on central time, so it was only about 10:35 in Dallas. She'd be awake, likely watching the news and the late-show monologues before she turned in. As she'd e-mailed Sawyer yesterday, he knew Craig was out of town until Friday.

She picked up on the second ring, probably answering the phone that sat on the nightstand beside her bed. "Hey, Sawyer," she greeted, obviously having recognized him from the caller ID.

"Hi, Penny. Thought I'd call and check in and see how you're doing. Been thinking of you."

"It's getting a little easier," she said, and Sawyer heard the bed coverings rustle. "I take life one day at a time. What can be worse than Alyssa's publicity?"

"I'll be done this weekend," Sawyer told her.

"Done?" she asked, as if uncertain she'd heard him correctly.

"Yes. With the gambling."

He heard her resigned sigh. "Sawyer, you can't just break an addiction by going cold turkey. It's simply not possible."

He tightened his grip on the phone, willing her to be open and finally understand. "It's not an addiction, it's a card-counting scam that's part of my friend's dissertation. I know you don't believe me and think that I'm in denial, but I'm not. I'll be in town Monday and am stopping by to see Mom. Just tell Craig not to worry. I've got things in place and am going to pay off the loan."

"I just don't want to see this financial situation get messier than it is. Dad already messed us all up."

"*He* did but *I* won't. You'll have to trust me. Have I ever truly let any of you down?"

"You were out gambling when Craig called for the family meeting," she reminded him.

"Penny, I'm telling the truth. I told Dad, but it's not likely anyone would believe him if he showed his face and backed up my story."

"So, Monday?"

"Yeah. Just a quick stopover."

"When's your presentation for your doctorate?"

"Wednesday. I'm almost done, sis. Just a few more days and it'll all be good. I'm not a screwup anymore. I'm even dating someone special."

She shrieked a little at that. "Do you think she's the one?"

He chuckled. "Don't get all spastic and go pick out invitations yet. We're still dating. But, yeah, she might be. We're taking things slow." Or as slow as one could get spending as much time together as possible.

"Do you love her?" Penny seemed awed by the prospect of her brother in love.

"I think so. I've never really been in love, so heck, I'm not really sure I even know what it is."

"It's wonderful," Penny said. "Your whole world seems to light up when you're with the person."

"Is that how you feel about Craig?"

"Absolutely. But it can be scary, too. Love's not always smooth. Have you told her about the gambling?"

"I can't," Sawyer said. "I don't want to lose her and she won't like it. And I'm quitting. I told you that. It'll be a nonissue."

"Secrets are always deadly," Penny warned. "If she's the right woman for you she's going to be there through thick and thin. She'd better hear about this from you rather than from someone else."

He bristled, unhappy with the idea. "Who else will tell her? Dad didn't tell Alyssa or she would have shouted my indiscretions to the world by now. It's too juicy of a secret for her to keep. She's such a media hound. My family and Anita Wolcott are the only ones who know about my so-called problem. So unless someone's spilled, I'm fine. Tuesday this entire situation will all be behind me. I promise."

Penny sighed slightly, sounding more like she'd yawned. He could picture his sister, covers up to her chin with the TV volume low in the background. "I'm going to hold you to that," she said.

"Do," Sawyer encouraged. "I have too much at stake to screw up now. And I don't want to lose Lucy."

"She's that important?"

He could say the words honestly. "Yes, she is. I've never felt like this before. I saw her long ago and liked her, but she was with someone else. Yet I knew that someday we'd be together. Does that make sense?"

"Yes, it does," Penny said. Unseen by Sawyer, she was gazing at the new ring on the third finger of her right hand. Before Craig had left, he'd given Penny his grandmother's garnet as a symbol of his love and his continued commitment.

"So, I'll call you later? Give Mom my love, will you? Tell her I'll see her soon."

"You should call her," Penny chided. "Telling her about Lucy will make her day and help keep her mind off the mess Dad made."

"Not until I get my finances straightened out, which I hope to do this weekend."

"I'm telling her about your girlfriend," Penny taunted playfully.

"Feel free," Sawyer said, and he and his sister chatted for another minute before hanging up after saying their goodbyes.

Sawyer hit the remote and opened the garage door to his condo. He parked the car, and as he entered the house, turned and stared at the Corvette for a minute.

Could he win enough this weekend to pay the loan and put himself on easy street? He had forty thousand in his bank in Charlotte. He had another ten in Dallas, the seed money for the gambling trip this weekend. His retirement accounts were untouchable without paying a prepayment penalty to the IRS.

And, unlike the MIT group that had formed a corporation and had a group bank account, Jake's theory operated on everyone keeping his or her own stake. That meant Sawyer still needed fifty thousand to clear off the loan. Easily doable. Jake's formula had been pretty consistent. Anything won over that amount would be gravy.

So come Tuesday, the gambling debt would be paid in full. The thrill from playing blackjack was gone; the college card-counting scam that they'd perfected and gotten away with ready to be ended while they were kings on the top of the mountain.

Thankfully he and Jake had stopped that other stupidity, before things had gotten too serious. Sawyer didn't think Lucy would forgive him if she knew the truth.

He was Kent Grosso's blackmailer.

CHAPTER THIRTEEN

SUNDAY DAWNED ONE OF THOSE picture-perfect weather days, adding dramatic irony to the melancholy Lucy was feeling. Lucy sighed and gazed upward. The sky was a rich cobalt-blue and the high cirrus clouds so wispy they appeared painted on like feathers. The temperature was made for racing—like Goldilocks's third bowl of porridge, it was just right.

But life wasn't—she hadn't seen Sawyer since Wednesday night.

They'd intended to get together before he left, but his doctoral presentation had been moved up to Friday. He'd left a message on her work answering machine early Thursday, saying he'd make it up to her.

Lucy followed Tanya out of Kent's private plane at a little after ten that morning. She'd risen early to catch the flight, and a renewed sense of raw determination overtook her. She was going to have fun today.

Oh, certainly she was going to keep her ears open for any additional information about Sawyer and his gambling problem, but tomorrow was Monday and she planned on them clearing the air once and for all. She clung to her last hope that he would come clean, and then like Tanya and Kent, all would be well.

By the time they arrived, the race track had come to life. Vendors cooked food. Merchandise trailers opened to sell wares to fans who arrived a few hours early. Parking lots filled as people competed for close spots. Tanya showed her and Lucy's credentials to Security and soon both women were in the infield and driving toward the motor homes.

"Are you sure you want to go and hang out by yourself? Kent and I don't mind you spending the morning with us," Tanya insisted.

Lucy shook her head. "I'll be fine." This wasn't an impound race, so the teams were already at the garages. "I'll wander around and see the sights. I don't want to interrupt your and Kent's reunion."

"It's not like we're going to do anything," Tanya said with a light laugh. "The team would kill me if I tired him out before he got in the car and drove. He's got to be on top of his game. This five-hundred-mile race is brutal, especially that tunnel turn."

"If you're sure I won't be in the way," Lucy said, still a tad uneasy.

"I'm positive. Come with me. You at least must say hello. I already warned him you'd be with me and told him to be decent."

Parts of the Drivers' and Owners' lot bustled by the time they arrived. A few teens were playing a pickup basketball game. One five-year-old raced his tricycle while his mother watched from a nearby lawn chair. Some single drivers' motor homes stood dark and silent as their occupants wouldn't face the day for at least another hour—the mandatory NASCAR driver/crew chief meeting not starting until a little before one.

Tanya parked her rental car next to Kent's. "We're here."

Lucy had never been inside Kent's motor home. Fitting the current reigning NASCAR Sprint Cup Series champion, Kent's digs were impressive, even more so than Bart's had been. She took a seat on the leather couch and waited while Tanya retreated to the rear bedroom.

Tanya came out a few minutes later. "Kent's up. He's getting a shower. What can I get you for breakfast?" She opened the refrigerator door. "Oh, Jesse baked a coffee cake and there's still some left."

"Jesse?" Lucy queried.

"Kent's coach driver. He's a godsend. This place would get pretty bare without his shopping skills. Kent's idea of cooking breakfast involves either powdered doughnuts or sugary cereal."

She pulled out the coffee cake, some cream cheese, some bagels and a grapefruit. "We've even got fresh orange juice. Jesse's the best. He's this retired army vet, and you'd never know he loves to bake from looking at him. He also makes sure to have fresh flowers on the table."

Lucy followed Tanya's gaze over to the kitchen table, where a batch of white daisies resided in a blue vase.

Having eaten a bowl of cereal before the flight, Lucy still indulged and had half a bagel and a slice of homemade coffee cake. By the time Kent came out, Tanya had cooked him some eggs and bacon and sliced the grapefruit. He wore a T-shirt and jeans and kissed his fiancée gently.

"You look tired," Tanya remarked.

"My nose is a bit stuffed up. I'm hoping I'm not coming down with a cold," Kent said, reaching for a tissue.

While Tanya fussed over Kent, Lucy made her excuses and a few minutes later stepped out of the motor home. As much as Tanya had insisted she wouldn't be, Lucy didn't want to be a third wheel. There were plenty of race preparations going on so she headed toward the garage. Since Tanya had invited Lucy to watch the race from Kent's pit box, she'd promised to meet Tanya at twelve-thirty.

Lucy wandered through the garage area, making mental notes. Prerace activities started at one. The teams had all practiced and qualified, so once they'd been introduced, the drivers would climb in the car and go. Members of the media moseyed around, filming pieces of footage they might use later.

"Lucy?"

Lucy turned, seeing Anita Wolcott step out of the back of Bart's hauler. "Hi, Anita."

Anita's face had paled slightly and she appeared shocked to see Lucy. "I thought that was you. What are you doing here?"

Lucy frowned. "I'm Tanya Wells's guest. Kent Grosso's fiancée?"

"I know who she is." Anita gestured and Lucy walked over. "I didn't expect you. Come inside a moment. I need to talk to you and no one's here yet except for some team members, and they're working in the garage."

Once safe inside the confines of the lounge, Anita faced Lucy. "So Sawyer isn't with you?"

Lucy didn't understand Anita's worried tone. Bart's P.R. rep was obviously upset about seeing Lucy alone. "No, he's out of town."

Anita exhaled, her tension visible. "He told Bart he was taking a romantic getaway with you. You're here without him."

The coffee cake Lucy had eaten felt like lead and she

couldn't help herself. Her jaw dropped open. "Anita, what exactly is going on? I overheard you and Sawyer talking on the plane. You need to fill me in."

"You'd better take a seat." Anita pointed to the sitting area and Lucy sat on one side of the booth.

"Okay, tell me. I'm trying hard to understand."

Anita sat across from Lucy. "Bart wanted Sawyer to attend this race as his guest. You were invited, too. However, Sawyer told Bart that he was taking you on a romantic trip this weekend. So imagine my shock to see you and not him."

"He said he's helping a friend," Lucy said. She stared at the silent plasma-screen TV inset into the wall across from her. "Look, I know you're trying to protect his family and so am I. You better tell me exactly what's going on. I keep hearing snippets about a loan Sawyer owes."

Anita frowned. "Sawyer hasn't told you anything?"

"You mean about his gambling? No. But I've overhead things, mostly from when you and Sawyer were talking. Also, Justin overheard you and Bart and he mentioned it to me."

Lucy watched Anita's face closely for a reaction. The woman's P.R. training had her maintaining a neutral facade, but Lucy could see in the slight way her lip quivered that she was deciding what she should do. Was this a situation requiring damage control or one where she had to confess?

"I know he owes a whole lot of money. Justin even warned me not to get involved with Sawyer," Lucy added, hoping this would help Anita in making her decision to fess up.

Anita rested her hand on her fingertips, her elbows

planted on the table. "I swear, this whole Branch family situation is going to do me in before the end of the season. Sawyer has a signature loan with his father's bank for the amount of one hundred thousand dollars. He needed the loan because he owed a Las Vegas casino. He'd lost the full amount of his yearly allowance in one weekend. I guess he expected Hilton to be around to bail him out, which, in a sense, his father did."

"So it's true." Lucy voiced the words aloud, for doing so made the enormity of it more believable.

"What, that he needs to pay this off quickly? Absolutely correct. Alyssa Ritchie had no idea of the loan or she'd have spread the news everywhere that Hilton's son needs Gamblers Anonymous. Now that Hilton's left her behind, no one in the Branch family is safe from her wrath. Like she has any reason to act like a woman scorned. I won't continue with what I'd like to do to her for hurting these people. But if this gets out…"

"So is Sawyer going to be able to come up with the money or not?" Lucy asked.

Anita straightened and shook her head. "I don't think so." She appeared tired, as if the weight of the world was starting to wear her down. "I wish I knew. The loan originated in early January, so Sawyer's had all this time to deal with it. He hasn't even made one payment. Hilton gave him seven months deferred before interest and payment begin."

"Nice terms," Lucy said.

"Exactly. Sawyer's not taken his debt seriously. His career isn't on the line like his brothers'. He's going to be a math professor. Who cares about that?"

Lucy did, but she bit back her retort.

Anita sighed. "I'd love to believe he'll follow

through, but I can't. I did some research. One of the main symptoms of a gambling addiction is denial that there's even a problem. The gambler lies to his family and friends. He also gets bailouts. Then there's the preoccupation with the game and the fact that the highs and lows provide an escape from reality. Sawyer has so many of the signs of a pathological gambler, and we're concerned that he'd be the last person to see that he has a problem."

"I did some research on my own, too," Lucy said. Worry mixed with anger. Sawyer had told her the truth about his travel, but omitted major parts of what he was doing.

Anita straightened. "He's willing to risk his relationship with his family over this. That's one of the huge red flags you have to watch out for. Gambling can be as addictive as any drug," Anita finished.

"Then what do we do?" Lucy asked, furious that Sawyer had lied to her. Still, if he needed help, she wanted to be there for him. As his friend, she at least had to try. She'd do the same for her family or anyone else she cared about. And she did care for Sawyer. She wasn't ready to give up on him yet.

"I don't know what we can do," Anita replied. "We've all been putting pressure on him, but it's not done any good. He doesn't seem to care. He keeps saying he'll take care of the debt, but none of us has seen any concrete evidence. Heck, now that you're here I don't even know where he is this weekend. At least when he's at the track we know he's not off somewhere playing cards. Do you know where he might be?"

"I believe he's in Atlantic City," Lucy said, trying to remember the exact contents of the e-mail she'd read.

"Yes, but where? He uses his cell phone when he calls

so you don't know where he's at. He could be in Monaco for all we know."

"Does his phone have a GPS feature? Could we have his provider track him down for us?" Lucy suggested.

Anita shook her head. "Even if I knew his carrier, that's too dangerous. This race track is so small that doing something like that would be all over the place before the cars got to Turn One on the first lap. You can't burp without someone overhearing it."

"Do you have a computer?" Lucy asked, ready to try the next thing she could do.

"I have my laptop," Anita replied.

"If it has Internet, that should work."

Lucy waited while Anita retrieved it. One of the things Lucy had been able to do when hacking into the State University math server was to learn Sawyer's user name and password. While Lucy hadn't checked his e-mail since that one time, she knew how to legitimately pretend to be him and access his account.

Anita placed the laptop on the table and hooked it up to the hauler's satellite connection. Once she'd brought up the Internet, she passed the laptop over. Lucy angled the screen so that Anita couldn't see what she was doing, and within a minute, Lucy had opened Sawyer's e-mail.

"I need a piece of paper," Lucy said.

Anita opened a drawer and took out a spiral notebook. She ripped out a sheet and passed it over. With the pen Anita handed her, Lucy began to jot down the information she found.

Jake had sent Sawyer an itinerary for the weekend. They had several stops, but today they were hitting the Zone Hotel and Casino in Atlantic City. Lucy logged off, cleared the history and deleted the cookies. She then went on the hard drive and made sure everything was gone. While someone could still retrace her steps, they'd have to be an expert to be able to access the computer's inner workings.

"Sawyer's here," she said, passing the paper to Anita.

"The Zone in Atlantic City? I've never heard of that place."

"That's where he's at."

"And you're sure."

Anita appeared shook up, and Lucy could imagine her trying to plan for the consequences. "I'm positive," she told her with a nod. "He's on a flight to Dallas around six tomorrow morning. He told me he plans to visit his mother before returning to Charlotte."

The pressure of Bart losing his sponsor, Richard's stroke and Sawyer's debt had taken its toll on Anita. She looked ashen, almost beaten. "So what do we do? I'm a P.R. person, but this one is way over my head. I have no idea how to spin this should it get out."

"You don't need to do anything," Lucy said as she made her decision. Her soul was sick with having to get the information this way. She was the one dating Sawyer, the one he'd made love to and then lied to. "I'll handle this. I'm going to need your help, but whatever you do, you cannot breathe a word of this to Bart or anyone else. Can you agree to do that?"

Anita debated and then she nodded. "If it helps Sawyer and protects Bart, you bet I can. But you'll owe me a full report."

Lucy's determination grew. "I can live with that. Now, this is what I need you to do. First, I'm going to need help getting to Atlantic City."

AN INTERESTING FEATURE OF casinos is that they are deliberately designed without windows. Three in the afternoon or three in the morning, a casino appears exactly the same. It's a place where day and night cease to exist, and the only thing a player needs to do is focus on the game he's playing and how much he is winning.

Not that the house ever planned to let a player win very much. Even those offers of free meals, drinks and shows were designed to lure the player into losing.

Sawyer glanced at his watch. He'd been sitting at the blackjack table in the same spot for the past two-and-a-half hours. So far he'd won some and lost some, doing a decent job of flying under the radar of the ever-present and watchful casino security.

When he'd hit the fifteen thousand mark in winnings, he'd been offered a free cocktail. Although the bar served alcohol twenty-four hours a day, Sawyer turned down the offer and stayed with water and the occasional cola for much-needed caffeine. The Zone was his last stop. He'd marathon here until he reached the goal he'd set for himself.

It wasn't as if the casino would be in any hurry to have him leave. He'd seen players sit at the tables for a day straight, only rising for the rare trip to the restroom. He'd seen the high rollers come in and win and win and win, and then lose everything in the last five minutes.

The State group hadn't played the Zone, a newer casino that had just opened a few months ago. It had highly sophisticated security surveillance, and the entire group who'd been helping Jake with his research was here, something Jake hadn't risked in the past.

But this was the end of their journey, the last hurrah, so they'd figured the odds of being connected to each other were low. Each of them had their own distinct mode of operation. Unlike the MIT team, the State group never used spotters and didn't keep a central bank. Any money won or lost was an individual responsibility. The group only met when they were on campus. Then they practiced Jake's formulas and presented him with their data. Those involved had made a fortune. The only one with debt was Sawyer, who'd taken out a hundred-thousand-dollar loan so he could pay medical bills for a needy family. He'd planned on his father's allowance to provide him the seed money to win everything back long before now.

Thanks to Hilton's actions, that hadn't happened.

"You're lucky," the dealer said as he again paid out to Sawyer.

"Not really," Sawyer said, not bothering to touch his new chips. He grinned, acting the role he'd chosen. "I'm trying to win enough for a wedding ring set, but every time I get close, I lose it all. I'm hoping today will be different. It has to be. Those jewelry stores are murder. You should see the rock she wants."

"Yeah, but Lady Luck can be fickle," the dealer warned as play resumed again.

As the players anteed up, Sawyer knew the casino was watching both dealers and players. One of the most common ways cheaters got caught was because of "rubbernecking." The cheater would look around, stare at the cameras in the ceiling and look for the security personnel on the floor.

Sawyer never did any of those. Card counting wasn't necessary illegal, but casinos didn't like it very much. They couldn't detect card counting as it was an entirely mental activity, impossible to prove unless a player moved his lips, scratched numbers on his leg or gave some other telltale sign.

Sawyer was an expert. His memory worked like iron. His posture was relaxed. When necessary, he kept up the correct amount of inane chatter. His brain worked the math and the probability scenarios, but his face never revealed more than any other recreational gambler.

He resisted the urge to check his watch or to glance around and see how his friends were doing. He adopted the posture of a man intent on winning enough for a ring for his very spoiled fiancée. He only had a little bit more to go and he'd stop.

Movements behind him made the hairs stand up on the back of his neck. He forced himself to stay composed. Casino security could not be deciding to harass him now, not when he was this close to the amount he needed. However, no one stepped into your space this near unless you were about to be escorted out....

"There you are. I've been looking for you."

His heart sank and he almost dropped his cards. Not casino security. But he *knew* that voice. The dealer looked at him expectantly, waiting for Sawyer's decision.

"This is my fiancée," Sawyer told him as he motioned for a hit. This time he should get the six he needed. He pivoted slightly and reached for Lucy, his black eyes shooting her a firm warning as he grabbed her hand. He had no idea how she'd found him or why she was here, but they could save that for later. She couldn't blow things for him. Not now.

"Hi, honey," he told her, ignoring the red-hot glare in her blue eyes. "I'm glad you finally arrived."

CHAPTER FOURTEEN

DURING THE FLIGHT FROM Pennsylvania to New Jersey, part of Lucy hadn't wanted to face the truth that Sawyer's problem might be insurmountable.

She'd harbored the slightest hope that when she got to Atlantic City, she'd find the casino and discover that Sawyer was doing some sort of covert work for the government. She'd hoped he'd have some reasonable justification for his gambling—that somehow he'd have a viable excuse that would show he wasn't simply a junkie who needed a weekly fix.

She'd strolled into the casino and immediately felt out of place. Oh, she'd been in a casino before, once when she and Justin had visited during a NASCAR Sprint Cup Series stop at the track in Las Vegas. They'd stayed an extra day and Justin had blown a small fortune, the low five-figure amount staggering to her sensibilities.

Of course, any amount over five hundred was mind-boggling. Five hundred dollars was more than the average car payment. How could people lose double, triple or even ten times that amount without blinking?

She'd caught the warning in Sawyer's black eyes and so she'd stood there, waiting, until play ended. He'd won again as the dealer busted.

"I guess she wants me to quit while I'm ahead," he told the dealer. Sawyer placed all his chips on a tray and rose to his feet.

"Come on. We're cashing out," he told her, and she followed him to the teller window, where Sawyer filled out a tax form, took his winnings in the form of a cashier's check and then walked out with Lucy at his side.

She was aware of quite a few interested gazes following them, and despite herself, she looked back, seeing several people she recognized from that day in the math lounge. Could it be even worse than she'd imagined? No wonder Sawyer denied he had a problem if all his friends gambled, too. They might not have been playing for money that day, but they were playing for big bucks today.

Sawyer grabbed her hand so that they appeared like a happily engaged couple, and together they walked out of the casino and toward a bank of hotel elevators.

"I have a room upstairs," he told her.

"Look, I…" she began, a small part of her suddenly a little bit nervous to go anywhere. She'd spent Friday night watching gangster movies, which was proving to have been a major mistake as her paranoid brain was now working overtime.

"We'll talk in private," he said, his sharp tone making her aware of the black camera domes hanging from the ceiling, recording their every move. The domes were everywhere, even in the lobby and the elevator.

They exited on the fifteenth floor and Sawyer slid his passkey into the door handle of room 1510 the moment the light turned green. They stepped inside into a typical, nondescript hotel accommodation with a king-size bed.

"So let me guess, Bart sent you," Sawyer said. His earlier anger in the lobby seemed to deflate.

"Actually, I sent myself," Lucy said, gaining sudden insight into the phrase "walking on eggshells." "I was at the track in Pocono when I heard you were out of town. Anita told me we were supposed to be on a romantic holiday, or at least that's what you told Bart we were doing."

He gave a harsh, bitter laugh. "I probably should have used a better excuse. Left you out of it."

"Do you have an excuse?" she asked, for turning the inquiry around seemed like a logical way to proceed. She had to make Sawyer see the truth, get him to take off the blinders and reach his own conclusions and revelations.

"Actually, no. I don't have a gambling problem. I keep telling my family that," Sawyer said. He took his wallet out of his pocket and sat with a thump on the bed. He slid the check inside the billfold.

Lucy sighed. Anita had told her that Sawyer had denied the problem for months. "Then what would you call my finding you in a casino with all your math buddies?" Lucy asked from where she remained standing by the closet.

"Blackjack's a way to make a lot of money very fast, and my family wants me to pay off my debt," Sawyer replied. He glanced up and noticed her location. "You can sit in the chair. I won't bite. Have I ever mistreated you?"

He'd lied, yes. But he'd never treated her with anything but TLC. She eased toward the wooden hotel desk and sat in the chair. She was physically closer to him now, but still five feet away.

She had to know the truth. "Okay, I'm listening. Tell me your side. Start at the beginning. Explain why you're here and why everyone thinks you have a problem. Why is it that you owe one hundred thousand dollars?"

"Ah, so they told you about that, too? Why am I not surprised?" He reclined against the decorative bed pillows and stretched his legs out, dress shoes still on his feet. "What if I told you this was all some big math project? Like that MIT card-counting ring?"

"Those are impossible these days," Lucy said.

Sawyer leaned back. "Yeah. That's why you can take classes, buy books and train on the Internet."

Lucy wanted to throw her hands up in frustration, so she shoved them under her legs. "Those sites are like those companies that tell you to sign up for their seminar so you can make six figures in a week buying real estate. The only people who make money are the people selling the tapes."

Sawyer's lips puckered slightly and he moved them from side to side before he sighed. He reclined further and put his hands behind his head. "And you know this because…"

Because she'd done her research? A desperate sensation consumed Lucy. To tell him why, to convince him she was right, would mean revealing she'd violated his trust by accessing his e-mail.

"Look, I'm not on Bart's side. For all I knew you were out with someone else. Tell me what is going on," she told him.

"I did."

"What? A gambling ring?" She tried not to sound mocking, but the thought was simply ludicrous. He'd said he was helping a friend, but gamblers lied. She'd researched. Read up on the symptoms.

His gaze narrowed, his disbelief obvious. "See, you

don't believe me, either." He released his arms, dropped them to his side and began to tap his fingers on the bed-spread, the cloth muting the noise.

"I'm trying hard to believe you," Lucy said, her anger beginning to boil.

"No, you're not. You're judging me and prying. Is it because we made love all those times? Do you think that gives you the right?"

She steeled herself. She'd seen an intervention on a TV talk show once but it hadn't prepared her for this. "I'm here because I care. I'm hoping you care enough about me, and any future we might have, that you won't throw it away."

"Do we have a future? You once told me that you'd never put up with someone who gambles, which is why I never told you what I was doing. So what hope do I have? You caught me red-handed. Is telling you that I'm finished as of today going to be believable when you don't believe why I'm doing this? Are you going to trust me or will this always be a black mark hanging over my head?"

His bitterness was obvious and Lucy's frustration continued to mount. Her fights with Justin had less verbal wrangling, and she hadn't yet gotten a handle on her current situation.

"Sawyer, stop fighting me. I am not your enemy. I care about you deeply or I wouldn't be here, worried about you. I left Pocono to come here."

Sawyer exhaled, as if tired and beaten down. "I haven't eaten in hours. I need some food. Are you hungry? What do you want? The room service menu is over there in that folder. Pick something out."

She flipped the packet open, eager for something to view as she tried to determine how to best deal with

Sawyer. This whole situation was freaking her out, making her wonder if she should simply cut her losses and run. She'd held on to the relationship with Justin for far too long. Maybe she was doing the same thing here. She closed the menu, determined to give him some time, at least through dinner. "I'll take the chicken Caesar salad."

She handed him the menu and he made the phone call and placed the order. Then he studied her, taking in the polo shirt and khaki pants she'd worn to the track. She'd flown straight out, arriving a little after three-thirty.

The whole afternoon had been a bit of a whirlwind. Anita had arranged to get Lucy on the next commercial flight and hired ground transportation. Lucy hadn't wanted to tell Tanya anything, and had called her friend and said she had a sick family member. Tanya had offered Kent's plane, but Lucy had turned that down since she didn't want Tanya to be able to ask the pilot about Lucy's destination.

So here Lucy was, in a hotel room in Atlantic City with Sawyer. "Okay, please tell me what's really going on. Make me understand."

He stared at her a moment and then nodded. "I don't want to fight you, Lucy. I care about you more than anyone I've ever dated. These past few weeks have been some of the best of my life."

He paused, she nodded, and he continued. "I'm not a gambler by nature. As I told you before, I'm helping out friends."

"Sawyer…"

"Hear me out," he grated, and Lucy closed her mouth. Whatever he had to say, she could do him the courtesy of listening, even if it was a big lie. She could always confront him at the end. "Sorry."

"Thanks. As I told you, I'm helping out a friend. You met him. Jake, he's here with me, as are a bunch of other guys from State…"

Lucy nodded. "I saw them downstairs."

"Anyway, early last year Jake got this idea and thought we could resurrect the MIT blackjack card-counting team that existed in the early 1990s. They were pretty prolific and notorious at cheating the house. They used mathematical statistics and computer programming to win millions. They had quite a run until their greed, use of various aliases and casino profiling pretty much brought them down."

Lucy frowned. "We talked about this that day I came to campus."

"Exactly," Sawyer said.

She worked to tie up the threads. "One of the guys even went on to win the first world series of blackjack. I think he has a video."

"We've seen it."

"So you're doing the same thing or taking his advice?" Lucy asked, still not comprehending the complete picture.

He shook his head. "Not exactly."

She still didn't get it. He was sticking to this story, and in a skewed way, suddenly it seemed a little more plausible. He had told her about Jake. "Then how are you guys different?"

Sawyer folded his hands and rested them on his stomach. "Jake studied the MIT team's programs. He analyzed their strengths and their weaknesses. Aside from knowing how to count cards, the team's real problems came from being sloppy. They played well but they didn't master how a casino works. The money got to their heads and they fell into the traps of big winnings, taking the free meals and drinks, and living large. Jake's research and subsequent programming eliminated those weaknesses. He created ways around the casino's own mathematical engineering. He learned how to adjust the formula when the casino makes a table impossible to win on. He designed programs that one could do without assistance from someone else, meaning that each man was his own owner-operator, eliminating the central bank, investors and that sort of stuff."

"So this gambling, this blackjack, is all about doing math?" Lucy asked, incredulous.

Sawyer raked a hand through his dark hair. "Oh, no, don't assume we're that innocent. It was also always about the money. Jake's dissertation is about using the house's own advantage against it. But he's saved up a pretty decent nest egg. We all have."

"You're in debt up to your eyebrows," she pointed out, her tone shocked at his nonchalance. He was serious. He wasn't making up this story. It was too far-fetched to be an illusion, and it fit with what he'd told her before.

"The loan was an unfortunate mistake on my part," Sawyer replied.

She gaped at him. "One hundred thousand is a mistake? That's…" She couldn't formulate the words. "That's a huge portion of what my condo cost. Real people work their entire lives to earn that much money."

He gave a slight shrug. "Yes, they do, but gambling lets you get money quickly especially if you know what you're doing."

"You lost six figures."

"I stupidly banked on the fact that my father's quarterly allowance would arrive in time to bail me out. I didn't plan on discovering my father was an embezzler with a mistress on the side."

"Still…" One hundred thousand would pay off all her debt: her charge cards, her car and most of her home. The heck with winning the lottery; she'd be on easy street with that amount.

"I didn't play stupid. I established a budget. My college was paid for. I put a fixed amount aside for retirement each quarter. My allowance was twenty-five thousand per quarter, way more than I needed."

"So you gambled it away? To help Jake?" Jake had seemed like an okay guy, but to throw money away?

"No. I donated a lot of my winnings to pay the medical bills of some families whose children I was working with. You of all people should know how high those get at the hospital. Some parents have their houses mortgaged two and three times to pay for their child's medical care."

"I didn't know anything about this."

"Neither did they, and I'd like it to keep it a secret. All my donations have been sent anonymously. I also donated money to The NASCAR Foundation." He smiled slightly, remembering. "I admit, I felt a bit like Robin Hood taking from the rich casinos and giving to the needy. As for my loan with my dad, sometimes you have to lose big to stay above suspicion. But I used a lot of that money to pay for Johnny's treatment. His family was about to lose their house. I made sure that didn't happen. I wanted him to have a place to go home to."

"But you still owe that money," Lucy said, trying to process everything he was saying. The whole concept of Sawyer gambling to help others was simply incomprehensible. Not that his heart didn't care deeply. But people just didn't do things like this, did they?

Sawyer loosened his hands and toyed with the edge of the bedspread. "Everything would have been fine had my allowance arrived on schedule. That would have made a major dent in the loan. I'd planned on that money. Instead, I can thank my father, his mistress and his embezzlement for yet again another drama. All I've heard since February is how, if this gets out, it will ruin Bart and Will's careers. Funny thing is that it's my brother spilling the secrets."

She understood now. "So you have to get the money. Pay the loan and all's well."

"It would have been if you hadn't shown up. Because I can't finish playing, I'm short the amount I need."

He reached on the nightstand for his wallet and pulled out several cashier's checks that he had inside. He passed them over, and as Lucy thumbed through, she added up the numbers in her head. "You have $40,100 here," she said, awed by the amount she was holding.

He nodded, his mood embittered. "Yep. I'm approximately ten short of the fifty thousand I need. The rest is in my non-Branch bank accounts earning compound interest. Notice that I've already had the taxes deducted out of my winnings so that Uncle Sam's happy. He and I will straighten out who owes whom next April. As for the rest of the money, I'll get it somewhere. I've got some ideas."

"And you never told your family any of this? That you were donating all your earnings to charity?"

He held her gaze for a minute. "I explained I was in a gambling ring, but like you did at first, they didn't believe me. Their biggest concern is that my 'problem' might have a negative effect on Will and Bart. God forbid I embarrass the family any more than my father has. Not that I can blame my brothers for worrying. They've been through a lot."

She could hear the hurt and pain in his voice and her heart softened a smidge. "You've all suffered."

But that didn't mean she was satisfied yet with his explanation. "So you've got the money to pay it off," she probed.

"Yes. All but ten thousand. If necessary, I could sell the Corvette. While I love the car, I could use something that gets better gas mileage. Something with four doors might be more fitting for my upcoming role as a university professor, and, well, you can't fit four people in a Corvette. While sporty and fun, it's rather impractical for the next phase of my life. Maybe I'd feel a little better getting rid of my father's guilt gift."

A knock on the door indicated that room service had arrived, and conversation ceased while the waiter wheeled a cart into the room. He left after Sawyer signed the ticket. Sawyer had ordered a hamburger and fries and he balanced the plate on his lap, having set his cola next to him on the nightstand.

"So you'd really sell your car?" Lucy asked.

He arched an eyebrow. "Why not? It's just a car. I've enjoyed driving it, but basically all anyone really needs is a way from point A to point B. A Corvette is just a sporty way to get there. It's either that or sell my condo, which would take a lot longer than the car. I'd tap into my retirement accounts, but I'd have to pay a ten-percent early-withdrawal penalty and that'd be foolish. You could say that, despite my gambling, I've learned how to manage my money. Actually, I'm probably better at it than anyone else in my family, including my father."

They ate in silence for a few minutes as Lucy digested both her food and what he'd said. She could accept he was part of a gambling ring, but some things still didn't make sense. She'd been so deluded by the men in her life before. And there were too many holes, too many coincidences in Sawyer's debt, like his affiliation with Larry, Bart's need to win and the amount of Kent's blackmail.

She hesitated, then bit the bullet and thought of a wild idea. She could throw out a wild herring, place all her cards faceup on the table so that he would have to react. She opened her mouth and then closed it again. If she was right she'd ignite a powder keg. If wrong, she'd look like an idiot.

She'd promised Kent and Tanya she'd find the truth. Beyond that, she owed it to herself to put her suspicions to rest once and for all. She set her fork down, inhaled and, before she could talk herself out of her decision, said, "So if you had all the money covered, why did you send the e-mails blackmailing Kent?"

HER QUESTION CAME SO FAR out of left field that Sawyer almost spit out the cola he'd been drinking. He coughed for a moment and stared at her. She'd stopped eating and sat waiting for his answer.

Was there one to give?

She'd already demanded to know why he played blackjack. She hadn't believed him at first. She'd wanted the whole story. He had the suspicion that even though she'd heard the whole truth, she still thought he might have a gambling problem.

His biggest problem was that his past actions were about to bury him deep. The only relationship he'd really cared about, the one with the power to hurt him, had become a knife aimed for his heart. No matter what he said, he wasn't going to walk out of the hotel room unscathed or untouched.

"So?" she asked him. "You haven't said anything."

"I'm still trying to figure out how you found out about those."

Her mouth dropped into an O and Sawyer immediately realized he'd convicted himself. She'd only been fishing, groping in the dark. He'd just confirmed that he knew about them.

"No one knew about those except Kent and Tanya, who told me. You couldn't know about those unless you sent them."

Yep, he'd tripped himself up. Didn't matter what he said from here on out. From her aghast expression, he was history.

"Don't you have anything to say for yourself?" she demanded.

"What, and incriminate myself further? You're accusing me of blackmail."

"The e-mails came from the server in the math lab. I traced them back from Kent's computer. It's either you or Larry. You're the only two connected to NASCAR."

"Everyone in Charlotte's connected in one way or the other," he stated flatly.

"Yes, but you needed one hundred thousand dollars and you needed it quickly," she pointed out.

"The timing of the e-mails are off a bit," he said.

She banged her fist on the edge of her chair. "If not you, then who? Was it Larry? Does he have a reason to try and hurt his family? I assume the two of you are close. He's your mentor."

"What does it matter?" Sawyer responded, his shoulders

slumping slightly. "Kent never responded and the e-mails are over and done with. Dredging this up will only hurt people."

Her lips thinned and her eyes flashed angrily. "This is like playing twenty questions and getting nowhere. Just tell me the truth. You promised me you would be honest. No secrets, you said. You've explained why I came here and found you gambling—that you're part of a blackjack ring. Okay, I'll buy that explanation for now. However, you didn't blink when I told you about the e-mails. You know about them. The amount you owe is the same as what someone tried to blackmail Kent for. I'm not a big believer in coincidence. I'm sure there's some mathematical formula that would prove there are no such things as random occurrences like this. So if I'm not seeing things clearly here, make me understand."

He felt the noose tighten and lashed out. "You're right in that there are no coincidences. So tell me, who are you really, Lucy? Are you some sort of private investigator working for the Grosso family? What's in this for you? What are you getting out of this fact-finding mission? Why do you care so much about something that happened months ago?"

"I…" He watched as her offensive faltered and she took a drink of the iced tea she'd ordered with her meal. "I know everything. Tanya and Kent asked for my help in seeing if I could find the source of the e-mails," she admitted slowly. "I really didn't believe you had any part in them until you didn't play dumb a few minutes ago. You wanted to know how I knew, admitting you knew about the blackmail. You couldn't know about it unless you had a role in it yourself."

He gestured with a French fry, indicating she should continue. "Start at the beginning," he said, using her earlier words.

"You deny that you're involved with the blackmail e-mails Kent received?"

He hedged. So much hinged on these next few minutes. "I'll tell you everything once you tell me what you know."

She shook her head vehemently. "No. If I tell you what I know first, then you'll know where you stand. Forget it. You first."

The fight seemed to leave Sawyer. He felt a bit like a basketball player about to lose a championship game. "I guess I deserve that. I have lied through omission."

She seemed skeptical of his admission. "You haven't said a thing about your gambling the entire time I've known you. Except for getting mad when Jake taught me how to play." She paused, and he could read it on her face that everything had become crystal clear. "Jake."

"I knew you were clever." While proud of her detective work, Sawyer still could see the writing on the wall. He knew where this was going to end. He might win the money to pay off his debt, but he was going to lose Lucy. The thought chilled him, but like Titanic survivors in the icy water, he knew there was little he could do.

LUCY COULDN'T BELIEVE she'd figured the mystery out. "Jake's the blackmailer," she stated. Jake, who'd started the card scam that had gotten Sawyer so deep in debt. Jake, Sawyer's friend.

"I wouldn't go as far as to try to accuse Jake of blackmail," Sawyer said. "You have no proof of anything, and Jake's not one of those guys you want to mess with."

"Is that why you're protecting him? As I said, I tracked the e-mail back from Kent's computer to the State University math lab," she said.

"Which is extremely illegal and inadmissible in court even if you could prove he did it," Sawyer replied.

"Fine," she shot back, irritated at the whole mess. "Just tell me why you'd do something like this, and why you'd protect Jake."

"If someone would send those e-mails, and I'm not admitting either of us did, if you were a graduate student in math, you'd do it because of probability," he answered simply.

Had her ears heard him correctly? "You'd blackmail because of math?"

Sawyer sighed. "Everything always comes down to numbers. How cold it is. How much time you have. What percent off that sweater will be. The question you'd ask in this situation is just as simple. What is the mathematical probability that extreme bad news, in this case fear of exposure, could throw off an athlete's concentration? The formula you'd use is almost the same for predicting what card will be dealt next in blackjack."

"So this was all just a game? This was someone's life you were playing with!" She was shouting and she tried to calm herself. She couldn't believe Sawyer could be so callous.

"I think that overall, fate's a tricky thing to try and predict. Kent told me at dinner that night that he never would have won Tanya over had he not come clean and admitted what he'd done during his college days. I saw the interview he gave a while back."

"And Kent told you this willingly?"

Sawyer ate another French fry. "I'd asked him how you know the person that you care about is the one for you for the rest of your days. I figured he knew. He's pretty happy."

The few bites of food she'd eaten weren't sitting well. "You had dinner with the man. How could you sit there with him? I saw the butchered picture of Patsy Grosso. How could you look him in the eye? I find it despicable."

"Haven't you ever made a mistake?"

She clenched her jaw. "I'm starting to think I made one in dating you."

"Thanks. If you wanted to wound, you did." He'd become calm, almost apathetic.

She pushed her plate aside. "This is all very overwhelming. I don't know how much more I can take." She stood.

He sighed. "You might as well sit down if you came for the whole story."

She already felt unclean, but she sat. She'd come this far. If nothing else, when she walked away from Sawyer Branch, she'd walk away with all the answers.

CHAPTER FIFTEEN

As Lucy glared at him, for the first time in his life, Sawyer understood true loss.

Oh, sure, he'd watched thousands of dollars leave his hands in under two minutes. He'd had his father take off to parts unknown and destroy his family dynamic. Those had affected Sawyer, but he hadn't been mortally injured. He'd experienced anger and rage, but he hadn't felt the deep, searing pain that would never heal no matter how much time passed.

Lucy's rigid posture said it all. She'd never forgive him for his transgressions. Whatever they had was over. His greatest fear had become reality. The love of his life wasn't to be his.

He drew a long, deep breath. He'd never have the one thing he'd really wanted—true love. He could at least give her the truth.

"The picture was all Jake's idea," Sawyer said, not caring how lame that sounded. It was, after all, the truth, although Lucy probably wouldn't believe him after everything he'd done.

"Jake got greedy. It's his one flaw, which is why his card scheme was designed specifically to eliminate that variable while still paying a high rate of return. The first e-mail was sent for the reasons I already told you. I didn't think much of it. I mean, heck, messing with Kent's concentration could only help my brothers. It was also a way to test Jake's newest theory, help him narrow down the focus of his dissertation." He paused.

"Go on," she said.

He exhaled slowly. That saying, "the truth will set you free," was nothing but a lie. He could feel the chains tightening each minute.

"The second e-mail came about because, by Jake's estimations, we'd done such a great job in causing Kent's lousy finish at Daytona. I mean, here was the reigning Cup champion and all the media could report on was his lack of concentration. Jake took that as a cosmic sign."

Always the neat-and-tidy one, Sawyer took the silver dome and placed it over his plate. The remaining food no longer held any appeal as he'd lost his appetite.

"I learned about the picture after he'd sent the follow-up e-mail. I admit to being pretty angry. The first one was harmless. Heck, spammers send those chain e-mails all the time, we'd just taken it up a notch. But the second one went too far."

"They both went too far," Lucy insisted.

"I told him that. I also told him that if Larry found out…well, none of us likes to cross Larry. He's more than a mentor and professor, he's our friend. When Kent didn't respond to the e-mail, that ended everything. Jake backed down. His card playing and his dissertation are his main focus and the e-mails were a diversion. Aside from that, he respects Larry and didn't want to disappoint him."

"So Larry knows about the gambling?"

"Yes, Jake's dissertation has a title a mile long, but in

essence, it involves exposing house weaknesses. But as for the e-mails, Larry's not in the loop on those. Only Jake and I. No one else. Well, I guess besides you, Kent and Tanya."

She stared at him, her expression crushing any lingering hope that she might forgive him.

"I still can't believe you'd do something like this. Kent's been beside himself with worry. He's been highly troubled. He thought the blackmailer might be Justin, and if it was, well, what would that do to Sophia? It would crush her."

"And you care about that?" Sawyer asked.

"Yeah, I do. They're two people who deserve a chance. I've moved on. Justin's my past. I only want them to be happy. As I was. With you. Until." She stopped and glanced around the room. He got her point clearly. Until tonight. Until this damning revelation.

"So it was all a joke?" she said.

"Yep," Sawyer said. It seemed so silly now. However, even Bart and Will had never played a prank as horrible as this.

"You know, you still haven't explained one thing. How did you even know about Kent's cheating? I find it odd you knew, considering that Kent was long gone before you arrived."

Ah, so she'd come to that. The final nail on his coffin. Well, in for a penny…

"It's pretty simple, really. Jake, Larry, a few other guys and I had all gotten together for a few beers after a really long day. Larry doesn't usually drink, but it was his wedding anniversary. You know his wife died a few years ago."

Lucy nodded.

"Well, we'd all been together presenting our dissertation outlines and the work we planned to do for the semester. We all went to the bar and noticed he was out of sorts. We pressed him for the reason and he finally told us.

"We tried to cheer him up and bought him a bunch of gelatin shots. He ended up in pretty bad shape and Jake and I drove him home. While we were in the car he let a few things slip, mostly that not all drivers were innocent."

"That doesn't get you to Kent, though."

"No, not right away. I don't really remember the exact conversation. Larry mumbled something about being drunk and something about how we shouldn't take advantage of him. He said he wouldn't bail us out like he'd do his family. He never came out and said anything specific, but we assumed he meant something about either Dean or Kent. Since he also mentioned State, we did a little investigating and found out Kent had left State quickly. It wasn't too hard to put two and two together, and with a little hacking into school records, we found out the truth."

"So Larry told you about Kent." Lucy came back to that.

"Not exactly. He was rambling about all sorts of things. Heck, he doesn't even remember telling us anything and he never mentioned Kent by name. It was simply one of those nights where he was missing his late wife and didn't realize until way too late that he'd had too much to drink. Gelatin shots will do that to a guy. He forgot they're made with nothing but sugar and vodka."

Sawyer could remember the night pretty clearly, even if Larry couldn't. But who could blame Larry for letting loose for once? He'd loved his wife.

Neither Sawyer nor Jake had intended to get their professor drunk. They hadn't even known anything about Larry's wife until alcohol had loosened his tongue and he'd started talking about her. That had led to conversations about his family, then more specifically the allusions to cheating. To any untrained ear, the comments would have been irrelevant, just the drunken words of a lonely man whom graduate students were trying to console.

However, the more Larry had continued to talk, the more Jake and Sawyer had sensed a mystery—one they'd decided to solve.

Like he'd told Lucy, Sawyer hadn't minded the first e-mail Jake had sent. He didn't know Kent personally and his failure to drive well would only help Will and Bart. That had been the rationale behind Sawyer's actions, anyway. But the second e-mail had gone too far and Sawyer had told Jake to cease and desist, or else. Jake, in the midst of the gambling ring and in researching his own dissertation, had agreed.

So life had gone on. Lucy had broken up with Justin, and at the opportune moment Sawyer had asked her out. Never in a million years would he have guessed they'd end up in Atlantic City, dredging through secrets best left buried. The air conditioner hummed, the only noise in the room for several minutes.

She finally spoke. "Kent will be thrilled to know it wasn't Larry's intention to betray him."

"I wouldn't even tell Kent," Sawyer said. "Larry has no idea it was us who did this. It's been like a dark cloud over his head ever since Kent revealed his college cheating to his family and the world. Larry's innocent in all this. You'll just ruin more lives."

Lucy shook her head. "Perhaps, but Kent has the right to know why this happened to him."

"Yeah, and I guess he will once you tell him it's me,"

Sawyer said. "Actually, Jake, but I was there. I was the ac-complice to all this. You don't even have to say it. How could I? Why didn't I come forward? Stop him? Where are my morals?"

"You two hung out together," Lucy protested.

"Yeah," Sawyer said, stopping his fingers from fidget-ing. "Kent's a great guy. I'm sure that under other circum-stances we'd be friends, but that won't happen now. I think I'll take a page from you and stop going to the track. I don't need any evil looks inside the garage. Because of my father, I get enough attention from the masses as it is."

"That's it. Feel sorry for yourself," Lucy retorted. "You're the one at fault. You created this mess."

"So did you," Sawyer said. "Did you start dating me so that you could get close to me? Visit the math lab so you could see where the crime took place?"

She colored. He'd made her even madder. "You lied. You're despicable."

He was suddenly very tired. "Yeah, you're probably right."

She shook her head. "Justin told me about your gambling. He'd overheard Bart and Anita talking. Your brother and his P.R. people have probably done you more damage. Perhaps they can spin you a way out of this web you've woven."

"Doubtful." So Bart and Anita hadn't been the most discreet. No surprise there. Now that he had the money, or most of it, to pay off the signature loan, the whole issue would resolve itself.

Except for Lucy. His sister had been right. He should have told her long ago.

"So that's it," he told her. "The end. No more blackmail

attempts will ever be forthcoming. Jake and I are both graduating soon. We're about to go out into the real world whether we're ready or not. We're done gambling as well. After Jake's paper is published, neither of us will be welcome to play in any casino in the western hemisphere. We'll be targeted."

"You can't just quit gambling. It's an addiction," Lucy said, her brow creasing.

He shook his head. "No, not in my case. It's a game. It's been one big mathematical calculation the entire time. It's just another problem to solve. When I'm done, I'm done. I'm not an addict. Besides, isn't speed an addiction? Is that why all those guys climb into a race car every weekend? Are they addicts?"

"It's different," she tried.

"No, it's not. It's exactly the same. One day they climb out of the car and go on with their lives. They become car owners. Maybe crew chiefs. Perhaps sports commentators. They become fathers. Business owners. They move on. Well, so am I. It's not very hard. You just do it."

She jutted her chin forward. "So you say."

"I say," Sawyer replied. He sighed, and then realized there was one thing she hadn't told him. "By the way, how is it that you're here? How did you discover my location? Did you hack into my e-mail?"

She didn't hesitate. "Yes."

Wow. She had some nerve. Now it was his turn to be surprised. "I think you're just as despicable here."

"Perhaps," Lucy said.

"So the ends justify the means? You didn't trust me enough to call?"

Her lower lip quivered. "You lied to me. To others. I

showed up at the race track. You told Bart and Anita you were spending the weekend with me. Obviously not, as I was in Pocono and you were nowhere in sight."

He ran a finger over his own lower lip, rubbing it harshly as if to stop her from trembling. The motion didn't help. "How many times did you access my e-mail?"

"Just twice. The first was a few days ago. That's why I was so tired and called in sick. The second time was today, so I could find out where you were. Anita got me on a commercial flight and I took a cab to the airport."

At least she was being honest now. "Great. So how many other people know you're here?"

"No one but Anita, who promised not to tell Bart. I told Tanya I had a family emergency and I had to get to the airport. That's it. No more. No less."

"You've been just as underhanded as I've been," Sawyer said. "You broke into the State University's computer system."

"And you blackmailed," she shot back.

"Stalemate," Sawyer said. He'd smile but the irony was bitter, not funny.

"I guess the status quo is that nothing has changed but us and our feelings for each other," Lucy said. "You and I have both done something illegal."

"Which is why you're not telling Kent. It's done and it's in the past. Everyone's moved on. Just tell him it's not Larry or Justin and he'll be fine."

"But…" she protested.

"No. My life has been a nightmare these past six months and I'm about to be on the other side. I have the job I want lined up. I'm not having that ruined because you've decided to go all justice crusader. Sometimes meddling does more harm than good, and this is one of those cases. My life has been damaged enough by my father. I will not have my actions bring down the rest of the Branch family, especially Will and Bart. You've been just as guilty as me and I'll let everyone know it."

"That's blackmail."

"Life's full of irony." He gave a bitter laugh, one that belied the futility he felt. "If it helps your sensibilities, just tell them that you've hit a dead end. In a sense, you have."

"*We* have," Lucy said. She'd long ago set her mostly uneaten food on the desk and she covered the plate with the silver dome. "I thought I knew you, but I was wrong. I don't know you at all. You're not the man I thought you were."

He shrugged, refusing to let her know how much her words cut. Despite her own crimes, he deserved it. Worse, life wasn't something you could edit. You couldn't turn back time, take a mulligan and get a do-over.

At this moment, he'd love to take Lucy in his arms, tell her he was sorry and that he'd never meant to hurt her. But her angry expression told him that tactic wouldn't work. She might be hurting, but he was the last man on the planet she'd want comfort from at this time. Better to let her have her say, and let her go.

She stood, her body shaking slightly. "I wished...I hoped..."

She shook her head. The anger at herself came next.

"I always choose the wrong men. I thought I'd broken my pattern with you, but you've been the worst of all. I really hoped we might have a future. I think it would be best if we never cross paths again."

Her hand trembled as she grabbed for her purse and slid

it on her shoulder. He sat there, wanting nothing more than to get up, take her in his arms and sob that this was a mistake. He wanted to tell her that he'd never hurt her again. That he'd somehow make it all better. But it was far too late for that. He'd go on. She'd go on.

"I'm sorry," he said, the apology too little, too late and falling on deaf ears.

"I hope you are," she said. She stood there for a moment, staring at him with those pale blue eyes until she shook her head, her strawberry-blond hair forming a curtain around her face as if she erased him from her memory.

Then, her gait getting more purposeful with each subsequent step, she strode to the door, pulled it open and walked through. It closed with an ominous click; the only indication of her presence the covered plate, a half-empty glass of iced tea and the faint remains of her perfume in the sluggish air.

He stood, for a second rashly considering chasing after her and pleading with her, until he considered how unwanted and useless that action would be. So he simply sat back down, utterly defeated.

LUCY DIDN'T STOP SHAKING until she was safely in a taxi headed to the airport. She hadn't considered how she was getting home when she'd had Anita make travel arrangements. By now the Pocono race would be over, with everyone headed back to Charlotte.

For the briefest second when she'd stepped out of the elevator, she considered calling Tanya, but then Lucy had realized the implications of that, shut her cell phone and approached the concierge. He'd been wonderfully supportive, getting her on the next flight out.

She'd cringed at the amount she'd charged to her credit card, knowing she'd have to dip into her savings to pay the bill for both last-minute flights. But within two hours she was on her way home, seated next to a woman who promptly fell asleep.

Lucy glanced at the magazine provided in the seat-back pocket and then at the book she'd purchased at the airport. The thriller novel that promised plenty of action, adventure and death. She'd chosen it based on the dark cover, which matched her mood. Chalk up her life to just another boyfriend turned bad. Would she ever learn how to stop picking Mr. Wrong?

Sawyer, with all his promises of the future, had to be the biggest disappointment of all. Her head had wanted to believe in him so badly that she'd ignored all the warning signs that had been right in front of her.

He'd turned out to be the worst mistake of her life, her poorest choice in a man yet. She'd had such hopes…but perhaps marriage and romance weren't for her. She'd never picked a winner yet. She probably never would. Maybe it was time to get that kitten, or maybe an adult cat that needed a home. At least then she'd be able to love something and have it truly love her in return.

She leaned her head against the headrest and turned to stare out the window. The sky was black and the world below just a bunch of white lights that seemed the size of pinheads.

The flight attendant came by, a young man who asked her if she wanted anything to drink. Lucy requested a glass of water and then went back to staring out the window as she tried to put her life together one more time.

It wasn't until she reached her apartment, her credit card bleeding after the cab fare, that she allowed herself to break down and cry.

CHAPTER SIXTEEN

"SAWYER, WHAT A SURPRISE. It's so good to see you!" Gertie opened the front door and gave Sawyer a big hug before he even got inside.

At least someone still loved him, Sawyer thought as he stepped into the foyer. "My mom knows I'm coming, doesn't she?"

"She does. She can't wait to see you," Gertie confirmed. The housekeeper couldn't help herself and she gave Sawyer another hug before leading him into the house. "You don't come around as much as you should."

"I know." Even though he'd often stopped in Dallas to deposit his casino winnings, he wasn't a frequent visitor since the scandal broke.

Sawyer glanced around. The place still looked the same, he noted. Nothing had been stripped from the walls, no furniture had been moved or sold. He breathed a sigh of relief. He'd been worried about the feds taking any of his mother's personal possessions, like her artwork.

"Your mom's out in the greenhouse. She's been reading. Poor thing, she's been through so much," Gertie said. "Can I get you anything to eat or drink?"

"I could use a soda if you don't mind," Sawyer replied.

"Oh, you know I don't mind. It's the least I can do. She's

going to be so happy to see you. She needs all her family in times like this," Gertie said, gesturing toward the hallway that led to the attached greenhouse. While not technically manufactured as an actual greenhouse, the four-season room still contained plenty of plants, several of them rare tropical species. "Now, you go on and I'll bring your drink right out. Are you hungry? I'll bring you a snack, too."

Sawyer traveled the last few steps toward where his mother waited. He hesitated in the doorway. How did he face his mother after all he'd done? After all the people he'd disappointed and hurt?

She didn't see him immediately, giving him time to assess her. She had worry lines he'd never seen on her fifty-two-year-old face.

"Sawyer!" She saw him then and she set her book down and got to her feet. He noted she was reading *Night*, Elie Wiesel's memoir of his personal experience surviving the Holocaust.

She opened her arms and he stepped into them, hugging his mother fiercely for several moments until she finally drew back and studied his face. "It's so good to see you. Penny told me you were coming, but I refused to believe it until it happened. Too much of my life lately is hearing that there might be good news, and then it doesn't materialize."

Gertie arrived with Sawyer's soda and cookies. He took the glass and plate from her and she returned the way she'd come.

"Sit, sit," Maeve said, gesturing to a floral love seat near her chair. "Tell me everything. Penny said you'd found the woman you want to marry. When do I meet her?"

Sawyer's face clouded and for a minute he couldn't find the words.

She understood immediately. "Oh honey. Did something happen?"

"It didn't work out," Sawyer admitted. He took a big breath, tilted his head back and looked up at the glass ceiling. Maeve had left the blinds open and, outside, birds flew past, silhouetted against the bright blue sky.

She moved closer and gathered him into her arms for a mother's hug. "I'm so sorry," she said as he leaned his head down on her shoulder.

"It hurts," he told her. He'd said those words to her hundreds of times growing up. When he'd scraped his knee. When he'd blackened his eye. But none compared to this.

"Losing love always does," Maeve said wisely. She sat next to him on the love seat and grasped his hands. "You're strong. You'll survive. You're not a quitter, no matter how hard things get."

"What if I want to? Why can't I give up? Write my life off as a loss?" He voiced the words more to give them credence, to exorcise his demons once and for all.

"You can't because you've got my family's blood flowing in your veins. We dig in for the long haul." She glanced at her book. "I'm rereading that. He's taught me that we'll always be haunted by the personal choices we make. But we have to grow and learn from them or we're doomed to repeat our mistakes. Our lives have a greater purpose."

"Yeah, how?"

She appeared so earnest. "Your dissertation. All those children you helped. They might not know why, but you gave the doctors tools to save them. You made the world a better place just by being you."

"I screwed everything up," he said.

"No," Maeve continued. "You didn't. No matter what, your heart has always been in the right place."

How he'd love to believe that! "What if I broke someone's heart? Hurt them so bad that I doubt they'll recover?"

Maeve gave him a sympathetic smile. "You mean yourself?"

"I'm one of them," he said. "But Lucy. What I did to her is inexcusable. I treated her terribly."

"Tell me all about it. Let me listen and try to help. I'm tougher than I look. I can handle volunteering at the animal shelter, seeing those lovely pets who might never find a home. I've handled your father's defection and the fallout. Maybe not well, but I'm handling it. Nothing you will say can shock me. Unless you're going to prison."

He thought for a second about the e-mails. "I don't think so," he told his mother.

"Then begin," she said simply.

So he confessed. That was really the only word for it. He started at the beginning. Told his mother about learning of Kent Grosso's mistakes. Told her about the e-mails. The gambling and the loan. He filled her in about Lucy, managing to smile as he thought of the happier times.

He talked for almost forty minutes straight, and Maeve didn't interrupt him once. She patted his hand on occasion, waved off Gertie when she'd come to check if Sawyer needed more soda. His mother just listened.

When he finished, there were tears in her eyes.

"I knew I shouldn't have told you," he said, anguished that he'd hurt her as well.

"No, no," she said, wiping the tears away with the back of her hand. He saw a box of tissues near the book and reached for it. He handed her one. "Thanks."

"You're disappointed in me," he said. "I've failed you and for that I'll never forgive myself."

"It's not you. It's me," she said, blowing her nose. "I should have been there more for you. I should have trusted my gut and demanded you tell me your side of the story before I simply took Craig's word for it and Penny's advice that we had to get you help."

"I probably should have told you everything that was going on. I'm not sure why I didn't. It was a mistake."

"Which we've all been making a lot of lately," Maeve said.

"So you don't believe I have a problem?" he said.

She shook her head, the tip of her nose red. "Of course I don't. You're not addicted to anything. I gave birth to you. I watched you grow up. I know the strength of your character. I shouldn't have depended on others to make my decisions for me, which is why I'm taking better control now. Maybe it was the shock of learning the past twenty years of my life have been a lie that I simply didn't look past the surface. Learning about your father was quite a shock."

He grabbed her hands and squeezed them. "Do not blame yourself. I should have come to you and given you an opportunity to ask me what was going on. My pride… I've been foolish. It's my greatest weakness. I'll probably fight being stubborn and mulish the rest of my life."

"You will, but recognizing that's your problem is half

the battle. I'm proud of you, son. You're going to get through this and I'll be right behind you the entire way."

He shook his head. "Yeah, but I won't escape without scars."

She lifted his hand, showing him the thin, half-moon-shaped white line visible on his forefinger. "Remember this? You needed stitches because you cut yourself with the end of an antennae."

"I was running and the safety tip had broken off long ago. I figured once broken, might as well tear off the rest."

"I believe you were chasing one of your brothers with it, pretending it was a sword. Instead, it got you," Maeve said. "With four children I visited the emergency room a lot. The point I'm trying to make is that life gives you scars. They remind you of the foolish things you've done and teach you not to do them again."

"Ever since I started walking I made at least a trip a year to the ER until I was ten," Sawyer pointed out.

Maeve smiled at the memory. "Sometimes the learning curve takes some time. Maybe your whole life. I mean, look at me, I'm still learning. I'm going to get through this current debacle and come out fine. It's just not going to happen overnight."

"I guess there are some things you can't put back together," Sawyer observed.

"No, and in this case, the destruction is complete. I don't want your father back. I'm not sure I want to be single at my age, but that's going to be my lot. I've screamed and ranted. I've cried and sobbed. But in the end, those do nothing. I simply have to put one foot in front of the other and move on. Not that it's easy."

"I think the chasm between me and Lucy is pretty deep,"

Sawyer said. He raked a hand through his hair. "I've gone over every possible scenario. I can't find one that works. I can't find a way to win her back."

"You always told me that every problem has an answer," Maeve reminded him.

"Yeah, but those answers may not be the ones you want," he replied.

"Well, then I guess you have to change the variables. That's the biggest thing I've learned these past few months."

"You can't change what Dad did," Sawyer said, recognizing the math analogy.

She gave him a sad smile. "How true. But the thing I can change is me."

Sawyer sat there for a moment, absorbing what she'd just said. Could it really be that simple? He'd been manipulating external variables for so long that he'd forgotten the only one he had the most control over. The only person he truly could influence and force to transform.

Himself.

He was the variable. The one who could change.

He could stop reacting to this current situation, take his lumps like a man, and choose to find happiness no matter what his lot in life.

He'd always poked fun at his sister for suggesting he attend a self-help group meeting. But for a lark he'd visited the Web site, following the link she'd sent. The very first step they'd listed was to admit you were powerless—that your life had become unmanageable. Until yesterday he never would have assumed his life had hit rock bottom. He'd been in control. Powerful. Despite his brothers' financial ills, Sawyer had had it all. Money. Security. The girl. How fast that had changed.

"So when do you hear the results of your dissertation?" Maeve asked.

"I presented this past Friday. The official results won't be posted for another week or two, but Larry gave me a thumbs-up before I left, so I'm positive everything went well and that I passed."

"I'm so glad," Maeve said. "Congratulations. You've done it. Dr. Branch. How formal and distinguished-sounding."

"Yeah," Sawyer said, his mind elsewhere. His thoughts raced now that he'd found another path, one he hadn't discovered on his own. He'd been blind to an essential, but his mother had pointed him in a new direction.

He was the variable.

That concept changed the whole equation. The black cloud of doom lifted slightly, offering a sliver of hope. Yet he knew it wasn't going to be easy. He might discover he'd opened up a can of worms, and that life would get worse before it got better.

Was he ready for that? Could he stand any more pain? Could he live with the fallout of his actions?

He had to try.

"So you think it's hopeless with this girl you love?" Maeve asked, breaking into his zinging thoughts.

"I don't know," Sawyer said slowly. "Probably. Maybe. I really have no idea. I thought so but there could be a chance. I'll probably have to grovel and it might not work."

She tilted her head, studied him. "You have that look about you. I've seen it before, usually before you'd go process a bunch of facts and figures or have a problem to solve and you found an idea how to proceed. Like the time you made Bart's car go faster."

"This is somewhat like that," Sawyer agreed.

"If she truly loves you, she might forgive you," Maeve encouraged.

He had to know. "Would you forgive my father?"

"I don't know. I'm not there yet," Maeve answered honestly. "I definitely wouldn't take him back as my husband. That part of my life is dead. But forgiveness is another thing. You can't live your life consumed by hate or bitterness. I certainly don't want to live with a black cloud for the rest of my days. I want to be happy. I choose to be happy. It's just taking a while to get there."

"I don't know if she'll forgive me or take me back," Sawyer said.

"It's a risk you have to take."

"Yeah." He sighed. "The numbers are against me. The probability for my success is pretty low. Maybe less than one percent."

Maeve smiled encouragingly. "You'll just have to do something to increase your odds."

"Perhaps. But I'm not doing this for her. I'm going to do it for me. That's got to be my motivation."

"Then you're doing it for the right reasons," Maeve said, and he could see the love his mother had for him shining in her eyes.

"I'm going to have to leave soon so I can catch my plane," he told her.

Her expression was tender and bittersweet. "I know. Your life is in Charlotte now. I'll admit it's sometimes hard to deal with, but I knew when I gave birth to each of my children that someday I'd have to let you all go and be your own persons."

"You did great with us," Sawyer told her. "I don't think

I could have asked for a better mother. You've been the best."

He was ready with the tissue when she burst into happy tears. "You don't know how much that means to me," she said.

"I love you and I always will. I just want you to be proud of me," Sawyer said.

"And I am," she replied. She touched his cheek gently.

He hugged her tightly for the longest time until, with the promise not to be so much of a stranger, he left and drove the rental car back to the airport. He bought a notepad in the bookstore, and since the flight was half empty, he had space to spread out. He began by making a list of everything he needed to do when he arrived home. He had at least ten items and he prioritized those.

He'd left Lucy off the list. At this moment he had nothing to offer her. Nothing to prove to her he'd changed or was even worthy of her attention. Seeing her now, and begging for her to return to him would be idiotic and futile.

He'd actually do more damage than good, killing his chances before the battle to regain her heart began. That chance he wasn't going to take.

CHAPTER SEVENTEEN

IF TIME WAS SUPPOSED to heal all wounds, it sure wasn't doing a good job. Home from work, Lucy pressed Play on her home answering machine. Tanya had left another message beseeching Lucy to call.

Guilt began to creep in and Lucy sighed as she erased the message. She'd been ignoring her friend since Monday morning when Tanya had called at work. All Lucy had told her friend was that she'd broken up with Sawyer. Now Wednesday evening, the whole situation was still too raw to discuss.

Telling Tanya the details would entail confessing the whole story, and Lucy couldn't stomach saying that Sawyer was the blackmailer. Her anger and rage still bubbled. Her frustration remained high. Her disappointment in herself was off the charts for picking another loser.

Maybe this weekend she'd be able to talk to Tanya and tell her everything. Right now, Lucy preferred to lick her wounds in private. Her cell phone beeped, indicating she had a message. She checked—that was from Tanya as well.

Sawyer hadn't called.

Not that she'd expect him to. Okay, maybe part of her wanted him to call and apologize, perhaps grovel a little bit. But she was better off without him. It would just take time to let go of the idea that she'd find Mr. Right. But she could do it. Starting now.

ON THURSDAY, SAWYER hesitated outside the classroom door, savoring the brief reprieve from the task ahead. He waited until the last of the undergraduate students filed out of the lecture hall after Professor Grosso's seminar ended. Larry had taught a rare one-day symposium and the room had been at capacity.

Sawyer watched as persons of all ages and ethnicities walked up the steps toward the exit. As the last person passed by, Sawyer stepped into the room.

"Sawyer! Sorry I haven't been able to meet up with you until now. I've been busy wrapping things up. How's my favorite graduate?" Larry greeted as Sawyer began to descend the stairs.

Sawyer paused halfway as Larry's words sunk in. "Is it official?"

The posting of the Ph.D. committee's decisions wasn't to occur until next week.

Larry grinned. "Oh, it's not official yet, but I have it on very good authority that you skated through with one of the highest grades."

"Yes!" Sawyer made a fist and jerked his arm backward. That was some of the best news he'd heard. Then again, he hadn't heard much since his return. He'd been holed up in his condo, working on the problem that was known as his life. Bart had even called and left a voice mail saying Tanya had told them that Lucy had dumped Sawyer. Bart had asked Sawyer to call him, but so far he hadn't felt like talking to his brother except to text him and say the loan was paid in full.

He gave a sigh of relief as he realized that at least something had worked out, although maybe not for long.

"To celebrate your success, I've arranged the interview for one of our open faculty positions. Your time slot is next Monday at two," Larry said. "Everyone's very impressed with you. While I won't be there since I'll be on vacation, I can assure you it's just a formality. One of those jobs is yours should you choose to take it."

For a moment, Sawyer allowed himself to taste the elation. He'd been anticipating the official interview, that next step on his career plan.

He sobered as he reached the lecture stage. Larry had almost finished disconnecting his laptop and Sawyer moved closer to the podium.

"I wanted to talk to you about the interview," Sawyer said.

Larry paused, black power cord in hand. His gaze narrowed. "Don't tell me you're having second thoughts about joining the faculty."

Sawyer shook his head. "No, that's still my dream. But you might not want to recommend me after I tell you what I'm here to say."

Larry's brow creased. "This sounds serious. Don't tell me you've cheated, that is aside from Jake's card counting. He's been having a little bit of trouble with refining his presentation and I won't be here when he goes before the committee."

"No." Sawyer replied. "I promise it's not cheating or anything like that."

"Good." Larry packed away the power cord. "I suffered enough grief back in January trying to get Jake's crazy idea through the committee. Only when I showed them the end application, as to how casinos could use his card-counting formulas to improve their own security, did they bite and say yes. Hopefully he hasn't forgotten that part. He's been getting off track. If you talk to him, make sure he stays on it tomorrow afternoon when he presents."

"This does have a little bit to do with Jake," Sawyer said. He gestured toward the desks arranged in auditorium-style seating. "You'd better sit down."

Larry slid the laptop in its carryall and zipped the leather bag closed. "Okay. Shall we go to the Underground?"

Sawyer shook his head. "Here's fine." He pressed a button on the podium, shutting down any microphone and audio feeds.

"Well, then I guess we'll use the front row," Larry said. He followed Sawyer off the stage and they took seats, leaving one empty desk between them. "So tell me what's going on."

Sawyer took a deep breath and resisted the childish urge to cross his fingers behind his back. "I'm the one responsible for forcing Kent to have to reveal the cheating scandal," Sawyer said, watching Larry's face.

Larry quickly masked his many emotions. He drew a breath. "Okay, I'll bite. Explain?"

"I blackmailed him," Sawyer said quietly. He then explained the two e-mails.

Silence descended in the room until Larry finally said, "I see."

"I'd understand if you'd like to withdraw your support of my candidacy and cancel my interview," Sawyer said. The words pained him, and despite a great desire to glance away and look at anything—the LCD projector, whiteboard, boring beige walls—Sawyer kept his focus on Larry. He met his mentor's scrutiny like a man.

"I see," Larry repeated, a bit at a loss for words.

"I just wanted you to know," Sawyer said.

Larry frowned. "And that's it? No explanation?"

Sawyer shook his head. "I don't really have one."

Larry tapped his fingers on the arm of the chair. "I have to tell you I don't buy that. I've known you a long time. I'm fifty and I've seen and heard a lot. You can't fool me on this one, Sawyer."

"It doesn't matter what my reason was," Sawyer tried. He hated disappointing Larry, but he'd chosen his path and was determined to follow it through. "I'm responsible. I plan on telling Kent the truth and I wanted you to know first so you weren't caught by surprise."

"Are you planning on telling Kent where you learned the information? You did get it from me, didn't you?" Larry said, his face a tad remorseful.

Sawyer used his teeth to pull his bottom lip under before replying. "In a roundabout way."

Larry sighed. "Sawyer, be straight with me. I'd say my tongue was loose the night you, Jake and I had all those gelatin shots. Although most of the night is hazy, I have a vague recollection of saying something about cheaters, although I don't know exactly what words came out of my mouth."

Sawyer didn't want Larry to blame himself. "You never mentioned any of your family members by name. Except your late wife."

"Libby," Larry reminded Sawyer. "So you heard my ramblings and you added it all up. You always were clever. Give you a problem and you're like a dog with a bone. I always admired that quality about you. You never quit on anything."

"You'd given me enough to go on and I was curious. I did some digging after that night," Sawyer said.

"Probably none of it legal," Larry said with a wry nod. "I could see why. I probably would have done the same."

"Yes, but you wouldn't have sent anonymous e-mails threatening blackmail. I never meant to hurt you or any member of your family. But I have. Seems like I'm doing a lot of that lately."

"What do you mean?" Larry queried, wanting further clarification.

"Hurting people I care about," Sawyer said.

"So why did you do it?" Larry asked. "Why was it so important that you blackmail Kent?"

Sawyer found himself surprised. He hadn't planned on this. "You really want to hear my reason?"

Larry nodded. "Yes, I do. Kent's been through a rough patch. I've been racking my brain trying to figure out who could have done this, and when I could have let his secret slip. Now you tell me it's you and I'd like to hear why. I mean, besides our mentor relationship, we're friends. I think I deserve the truth, don't you?"

"Yes, sir," Sawyer replied. He'd planned on coming in here, confessing, taking the entire blame and apologizing. He didn't think Larry would want the specifics.

"So?" Larry prodded.

"I…" Sawyer struggled, and then said, "They were both jokes. The first e-mail was simply to see if w…I could disturb Kent's concentration. You know, help Will and Bart. The next one, well, I needed the money. I told you about my father and his situation. Well, he'd given me a signature loan from his bank and I was under pressure from my family to pay it off immediately."

"And have you?" Larry asked.

"Yes. On Monday. Paid in full."

"So this loan payment, is it one of the reasons Jake's driving around in his new Corvette? A car he bought off you?"

"Yes," Sawyer said. "I sold it to him."

Larry didn't seem too interested in the logistics of title transfer. "So if I gave you a picture of me and a picture of Libby, could you add her in and make one photo? I'd like one of both of us. Could you do it?"

"I could try," Sawyer said.

Larry craned his neck slightly, leaning so he could study Sawyer. "You might be great at playing cards but you'd be terrible on the witness stand. You just revealed yourself. You don't know how to use Photoshop at all, do you?"

"No," Sawyer admitted, realizing Larry had busted him just as Lucy had.

"Then stop trying to protect Jake," Larry said. "I know he's the one behind this. I just didn't have any proof so I kept my mouth shut."

"I owed the money," Sawyer defended, trying to protect his friend.

"I have no doubt you did," Larry said. "But you aren't the kind of guy to blackmail someone."

"I hate to disappoint you, but I am," Sawyer insisted.

Larry shook his head. "I spoke with Kent just a few days ago and he told me about the e-mails and I promised to keep it a secret. He's never mentioned the blackmail to the family and probably never will again.

"But once he told me, I recognized Jake's handiwork. The probability formulas between seeing if blackmail would work or if the two of spades would be dealt next are way too similar so I clobbered Jake with my suspicions Tuesday during our final review. Told him if he ever sent any e-mail to my family again that I'd work until the end of my days to discredit any future math work he did, starting with sabotaging his presentation tomorrow morning. His dissertation is my last official duty before fall semester."

Sawyer's mouth formed a large O.

Larry chuckled. "I can see you're surprised. I didn't think Jake would tell you. He told me you'd been the one to force him into submission after the request for one hundred thousand. Well, I can be good at blackmail when the situation warrants. It's useful for keeping the status quo."

"Did you tell Kent, Jake was involved?" Sawyer stuttered, unprepared for this turn of events.

Larry shook his head. "No. It was my fault that his secret got out. I figured once I dealt with Jake, I'd ended the situation once and for all. It's over for good."

"But it's not," Sawyer said, realizing that the situation was totally screwed up. He'd planned on taking the fall, but Larry had already known.

"Why not?" Larry asked.

Sawyer winced. "Kent and Tanya asked Lucy Gunter to find the source of the e-mails."

Larry seemed puzzled. "Lucy? Wasn't that Justin Murphy's girlfriend pre-Sophia?"

"Yes. She and Tanya are friends. Kent and Tanya were worried the e-mails might be from Justin, and if so, then the truth would devastate Sophia. Lucy's a computer guru and she tracked the e-mails back to the math lab."

"Oh," Larry said, processing it all. "Is this the girl who came here? The guys mentioned it."

"Yes. We were dating. But no longer. Not after this weekend." Sawyer told Larry what had occurred on Sunday.

"You made a mess of things," Larry said once Sawyer had finished.

"Big time," Sawyer agreed. "The only silver lining I've seen so far is that my mother and I have cleared the air and the debt is paid in full."

"Yet you're without a car. You gave up a Corvette. I like those cars. Pretty sharp."

Sawyer shrugged. That night he'd told Lucy that he was done gambling and he meant it. Even with being ten thousand short, he wasn't about to go back down to the casino and win the money he needed. Instead, he'd called Jake. Flush with his winnings, which were twice what he'd hoped, Jake had bought Sawyer's car.

"I'm driving a rental while I research what to buy next. As for the Corvette, my father paid for it, so Jake's fifty thousand was like found money. I didn't lose a thing by selling and he got a deal. There's only four thousand miles on the thing. Believe me, we checked the value on one of those Internet sites before he passed over the cash and I handed over the keys. Now I've got a nice nest egg even after paying everything back."

"So what are you planning to do next?" Larry asked.

"I guess with your permission I go talk to Kent," Sawyer said. "Tell him what happened. Apologize. Deal with the fallout. No matter what, I think I need to do that and put things right, at least to make peace with myself."

Larry nodded. "I'll probably need to speak with Kent as well. This is going to be mighty awkward, but maybe it's all for the best. My family can have way too many secrets sometimes. This is one situation that might be better if everything's let out and allowed to evaporate into nothingness. Might give everyone a huge sense of relief."

"Thank you," Sawyer said, relieved.

"You're welcome. Before you go, I do have to tell you, I like this new maturity I'm seeing. It's impressive. I'm sure you'll dazzle the committee next Monday. Don't forget, 2:00 p.m."

"You're serious? You'll still recommend me?" Sawyer couldn't believe it. After everything, Larry was still standing by him.

Larry smiled. "Very much so. Now, if you were Jake, it might be a different story. But luckily you're not."

"No, sir," Sawyer said.

Larry reached over and shook Sawyer's hand. "Now, get out of here. What was I thinking, having you two graduate at the end of July? Makes more work for me. I could be fishing or something. I'm definitely ready for a good vacation."

Sawyer rose to his feet. He'd just gotten a new lease on life and he took the stairs out of the room two at a time.

Next stop, Kent Grosso.

CHAPTER EIGHTEEN

LUCY COULDN'T CONCENTRATE. She whirled her chair around and stared out the window at the parking lot. Like the creatures of habit that they were, most people parked in the same spot every day. Perhaps there was comfort in ritual.

Although she was in her climate-controlled office, it wasn't hard to tell it was summertime. Visible heat waves radiated off the pavement. School had dismissed until fall and her condo's pool complex had opened. Even Michigan was having great weather, not that she'd been there this past weekend for the races.

Maybe her "I'm giving up NASCAR" had finally come true, for she'd been unable to bring herself to turn on the TV and watch the race. Marcie had been the one who'd finally told her later who'd won, and that Justin had had engine problems again.

It was now Wednesday and she'd determined it was time to dig out of the big funk into which she'd slid. Just a short time ago she'd been standing on the precipice of a lifetime of promise. Now she was realizing that maybe she and Mr. Right weren't ever going to connect.

Worse, Sawyer Branch wasn't going to be easy to get over, no matter how mad she'd been at him.

Part of her, despite all his sins and transgressions, still cared. When things had been going right, they'd been almost perfect. They'd connected on many levels, had been as physically close as two people could be. It had been more than just sex.

She'd racked her brain trying to understand the reasons for why he'd done what he did. The more she analyzed the situation, the more her anger lessened.

Not that she forgave him for any of his lies or omissions. But she could comprehend the catalyst and pressure he'd been under. Why, just yesterday the Charlotte newspaper had given Alyssa Ritchie a full-page interview in the life-style section. Lucy had read the article, wadded up the paper and dashed off a nasty letter to the editor.

In her opinion, the woman was poison. No wonder Sawyer and his family were so messed up. Best for everyone if Alyssa became a has-been and disappeared, quickly.

Lucy swiveled and glanced at the clock. Not even three. She had at least another hour and a half before she could reasonably go home without any raised eyebrows.

Her charge-card statement had already arrived and her stomach had dropped when she'd read the bill. Living and learning could be expensive, and she'd already burned two of her vacation days calling in sick over the past two weeks.

Her phone shrilled, breaking the eerie silence that had settled. Lucy reached for it, checking the caller ID. It read "Unknown."

"Lucy Gunter," she answered.

"Lucy, it's Tanya!"

"Hey," Lucy said, realizing that at some point she had

to talk to her friend. Knowing Tanya would want to sympathize, Lucy hadn't picked up the last few times Tanya had called as she'd recognized the number.

Tanya breathed a sigh of relief. "I am so glad I finally caught you. You won't believe what I have to tell you. We know who the blackmailer is."

"What?" Lucy sat up so fast that the back of her chair hit her with a thump. She leaned forward. "You're kidding me."

"No, I'm not. Sawyer came to see Kent last week and told him everything about how he was involved. He took responsibility and apologized. After that, Kent had a long talk with Larry. I've been trying to reach you and tell you the news for days. This isn't something you can leave on an answering machine—and you've been avoiding me."

Tanya's voice had come through loud and clear and Lucy glanced around her office. Her diplomas hung on the walls. Her Beanie Babies were in place. She hadn't entered a twilight zone or alternative reality. "I don't understand. Sawyer confessed?"

"Yes. I don't really understand parts of this, either, but the story in a nutshell is that Larry let something slip by accident, Sawyer and his friend picked up on it and the friend sent the e-mails. Larry confirmed everything. He feels terrible about the whole debacle, as does Sawyer. Anyway, Larry and Kent decided to keep this just between them for now. No one else in the family needs to know. Everyone has too much else to worry about right now. As for me, I'm just glad we got some closure."

"I can't believe Sawyer came forward," Lucy said, shock settling over her. She didn't know whether to laugh or cry or reach for something to smash.

Of all the nerve. He could have told her what he'd planned or that he'd changed his mind! Fury bubbled. She'd been stressing and fretting, hating and caring…

"Are you still there?" Tanya asked.

"I'm here," Lucy replied, focusing.

"Are you okay?" Tanya asked, concern lacing her voice. "You haven't talked to me and I've been really worried about you."

"I'm fine," Lucy lied.

"You don't sound fine," Tanya said, calling Lucy's bluff.

"I'm a little shell-shocked," Lucy admitted. He could have let her know. Then again, she had told him never to contact her again. Why did he have to be the one guy she'd dated who followed her directives?

"You knew he was involved in all this, didn't you?" Tanya asked.

Lucy exhaled. "Yes. I had some suspicions before Pocono. But I didn't know for sure he was involved until I left the race and went to Atlantic City. I didn't have anything to connect him to Kent except that the e-mail came from the math lab. However, I kept hearing rumors that he had a gambling problem and that he owed one hundred thousand dollars to his family bank."

Tanya whistled at the amount.

"Yeah. Exactly. Even Justin knew about the debt. He'd overheard Bart and Anita talking and tried to warn me. But despite owing money, the more I probed, Sawyer didn't seem to show any signs of being the person behind the e-mails. He met you and Kent and they got along famously and had no issues."

"Kent really liked Sawyer. Amazingly enough, he still does. So how did you find out?"

"I broke into Sawyer's e-mails and read them, which is how I found the truth about the money. But there was nothing there about any blackmail. So I didn't deliberately keep you in the dark. I didn't want to come to you with only suspicions. What if I was wrong? I had no proof."

"Does he know you accessed his e-mail?" Tanya asked.

"Uh, yeah. That was a part of our fight."

"So you did fight. You were pretty short with me on the phone."

"I know and I'm sorry. I needed alone time."

"I'll forgive you, this time," Tanya joked to make the moment lighter. "But you had me concerned. You left Pocono so fast and Atlantic City must have been rough."

"It wasn't pleasant. After I found him in the casino, we went upstairs. After he told me about the gambling and money, I just came right out and asked him why he'd sent the e-mails. He didn't deny knowing about them or ask me what I was talking about. I mean, there was truth and things went downhill pretty quickly from there."

"Wow."

"You're telling me. It's been hell. I didn't expect him to visit Kent or come clean. This is a surprise. He told me he wouldn't say anything and he was pretty adamant about it." Lucy sighed.

"You still like him, don't you?"

Tanya's question caught Lucy a tad off guard and she took a pencil and jabbed the lead down on a piece of scrap paper until it broke, leaving a gray smudge. "I thought he might be the one, but I've been wrong before. Many times, in fact. So I've quit searching for a man. I went to the local animal shelter this past weekend and adopted."

"You got a kitten?"

"No. They had a few there, but they told me kittens always find homes. It's the adult cats that no one seems to want. So I took home two."

"Two cats?" Tanya squeaked.

Lucy smiled as she thought of her new "children." "They were inseparable and they really are the sweetest things. They're littermates and they sleep together and everything."

"Fixed?"

"Of course. They don't let animals out of the shelter without being neutered."

And while she was thinking about it, Lucy made a mental note to take pictures and put a few on her desk. Already she'd fallen in love with Butch and Sundance, her "boys."

"So you can see I'm doing as well as can be expected and time will heal all wounds," she told her friend. "I'll be fine."

"Lucy…" Tanya protested.

"Seriously. Hey, come on. If it comes down to it, I can just be a crazy cat lady like my sister. She's got four."

"She lives in a huge house with acreage. She's also happily married with kids," Tanya said, pointing out the flaw in Lucy's logic.

"Yeah, well, I didn't say I'd become one overnight," Lucy said.

"You sound to me like you're still hurting. I think you should talk to Sawyer," Tanya suggested. "Maybe clear the air now that each of you has calmed down."

Lucy made a face. "Why would I want to do that?"

"Because you still care for him. Because maybe the two of you can put this behind you and regain the love you had."

"I doubt that's possible. We said some pretty terrible things. I told him I never wanted to see him or talk to him as long as I lived. And we weren't in love."

"Maybe not, but you two were certainly faking it pretty well. As it is, the ball's in your court. Knowing Sawyer, he'll abide by your wishes."

Yeah, he had. He'd confessed to Kent and not contacted her. Then Tanya's words dawned. "Knowing Sawyer?" Lucy parroted. "How do you suddenly know Sawyer?"

"He was at the track all weekend as Kent's guest. I had a wedding. Kent told me Will and Bart had a bit of an issue with their brother hanging out with Kent at first, but then Sawyer fixed Bart's radio-controlled car so it defeated everyone else's and all's well. As for his brothers, I overheard them talking on Sunday. Something about not being able to play any more jokes on Sawyer now that some debt is paid. Maybe that's the money Sawyer owed, but I don't know. What I do know is that they all seemed pretty happy if slightly miffed at the same time, so I'm thinking everything's great."

Lucy hadn't yet been able to suspend her disbelief. "So after everything that's happened, Kent's befriending Sawyer?"

"They really do get along. It's amazing. Now, if you just get back into the picture we'll be a fearsome foursome. We can hang out. Play cards and eat more barbecue."

"This is all a bit overwhelming," Lucy said, trying to take it all in.

"Well, I just wanted to call and let you know what happened. I would have told you earlier, but…"

"Yeah, I've been ignoring everyone," Lucy said, absorbing the implications of her actions.

"Yep. Now, I've got another wedding this weekend so I'm not flying to New Hampshire until Sunday. If you need anything or want to talk, call me. I'm here. Oh, and I got a new cell phone number. Let me give it to you."

Lucy grabbed a fresh pencil and jotted it down. "Thanks for calling," Lucy said before she put the handset back in its cradle and swiveled around. While the weather and seasons might differ, parts of her view never changed. The parking lot was always full.

Could Sawyer really have changed? He'd come forward. Apologized. Owned up. Before he'd left for Atlantic City on that fateful trip, they'd planned to talk upon his return. Would he have told her all about his gambling and the e-mails, once the debt was paid and he'd made his last trip?

Would it have mattered if he hadn't?

Yes, it did, she chided herself. Couples shouldn't keep things from each other, except for what you were getting the person for his birthday or Christmas. Then again, she had to be honest with herself. She'd kept secrets from him. She'd been working for Tanya and Kent. When she'd first had her suspicions, she should have should asked him, taken him into her confidence.

Would he have told her the truth then?

Maybe this was one of those problems that had multiple solutions. There were too many paths, too many different probable outcomes. So she could continue to beat herself up by asking questions that would never be answered or she could be like Kent Grosso and put everything behind her and move on.

Her phone rang again and Lucy glanced at the ID and picked it up. "What'd you forget?" she asked Tanya.

"I know what's going on with you. I should have

realized it sooner. You're mentally kicking yourself. The reason I know this is because I did the same thing. It's hard to have faith and trust in someone when that person hasn't demonstrated he's worthy. We want a crystal ball to see into the future and to tell us that it will be exactly what we want. In the end, I learned that it came down to one question, the most important one of all."

"What's that?" Lucy asked, curious.

"Do you care about him enough to forgive him and start over?"

"I don't know," she said honestly. Part of her might want to start over, but the rest of her couldn't abide setting herself up for any more disappointment or hurt.

"Well, that's the only question you need to be asking yourself. Purge all the others from your mind from this minute forward and focus on whether or not your feelings are deep enough. If the answer's no, then move on. If yes, then you know what you have to do. Either way, it's not going to be easy."

"It never is," Lucy said.

"It all comes down to you. Don't worry about anything else or what your brain says. Trust your heart."

"It's been wrong so many times before."

"Maybe you weren't listening hard enough. Dig deeper this time. I've got to run, but I wanted to leave you with that advice. It really helped me. See ya." Tanya disconnected.

Once again Lucy hung up the phone. She stared at it, as if somehow the black plastic device would give her the answers she needed.

Listen to her heart, Tanya had said. Lucy's heart had been exposed, stomped on and shredded so many times she didn't even know if it had a voice of its own anymore. But one thing was for certain, she should at least talk to Sawyer. She lifted the phone to call him, but upon getting his voice mail, disconnected without leaving a message.

"Lucy." Marcie stood in the doorway. "I just fielded a call from geriatrics. Their entire network platform crashed. I've sent Bill but thought you should know."

"I'll go check it out," Lucy said, grateful for the diversion. She'd worry about Sawyer later.

"WAS THAT YOUR CELL PHONE?"

"Yeah, I think so." Sawyer removed the phone from his clip and glanced at it. Then he cursed slightly as he recognized the number.

"So who called?" Bart asked. He and Sawyer were sitting in one of the conference rooms of the race shop.

"They didn't leave a message," Sawyer said, not wanting to discuss Lucy. He grabbed the stacks of data Phil Whalen had provided. Sawyer had offered to analyze the numbers, see if there was something in the figures that would help Bart do better on the track. His brother really needed to turn things around, and soon. "I'll take this with me. Have it back to you Monday."

"We'll be leaving for New Hampshire pretty early tomorrow. You coming and hanging out with me and Will this time?"

"No, I won't be there this weekend," Sawyer said, suddenly itching to leave. Lucy had called.

"No?" Bart asked.

"Nah. I've got some things to do, including all this work and buying a car. I told you I got the teaching job."

Bart smiled. "You did. Congrats again."

"Thanks." Sawyer stood. "I'll catch you later."

Sawyer left quickly, pressing the remote once he reached the lot. This morning he'd negotiated his salary and signed his university contract. It was all a done deal.

Life had a way of working out, but one thing remained missing. He still had a huge hole in his heart. He missed Lucy. He wanted her in his life. That hadn't changed.

He prayed it was a good sign that she'd phoned.

About twenty minutes later, he'd reached her floor and he stepped up to the reception desk. Marcie's eyes grew wide as she saw him. "She's not expecting you. She's not here…"

"Then I'll wait," Sawyer said, taking a seat in one of the uncomfortable plastic chairs.

Marcie seemed defensive, rightfully so, Sawyer conceded. "She could be a while. There's a crisis in one of the departments."

"I'll wait," Sawyer repeated. He didn't even glance at his watch. Nothing else was more important.

His patience was rewarded about forty-five minutes later. By now his body had tightened and his joints were stiff. Lucy strode by him, wearing one of her floral skirts. She didn't see him immediately, not until Marcie pointed and she whirled around. By that time, he'd stood.

"Hi," he said.

"Hi," she said slowly.

"Can we talk?"

"I…" She glanced at Marcie and then toward her office. "I was about to leave."

"Then I'll walk you to your car," he offered. "I noticed you called. I'd like to speak with you for a minute if that's okay."

She seemed hesitant, but she said, "Give me just a minute to grab my purse."

Sawyer nodded and soon they were heading across the parking lot. Even though it was quitting time, the sun beat down and a bead of sweat formed on Sawyer's brow. He knew Lucy had to be hot. "Look, would you agree to meet me somewhere? For coffee? Would it help for me to tell you I'm terribly sorry and there are more things I'd really like to tell you?"

She drew a deep breath and exhaled slowly. He could sense her uncertainty, and then she finally said, "Okay. I actually have to get home. You can meet me there. Give me at least ten minutes."

"I will. Thank you." He stood there, watching as she got into her car and drove off. Then he walked the short distance to his rental and climbed in.

"HELLO SWEETHEARTS, I'M HOME," Lucy called as she stepped into her kitchen. She waited for a minute and then set her purse on the counter. Cats weren't like dogs. They didn't come when called. She made her way into her bedroom, where she found both of her new charges sleeping in the middle of her bed. Butch, the black fluffy one, opened one eye and glanced at her before dozing again.

"Hello to you, too," she said, making her way into her bathroom. She had just enough time to change and freshen up before her doorbell sounded, indicating Sawyer had arrived.

"Hi again," he said as he stepped inside. His hands were behind his back and he brought them forward, one of those grab-and-go rose bouquets in his grasp.

"These aren't as nice as the ones before, but I didn't want to arrive empty-handed especially when I'm very sorry, sorry for everything."

He held the bouquet out and Lucy took it from him, the cellophane rustling in her fingers. "Thank you. I'll put these in the refrigerator and put them in some water later if you don't mind."

"That's fine," Sawyer said, following her into the kitchen. "I've been horrible to you. I'm sorry that I've been the world's worst jerk. Thank you for seeing me tonight."

She nodded and his gaze landed on the plastic mat on the floor and the bowls on top. "You got a cat?"

"Actually, I adopted two," Lucy said, opening the refrigerator door. She set the flowers inside and removed a bottle of cola and handed it to Sawyer.

He seemed surprised. "You remembered."

She hadn't realized she'd made the rote motion. "I guess all that time we spent together made getting you a drink after work a habit."

He uncapped the twenty-ounce plastic bottle and took a sip. She watched him drink, reminded of the way his lips had touched hers.

"I went to see Kent Grosso," he said.

Talking was good. Lucy thought. He'd been tense in Atlantic City, but this was almost worse. "I heard. Tanya called me today. She said you were at the track with him this past weekend."

"I was." Sawyer set the bottle on the counter. "I'm going to pray this comes out correctly. You were right. I had a big problem."

She sat at her kitchen table, and after grabbing his cola, Sawyer joined her. "Go on."

He glanced around before focusing on her, his eyes intense. "My problem isn't gambling. But it is being stubborn. If I were to analyze myself, which I've been doing a lot since Atlantic City, I'd describe myself as being self-righteous and self-serving. I've been giving myself a pity party since February."

He paused, then drank more soda as if it were the water of life. "The irony is that it took a conversation with my mother to realize that the only person who could change my outlook was me. I can't control anyone else or how people react to the Branch scandal. But I can choose my response and how I present myself. I'm the variable in the equation. Once I understood that, I recognized that my life had gotten out of control and I'd hurt people who didn't deserve it. I also knew I needed to make amends."

"So, twelve steps?" she asked.

The corner of his lip lifted, as if he'd been expecting her to be skeptical. "Not exactly, and without attending any meetings. I've been pretty judgmental my whole life. You bore the full brunt of my typical behavior. I was wrong for speaking to you the way I did. I'm sorry I hurt you."

She waited, sensing there was more.

"I lied and I was a jerk. I know I don't deserve your forgiveness and I have no right to ask for it. But I wanted you to know how sorry I am and that I hope you'll be able to be happy. I never meant to rob you of that."

Her mouth dried and she wished she'd grabbed a glass of water. Anything to help keep her composure. One of her cats brushed against her leg and she jumped, not used to the stealth of her new pet.

"Are you okay?" he asked.

"Yeah, I'm fine," she said as she struggled with his apology. She could sense that he'd changed. But could she trust him?

"I don't want to take up any more of your time," Sawyer

said, rising to his feet. He went and placed the bottle on the counter. "Thank you for listening to me. I'll show myself out."

He'd made it several feet before she found her voice and cried out, "Stop!"

He froze and turned back around.

"Is that it?" She gazed up at him. "You've said your piece and now you're going?"

He nodded. "Yes. I realized something. I love you, Lucy. I can say those words because they come from my heart, and I don't think how I feel for you will ever change. I liked you even before I got to know you. Somehow I just knew you were the one for me. But I've hurt you badly. I don't deserve your love or your forgiveness. It would be rude and presumptuous of me to come here and expect you to fall into my arms after some gas station flowers, a declaration and apology. I love you enough to want you to be happy."

"Even if it means without you?" she queried, incredulous. If Sawyer cared enough to let her go, that spoke volumes.

"Yes. I'll wish you the best just as you did Justin."

His posture didn't change and she could tell he meant it. He stood there gambling with his life. Yet he'd walk away if that made her happy.

She decided she couldn't lose him again, like she had in Atlantic City. She had to trust her heart, as Tanya said. Her heart was saying not to let him go. Lucy had to trust what she found.

"We both said some terrible things that night," she said.

"Yes, but yours were justified," Sawyer replied.

Lucy shook her head and rose unsteadily to her feet.

"No. My words weren't. I didn't trust you. I was so afraid of losing the one person whom I hope is my destiny that I let my insecurities get in the way."

"I may not have told you the truth when I came back. Just a version of it," he said. "I'd been lying to you."

"And me you. Maybe we needed this to happen to us in a horrible, convoluted way. Fate's a tricky thing. Maybe fate did a number on us."

"But I lost you," Sawyer said, as if nothing could change that.

"You did," she said, reaching inside herself and finding the forgiveness that begged to be let out. She could love this man. Part of her already did. He was her other half. He'd come here with nothing but himself. She didn't have to take him back, and he'd leave, let her make her own way uninterrupted.

She no longer wanted to be alone. She wanted Sawyer and the passion and joy they'd shared. As Tanya had said, the ball was in her court. She could choose to start over.

"Sawyer, you came clean. You made a mistake. You hurt me terribly. But you owned up to that mistake. You admitted what you've done and made amends, even to Kent. That proves how selfless you are. You risked a lot by telling the truth and coming forward. So doesn't everyone deserve a second chance at happiness? I mean, look at these guys here."

Both of her cats had come into the room and they strutted, tails high. "They weren't going to have much of a future until I came along and took them home. Now they're spoiled rotten."

"They're very lucky to have you."

Lucy lifted her right hand, making a gesture as if she were holding an invisible baseball. "You broke my heart, but as much as I already love my cats, they can't fill the hole you left behind. Only you can do that."

Sawyer closed his eyes for a brief moment. "I'll never hurt you again. I berate myself every day for the way I treated you."

"If we're to make this work, we need to be honest with each other from here on out. No secrets. Nothing hidden. I want to believe and trust you in everything. I'm in love with you and I lied that night when I told you I hated you. But I can't hurt anymore."

"And you won't," Sawyer reassured, crossing the space between them and gathering her into his arms. He touched the side of her cheek tenderly. "I want to be the man for you until the end of time. I'm never going to do anything ever again to jeopardize that. You mean the world to me."

"Promise me," she said.

"My solemn vow," Sawyer said, bringing his lips to hers. He kissed her softly at first, deepening the kiss for a long time before breaking it off to allow both of them to catch their breath.

"I only want you to know a few more things. I'm never going to be anything but a college professor. It's all final. And I got rid of my car. Sold it to Jake to pay off the debt. I need to go buy something else less flashy this weekend."

"You're man enough to drive something sedate and four-door. You don't need a big engine to impress me," she said, pressing her palms to his rock-hard abs. "I've got everything I want right here. The whole package."

"As long as you know my full intentions. I'm not here for the short term. My goal is to have it all. White dress, tuxedo, a yard full of kids, the works. Not necessarily this instant, but all those things are on my radar for the future. And I want them with you."

"Demanding, now, aren't you?" she teased, reaching up to nip his lips with hers. As he kissed her back, her heart overflowed. Could anyone be this happy?

"I love you." He kissed her once more, pausing to glance down as a white cat with yellow markings brushed up against his leg.

"That's Sundance," she said. "The black one by the oven is Butch."

He arched an eyebrow. "You named your cats after a bunch of outlaws?"

She giggled. "Well, they did steal my heart the moment I saw them at the shelter," she said, tugging on the fabric of his tight T-shirt. "And since I have this thing for a former card player gone straight, it just seemed to fit."

He grinned. "Well, I guess that's fine as long as they know I'm going to steal your heart back."

"Oh, you are?" she teased.

He nodded. "Uh-huh. It belongs to me and I'm not afraid of a little cheating, either, to get it. I love you, you know that?"

"I believe you," she said, enjoying hearing him repeat it.

"You can always believe me from here forward."

With that, he swept her high up into his arms and carried her toward the bedroom, leaving the cats behind.

* * * * *

*For more thrill-a-minute romances set against the
exciting backdrop of the NASCAR world, don't miss:*

HITTING THE BRAKES by Ken Casper
Available in June 2008

For a sneak peek, just turn the page!

For a sneak peek, just turn the page!

"You issued a press release this morning," Jim stated, "disclosing my uncle's medical condition."

"Yes, I—"

"And last night you contacted Bart Branch and his crew chief, Philip Whalen. They called me this morning."

"Yes." Anita was about to elaborate, but he again cut her off.

"Let's get something straight, Ms. Wolcott. Until my uncle wakes and demonstrates his competence, I'm the team owner, the person in charge. I run PDQ Racing. In the future, if MMG wants to continue to represent this team, you will confer with me before you notify the press on any matter, and you will not communicate information to team members behind my back."

Her heart pounded, as insult and fury battled inside her. Yesterday Sandra had given her carte blanche to issue the very press release he was now complaining about. As for the comment about communicating information behind his back, she regarded it as a direct assault on her integrity and professionalism, both of which she took great pride in.

Her instinct was to tell him to go to hell, to hit back as hard or harder than he had just assaulted her. But her sense of self-preservation, and maybe just the slightest twinge of guilt that she hadn't coordinated with him before releasing the notice, gave her pause. It wouldn't have been hard to do. She had his personal telephone number, after all.

"We're not getting off to a very good start, are we, Mr. Latimer?" she said, refusing to break eye contact with him. "For the record, I told you yesterday afternoon that we would have to issue a press release very soon in order to control the rumor mill. I gave you adequate opportunity at that time to object or to at least raise questions about it. You did neither. I took that as assent, as I would have with your uncle. You're correct. We need to establish some ground rules. In the meantime, I apologize for stepping on your toes. I didn't mean to."

When he stiffened at the jab to his pride, she knew she should have stifled the last comment.

"As for talking behind your back—" she took a deep breath "—Bart Branch and Phil Whalen left messages on my cell yesterday afternoon. I returned their calls and told them exactly what you had told me. No more. I might also point out that they called me because they didn't know about you. They were able to phone you only because I gave them your number. I grant you, you didn't authorize me to pass it on, but then you didn't tell me not to, either. I saw no reason— you certainly hadn't given me one—to believe any harm would be done by keeping *your* team informed of Richard's health and the unlikelihood of his immediate return."

She started to take a sip of her coffee, realized her hand was shaking and released the handle without lifting the cup off its saucer. She could feel tears trying to squeeze out, but she wouldn't let them. One thing she was determined not to do was cry.

Another second slipped by. Then he blinked.

"I'm sorry, too," he said contritely. "I was out of line." He expanded his chest and huffed. "This is all very new to me." He let out a nervous laugh. "I guess that's pretty obvious." He raised his coffee cup and held it between them. "Truce?"

He'd actually apologized. That was something. Now if she could just get her heart to stop pounding. She hooked her finger into the handle of her cup again and was pleased when she was able to lift it without splashing coffee all over the table.

"Truce," she said, touched her cup to his and tried to smile.

They both sipped, settled and let a minute go by in silence.

"My uncle was very pleased with the job you and MMG have been doing for the team. I don't want to change that. All I ask is that you keep me informed about what you're doing and be patient with me if I keep asking questions."

"Ask all you want," she replied. "We're both on the same side."

REQUEST YOUR FREE BOOKS!

2 FREE NOVELS PLUS 2 FREE GIFTS!

SPECIAL EDITION®

Life, Love and Family!

YES! Please send me 2 FREE Silhouette Special Edition® novels and my 2 FREE gifts (gifts are worth about $10). After receiving them, if I don't wish to receive any more books, I can return the shipping statement marked "cancel." If I don't cancel, I will receive 6 brand-new novels every month and be billed just $4.24 per book in the U.S. or $4.99 per book in Canada, plus 25¢ shipping and handling per book and applicable taxes, if any*. That's a savings of at least 15% off the cover price! I understand that accepting the 2 free books and gifts places me under no obligation to buy anything. I can always return a shipment and cancel at any time. Even if I never buy another book from Silhouette, the two free books and gifts are mine to keep forever.

235 SDN EEYU 335 SDN EEY6

Name _____ (PLEASE PRINT)

Address _____ Apt. #

City _____ State/Prov. _____ Zip/Postal Code

Signature (if under 18, a parent or guardian must sign)

Mail to the **Silhouette Reader Service:**
IN U.S.A.: P.O. Box 1867, Buffalo, NY 14240-1867
IN CANADA: P.O. Box 609, Fort Erie, Ontario L2A 5X3

Not valid to current subscribers of Silhouette Special Edition books.

Want to try two free books from another line?
Call 1-800-873-8635 or visit www.morefreebooks.com.

* Terms and prices subject to change without notice. N.Y. residents add applicable sales tax. Canadian residents will be charged applicable provincial taxes and GST. Offer not valid in Quebec. This offer is limited to one order per household. All orders subject to approval. Credit or debit balances in a customer's account(s) may be offset by any other outstanding balance owed by or to the customer. Please allow 4 to 6 weeks for delivery. Offer available while quantities last.

Your Privacy: Silhouette is committed to protecting your privacy. Our Privacy Policy is available online at www.eHarlequin.com or upon request from the Reader Service. From time to time we make our lists of customers available to reputable third parties who may have a product or service of interest to you. If you would prefer we not share your name and address, please check here. ☐

SSE08R

Love Inspired SUSPENSE

RIVETING INSPIRATIONAL ROMANCE

Near her isolated mountain cabin, Martha Gabler encounters a handsome stranger who claims he's an ATF agent working undercover. Furthermore, Tristan Sinclair says that if she doesn't play along as his girlfriend, they'll both end up dead. So Martha calls up all her faith and turns her trust to Tristan....

Look for

The GUARDIAN'S MISSION

by Shirlee McCoy

Available August wherever books are sold.

Steeple Hill®

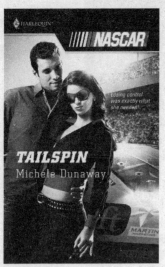